Love On My Mind

By Tracey Livesay

Love On My Mind
Pretending With the Playboy
The Tycoon's Socialite Bride

Love On My Mind

TRACEY LIVESAY

AVON IMPULSE
An Imprint of HarperCollins Publishers

Excerpt from *One Lucky Hero* copyright © 2016 by Codi Gary.
Excerpt from *Stirring Attraction* copyright © 2016 by Sara Jane Stone.
Excerpt from *Signs of Attraction* copyright © 2016 by Laura Brown.
Excerpt from *Smolder* copyright © 2016 by Karen Erickson.

EPub Edition July 2016 ISBN: 9780062497741
Print Edition ISBN: 9780062497819

To Trey.
Having you, loving you, and raising you
have enriched me in ways I'll never be able to quantify.

Chapter One

CHELSEA GRANT COULDN'T tear her gaze away from the train wreck on the screen.

She followed press conferences like most Americans followed sports. The spectacle thrilled her, watching speakers deftly deflect questions, state narrow political positions, or, in rare instances, exhibit honest emotions. The message might be scripted but the reactions were pure reality. If executed well, a press conference could be as engaging and dynamic as any athletic game.

But watching this one was akin to lions in the amphitheater, not tight ends on the football field. Her throat ached, impacting her ability to swallow. She squinted, hoping the action would lessen her visual absorption of the man's public relations disaster.

He'd folded his arms across his chest, the gesture causing the gray cardigan he wore to pull across his broad shoulders. The collar of the black-and-blue plaid shirt he wore beneath it brushed the underside of his stubbled jaw.

When he'd first stepped onto the platform, she'd thought he was going for "geek chic." All he'd lacked were black square frames and a leather cross-body satchel. Now she understood he wasn't playing dress-up. These were his everyday clothes, and as such, they were inappropriate for a press conference, unless he was a lumberjack who'd just won the lottery.

Had someone advised him on how to handle a press conference? No, she didn't think so. *Any* coaching would have helped with his demeanor. The man stared straight ahead. He didn't look at the reporters seated before him. He didn't look into the lenses. He appeared to look over the cameras, like there was someplace else he'd rather be. His discomfort crossed the media plane, and her fingers twitched where they rested next to her iPad on the acrylic conference table.

A female reporter from an entertainment news cable channel raised her hand. "Mr. Bennett?"

The man turned his head, and his gaze zeroed in on the reporter and narrowed into a glare. Chelsea inhaled audibly and leaned forward in her chair. His eyes were thickly lashed and dark, although she couldn't determine their exact color. Brown? Black? He dropped his arms, and his long, slender fingers gripped the podium tightly. The bank of microphones jiggled and a loud piercing sound ripped through the air. He winced.

"How does it feel to be handed the title by David James?" the reporter asked, her voice louder as it came on the tail end of the noise feedback.

The camera zoomed in and caught his pinched expression. "Right now, I feel annoyed," he responded sharply.

"Annoyed? Aren't you honored?"

"Why should I be honored?"

"Because *People Magazine* has never named a non-actor as their sexiest man alive."

"An award based on facial characteristics is not an honor. Especially since I have no control over the symmetry of my features. The National Medal of Technology. The Faraday Medal. The granting of those awards would be a true honor."

The camera zoomed out, and hands holding phones with a smaller version of the man's frustrated image filled the screen. Flashes flickered on the periphery, and he rubbed his brow, like Aladdin begging the genie for the power to disappear.

"How does one celebrate being deemed the most desirable man on the planet?" another reporter asked.

"One doesn't." His lips tightened into a white slash on his face.

"Is there a secret scientific formula for dating Victoria's Secret models? Didn't you used to be engaged to one?" A male reporter exchanged knowing looks with the colleagues around him. A smattering of chuckles followed his question.

"Didn't she leave you for another model six weeks before the wedding?"

"So you're single? Who's your type?"

"What's your perfect first date?"

"Can you create a sexbot?"

Questions pelted the poor man. The reporters had found his weakness: his inability or unwillingness to play the game. Now they would try to get a sound bite for their story teaser or a quote to increase their site's click-through rate. The man drove his fingers through his black hair, a move so quick and natural she knew it was a gesture he repeated often. That, and not hair putty, probably explained the spikiness of the dark strands that were longer on the top, shorter on the sides.

"This has nothing to do with my project," he snapped, then scowled at someone off-camera.

Chelsea glanced heavenward, grateful she wasn't the recipient of that withering look.

"Adam, what do you find sexy?"

The reporters didn't intend to give up easily. They circled, like shark to chum.

"This is why you called me away from my home? Do you have any idea what I'm working on? How revolutionary it is? You told me this was important. You neglected to mention I'd be subjected to idiotic questions by reporters from gossip rags." He continued talking to the person off-camera, raising his voice to be heard over the sudden uproar that resulted from his remarks. "I'm done."

He stormed off the stage, his exit allowing Chelsea to

see what the bank of microphones had hidden: an enticing bottom half, clad in well-worn jeans. In the wake of his exit, clicks and flashes were the only animation on the screen. A young man leapt onto the platform.

He was dressed in a sleek gray suit, his blond hair perfectly styled, his even, white teeth perfectly bleached. "Thank you all for coming today. Mr. Bennett had to hurry to an important meeting. We'll be taking no further questions." He smiled winningly and headed off, ignoring the torrent of questions.

Across from her, Howard Richter, her immediate supervisor, pressed a button. The image froze on the enormous screen and the lights came up. The blackout curtains whirred along their track, unveiling the unusually rare, smog-free, sun-drenched view of downtown Los Angeles, the famous Hollywood sign a name tag in the distance. Silence blanketed the room.

Chelsea shook her head slightly, as if awakening from a daydream, then stared at the two people who controlled her fate at Beecher & Stowe.

"That was a disaster," she said bluntly.

When the silence continued, Chelsea leaned back in the white leather chair, shifted on one hip, and crossed her legs, her beige Louboutin-clad foot dangling. "I'll admit it was entertaining, in a TMZ sort of way, but what does it have to do with my performance review?"

"What would you have done differently?" Rebecca Stowe asked, ignoring her question. The older woman, and named partner, was a legend in the PR community, being one of the first to understand and predict the impact digital marketing would have on both organizations and consumers as early as the late nineties.

"I would've told him why he was at the press conference, I would have prepped him for the type of questions to expect, and I would've guaranteed that he was dressed properly," she said, extending a finger to emphasize each point. "Publicity basics that eluded Peter Sonic from Kellerman." She waved her hand dismissively, thinking of the man who'd tried to regain control after his client had stormed off.

"What do you know about Adam Bennett?" Howard asked, shifting directions.

Chelsea shook her head. "Not much. That press conference was a year ago, right? I remember all the hype surrounding a non-celebrity on the cover. He's CEO of Computronix and a wunderkind in the tech community. He's known for creating both hardware and operating systems that I use on a daily basis."

"You heard him allude to something he was working on?" Howard asked. "Since the press conference, he's been holed up in his house in the Santa Cruz Mountains and no one has heard from him. Until two weeks ago."

"He contacted us?"

Not surprising. If the press conference was a sample of the type of representation he had with Kellerman, it was little wonder he was interested in Beecher & Stowe, one of the top PR firms in the country.

"No, I did." A voice from behind her.

Chelsea turned her attention to the fourth person in the room, a handsome, sophisticated, and stylishly dressed man, who exuded an air of authority that commanded respect. She'd immediately noticed him sitting at the back corner of the table when she'd first entered. She was sure she didn't know him, and the lack of an introduction compounded by the press conference debacle had worked to dismiss him from her mind.

"Chelsea, this is Michael Black, COO of Computronix," Rebecca said.

Chelsea held up her phone. "I'm a huge fan of your work."

He smiled, his light blue eyes dazzling. "Likewise."

She tilted her head to the side. "You know my work, Mr. Black?"

"Please, call me Mike," he invited. "And I do. What you pulled off with Ellis York was amazing. You took a girl heavy with talent but low on polish and turned her into a media darling in under two years. She wouldn't have won the Golden Globe without that transformation. And the fact that Leon Bush is now cohosting *Sports Talk Live* is due, in large part, to your handling of the whole cheating scandal last year."

Pride expanded in her chest. Receiving praise from a man with Mike's credentials and clout warmed her.

She loved her work. Controlling a person or product's image, dictating the way they were perceived—it was her reason for being. She believed she'd been groomed for it from a young age. Unlike many of her colleagues, she hadn't gotten into PR blinded by the glitz and glamour of three-hour lunches and red carpets. She'd been almost clinical in her decision, possessing that critical awareness of the burning need to have people view you differently while lacking the power to make that happen.

That insight kept her going when her entry-level salary was barely enough to cover her rent and student loans, when her workload was so heavy she barely had time for a three-*minute* lunch, and the only red carpet she walked was the one inside the Chinese restaurant around the corner from her apartment. Seven years later, that same insight was fueling her to the top of the industry.

"Thank you. Bush has oodles of charisma . . . and luck. As for Ellis, she deserves the credit for her success. She was willing to make the effort. Working with her was easy."

Mike sighed. "I wish I could say the same about Adam. He's going to be difficult."

She stiffened, her gaze swiveling between Mike, Rebecca, and Howard. "You want me to work with Adam Bennett?" Horror coated her words.

Only a rookie would find this assignment appealing. On the surface, it didn't seem like a hardship. The man *was* sexy. There was a roughness and edge to him many would find appealing, especially considering his intelligence. When she thought of computer geeks, the dangerous man she'd seen on the screen did not come to mind.

But his attire and mannerisms? The way he'd handled the reporters? Walking away from the press conference? This would be a nightmare of epic proportions.

As Executive Managing Director of the West Coast Entertainment division of Beecher & Stowe, Chelsea had earned the right to choose her own accounts, and she chose to work with clients who wanted her help, who were motivated but didn't possess the tools to achieve their goals. However, those who needed the help, but didn't want it? People like Adam Bennett? They were assigned to assistant account coordinators.

"Before we go any further . . ." Mike flipped open the cover on his tablet and tapped the screen. A few seconds later, he handed it to her. "This is a nondisclosure agreement. By signing it, you concede that what we talk about in this room, as well as any work you do for us, will be held in the strictest of confidence. You will not divulge it to anyone who is not working with you on this project."

Chelsea scanned it quickly before glancing up at her bosses.

"We've already signed it," Howard assured her.

Nodding, Chelsea wrote her name with the stylus he provided and handed the tablet back to Mike.

He glanced at it, satisfaction gleaming on his face, before continuing. "Adam has created a device that will change the face of personal computing. We'll be unveiling it at a special product launch on April eighteenth. Adam will be a major part of that launch and we need him to be ready. And that" —he pointed to the still image of an empty bank of microphones on the large screen— "is not acceptable."

She agreed. But this couldn't be *her* problem. She turned to Howard.

"I work in entertainment, not tech. I handle actors and athletes, people who understand the business. I've never handled 'real' people. Plus, that's only five weeks away. With the three new accounts I signed last quarter, there's no way I can fit this in."

"We'll reassign those projects to several of your account executives," Howard said. "They can take the lead for the next few months. Right now, Adam Bennett is your main priority. When you've worked your magic on him, you can catch up on the other accounts."

Chelsea's coffee and mid-morning snack seesawed in her stomach. They were pulling her off other high-level accounts?

Rebecca leaned her elbows on the table and steepled her fingers. "Chelsea, I know you came to this meeting expecting an offer of partnership."

Had she blown her chance by hesitating?

The pressure of unshed tears stung her eyes and panic clawed at her chest, threatening to erupt and decimate the mask of calm professionalism she always wore at work. She didn't want to make partner. She *needed* to make partner. There were times she'd thought she'd always be Dirty Diana's daughter. That her childhood, featuring an endless parade of her mother's men, bug-infested apartments, and a short stint in the foster care system, would twist around her ankle like a weed, impeding her efforts to rise above her formative years. Making partner in one of the top PR firms in the country would finally white-wash her past and confer her self-respect.

But if she didn't make partner at Beecher & Stowe, it was never going to happen. Since she'd already achieved upper management status, her options were to continue working for a company where there were no further opportunities for advancement, or leave and start over at another firm. A firm that would hire her for her contacts and skill and compensate her well, but would never offer her a partnership, assuming she was damaged goods because she didn't ascend the final rung on Beecher & Stowe's corporate ladder. Neither prospect came close to assuaging the remembered pangs of hunger that constantly reminded her of her upbringing.

"I've worked hard and paid my dues. I'm the youngest executive manager ever. In the past eighteen months, I've brought in business worth a quarter of a billion dollars." She jabbed her index finger into the conference table to emphasize her words.

"We are well aware of your contribution to Beecher & Stowe. When Mike approached us and requested the best for this account, we immediately thought of you. You've shown us your media relations savvy, marketing and business management skills, and a strong work ethic. Now we need to see your firm-first mind-set. Can you put the needs of the firm above your own? Of course you have the right to work on the clients you brought in. They're important to you. But Computronix is important to us."

A flush of giddiness tingled through her body, causing her hands to tremble. To cover, she pulled them down to her lap and twisted to stare at the abstract paintings on the wall, the only splash of color in the conference room's muted palate. She hadn't lost her opportunity. If she understood what Rebecca had intimated, Chelsea still had a shot.

"To be clear: If I make Adam Bennett presentable for the Computronix project launch in five weeks, you'll make me a partner?"

She held her breath.

Rebecca smiled. "How does Director of US Client Management sound?"

Chelsea exhaled. Like everything she'd been working for her entire adult life. She was so close the honeyed scent of success teased her nostrils. There was no way she would let an obnoxious tech geek prevent her from fulfilling her ambition. "You've got yourself a deal."

"Great." Howard beamed, offering her two thumbs-up.

"There's one small caveat," Mike cautioned.

It didn't matter. She'd do whatever it took to complete this assignment.

"Adam is a brilliant man, but he's . . . demanding. You're not the first professional we've hired to help him. He says we're trying to change him and he's refused to work with any of them."

That didn't sound good. "Isn't that why you need my help? Aren't you trying to change him?"

"No. We don't want to change Adam. I don't think anyone can. But we can't have him being surly and rude to reporters. Not in this day of instant uploads that go viral in minutes."

"So, what's the problem?"

"If he knows we sent you, he'll be resistant. You'll need to find another way to approach him."

This assignment had left strange in its rearview mirror and was hurtling toward bizarre.

She swung her widened gaze back to Howard and Rebecca. "Is that necessary?" she asked. "You're adding an element of espionage to an already difficult task."

A large part of her success at her job was her insistence on brutal honesty with her clients, a practice she'd embraced after emerging from a childhood of lies generated by her mother. She may spin stories for the media, but she always delivered the unvarnished truth to her clients. Always. She was often the only person who did.

Mike's lips tightened. "Trust me, we've run out of other options."

"We've always had faith in your abilities," Rebecca said. "This wouldn't be the time to make us question that belief."

My brother said your mother is a whore. She must be cheap, because you dress like shit.

Does your mother take food stamps? What about layaway?

She blinked away the taunts from her childhood. She'd do whatever it took to ensure she'd never end up poor, used, and disgraced like her mother.

"Consider it done."

AFTER THE ASSURANCES, handshakes and farewells, Chelsea took the elevator down to the twenty-third floor. Euphoria vied with frustration for ownership of her emotions. She didn't know if she should shimmy her shoulders and shake her hips in celebration of the opportunity before her or allow the awareness of another obstacle to hurdle to suffocate the burgeoning lightness in her limbs. When a triumphant smile snuck past her uncertainty to curve her lips, it immediately turned bitter upon reaching the air.

Director of US Client Management.

Partner in one of the top PR firms in the country.

A high six-figure salary and office suite on the top floor.

It would be vindication for all of her hard work and sacrifice. The missed vacations. The days she worked from home clocking a fever of one hundred and one degrees. Her anemic social life.

And all she had to do was make Adam Bennett presentable for the Computronix project launch in five weeks.

She slowed, her fingernails digging into her palms as she replayed the scene from the conference room over and over in her mind.

She should've gotten the advancement outright.

Is there any more she could've done to prove her suitability, her loyalty? Worked longer hours? Brought in more clients? Chosen more high-profile strategies?

No. She knew the work she'd done. She'd more than earned that promotion. But if she had to complete one more task to achieve her goal, she'd accomplish it with her usual skillful expertise. Then the partnership would be hers.

And her life would be perfect.

She detoured past the bright, airy loft space looking for her assistant. Jill's desk was unoccupied. Releasing an impatient breath, she perched on the edge of the rolling chair and opened her iPad. For most people, five weeks didn't allow enough time to tackle an assignment of this magnitude. But she'd spent her entire career proving that she wasn't most people. She'd maximize every moment she had, starting with research on both the man and his company.

And what a man he was. Image after image showcased a tall, strapping body, dark tousled hair and intense piercing eyes.

Heat coiled thick and heavy in her core. She shifted in the chair, pressing her thighs together, prolonging the sensation. The press conference may have been a fiasco, but *People Magazine* had gotten it right. Adam Bennett was the sexiest man she'd ever seen.

Which was all she could do. See him, look at him, and definitely don't touch. He was her ticket to the top echelon of PR professionals. He couldn't be more off-limits than if a neon *X* flickered on his well-defined chest.

Her gaze drifted to the time. Crap! She pushed to her feet and closed the tablet's cover with a snap. Hadn't she just complained about the lack of time she'd been granted for this assignment? She'd wasted precious minutes mooning over her client, and her assistant still hadn't appeared.

Where was she?

"Have you seen Jill?" she asked the person in the neighboring workstation.

"Not recently," the guy said, his eyes never leaving his computer screen.

Chelsea firmed her lips. She'd have to deal with her AWOL assistant later. She couldn't wait any longer. She had work to do. Her long legs briskly covered the distance to her office. By the time she was twisting the doorknob, she'd already formulated a preliminary plan of action.

"Congratulations!"

Adrenaline thundered through her body, causing her to stumble several steps back, rendering her unable to suppress the gasp that slid from her parted lips. She pressed a hand to her silk-covered chest and glared at the two women who stood next to her desk, their bright smiles already fading into frowns.

"I was just at your desk waiting for you," she said to the blonde woman on the left, letting her hand drift back to her side. She struggled to regain her composure. "Can you give us a few minutes? Then I'll need you back with your iPad."

Jill's gaze softened, but she straightened, nodded, and headed to the door. As she passed, she gently squeezed Chelsea's arm, before exiting the office, quietly closing the door behind her.

Chelsea turned to the other occupant. "Back so soon? You were here two days ago. I hope you're in a better mood this time."

India Shaw stared after Jill, a frown marring her perfect, tawny complexion. "Well, hello to you, too," she said, finally turning to face Chelsea. "I *was* here to celebrate your promotion by letting you take me to lunch, but there's no way we can make it to Primo's and back in 'a few' minutes."

She pressed a quick kiss to Chelsea's cheek and glided over to the Belgian linen sofa on the opposite wall. She sank down, slipped off her beaded flats and pulled her legs up under her.

Despite the confusing tangle of emotions Chelsea had experienced over the past hour, another one—deep affection—almost overwhelmed her as she watched her foster sister move with a natural fluidity she'd always envied. Years ago, she and Indi had been ships passing through the foster care system. For eight months they'd shared a room at a group home before Chelsea's mother had convinced someone—probably a man—that she'd gotten her act together and had reclaimed her daughter. Chelsea had been eager to leave, preferring to cope with a situation she could control versus one she couldn't, but she'd also been determined to stay in touch with Indi. Something about the younger girl had been like looking at a fun-house mirror image of herself.

Sitting in her own chair, Chelsea kneaded her brow and shook her head. "I'm supposed to celebrate *my* promotion by taking *you* to lunch?"

Indi held her hands up, palms facing outward. "I'm more than happy to treat. Since I'm saving up for my trip to Key West, I can probably afford the tacos from that food truck parked a few blocks away—"

Chelsea laughed. "All right, I get it."

"It's your celebration. I thought you'd rather go to your favorite place."

"That's very . . . noble of you, but it doesn't matter. I didn't get the promotion."

Indi swayed forward, her long Senegalese twists brushing against her face. "Are you joking?"

Heat swarmed Chelsea's cheeks and nape, prickling barbs of shame and frustration. "Do I look like I'm performing a set at the Laugh Factory?" As her sharp tone pierced the air, she closed her eyes and exhaled. "I'm sorry."

"You don't need to apologize." Indi jabbed her thumb over her shoulder. "Those idiots do. If they can't see that you'd make the best partner their stupid company has ever seen—"

"I wasn't denied the promotion," Chelsea said, her heart expanding at Indi's support. "It was . . . postponed."

"Oh. That's not bad news. What do you have to do to expedite the offer?"

Just take a challenging, exacting tech executive and make him presentable for a project launch in five weeks without telling him who she worked for and what she was doing.

She waved a nonchalant hand. "Handle a presentation for a very important client."

"Is that all?" Indi sagged against the sofa's back cushions and rolled her eyes heavenward: "Shit, Chels, you had me worried for a second. You've got this."

She did have it. "Thanks. I'll need to get started on this immediately, which means I'll probably be late getting home tonight and"—she grimaced—"we may have to postpone our trip to Napa Valley."

"Say no more." Indi unfolded gracefully from her lotus position and slid back into her shoes. "Actually, this presentation is coming at a good time. I got a call from a girl I went to college with. She lives in South Carolina."

Chelsea nodded, knowing what was coming before her sister uttered the words: Indi was pulling up her anchors and setting sail for another port.

And suddenly, the events of the past couple of weeks made sense. Indi's disproportionate outburst to her comment about rinsing her coffee cup before putting it in the dishwasher. Being awakened by noise at 3 a.m. and finding Indi mindlessly roaming the condo. Her sister's frequent visits to the office, "for lunch." All signs she'd come to recognize over the years that meant Indi was ready to roll.

Chelsea rested her elbows on the desk as stinging pressure began to build behind her eyes. "What happened to Key West?"

Indi shrugged. "I'll get there, by way of Charleston."

"When are you leaving?"

"That's what I was saying. At first I'd planned to stay another week. But now . . . I'll probably leave in the next couple of days."

"You don't have to rush—"

"I'm not. This works out for both of us." Indi came around the desk and pulled her into a hug. "I love you, Chels."

Chelsea held on to the other woman, inhaling her familiar vanilla scent. After another long moment, she extracted herself, dashing away the tears she'd failed to contain.

"You just love my Egyptian cotton sheets, stocked fridge and spa quality shower."

"Those things are nice, especially that showerhead." Indi exhaled and her gaze wandered upward.

"Ewww!" Chelsea slapped her arm. "I don't want to hear about that! Now I'll have to redo the entire bathroom."

Indi's light brown eyes widened. "Don't. Jeremy would think it was all his fault."

"Jeremy? Who's Jere— You named my shower head?"

"Of course!" She looked shocked. "I certainly hope you take the time to find out the name of your orgasmgivers."

"Ugh. Now I'm definitely getting rid of it."

Indi sobered. "Seriously, you know I'm allergic to staying in one place for too long. But it wouldn't matter if you lived in a shack. *You* are my home."

Chelsea wrapped an arm around Indi's shoulders. "I love you, too. And you always have a place with me. Don't ever forget that."

"I won't." She reached down and grabbed a small colorful bag covered in fringe. "Since you have your hands full here I'm going to head back to the condo and start packing."

"Text me later, okay?"

"Of course."

"And I'm calling the plumber as soon as you leave."

They hugged once more and Chelsea watched the closest thing she had to family walk away from her.

Again.

She gathered her hair back from her face, lifted the mass off her neck, and let the curls flow through her fingers. She understood Indi's wanderlust and missed her when she was gone. Chelsea knew she should wish for her to settle down close by, but . . .

A part of her was relieved that Indi was gone most of the year.

Chelsea swallowed past the thickness that developed in the back of her throat. How could she even think such a traitorous thought? And yet, having Indi close was exhausting. Always being on her best behavior. Looking the part, dressing the part, acting the part. The consummate professional woman. Trying to live up to the image that Indi had of her, expected of her, was tough.

She walked over to the window that afforded her a clear view of downtown. With its tall skyscrapers in the forefront and the mountains in the background, the city sat before her like a topographical tiara. Incredible weather, great beaches, world-class art, and the entertainment industry made LA one of the most powerful cities in the world. And she was thriving here. Her. Chelsea Grant. A woman who came from no money and even less pedigree. If she was truly making it here, did that mean she'd finally become the successful woman everyone believed her to be?

Or had she become really proficient at faking it?

A brief knock on her door preceded the appearance of Jill's round face. "I saw India getting on the elevator. You're not going to lunch?"

"No." Chelsea recalled her poise, headed back to her desk and sat down. Grabbing her iPad, she entered her password and frowned at the list already starting to read like a document that belonged in the National Archives. "I need you to make copies of our files on Portia Altman, Malcolm Murdoch, and the Glover Foundation."

Jill's brow lowered and her head flinched back slightly. "The three accounts you just brought in?"

"Yes. Email them to Stan, Fabiola, and Andrea, respectively."

"We've barely begun strategizing for them," Jill argued, closing the door behind her. "Is this a new approach? Are you planning on bringing in the other departments earlier than usual?"

"Plans?" She laughed, then wrinkled her nose at the

unpleasant sound. "I've recently discovered someone in authority laughs when I dare to make plans."

Jill crossed her arms. "What's going on? You were scheduled to meet with Mrs. Stowe for your performance review. I understand that your promotion means you have to be mindful of more eyes on you, but no reasonable person could possibly begrudge you showing a little excitement or taking the afternoon off to have a celebratory lunch with your sister." She hesitated. "Unless . . ."

Chelsea's chest tightened but she fought through it. This wasn't over. She still had a chance. She shrugged.

"You didn't make partner?" Jill asked in a tone that suggested the notion was absurd. "Are they crazy? You're the best publicity director in this company, not to mention the best boss. What happened?"

Although it was necessary, she hated re-sharing the tale. "They didn't deny me the partnership. They conditioned it upon my successful handling and completion of a high-profile project."

Jill sat in one of the two chintz-covered chairs facing the desk. "What project?"

Chelsea filled her assistant in on the assignment.

"You have the best job in the world," Jill screeched, her index finger flying high with emphasis. "You handle celebrities and athletes, and now you get to work with Adam Bennett. Sexiest Man Alive Adam Bennett." She leaned back, fanning herself.

He *was* hot, she thought, agreeing with Jill's assessment. Still . . .

"If you'd seen that *People Magazine* press conference,

you wouldn't be so excited to find out the fate of my partnership is tied to him."

Jill winced. "That bad? So it'll be a little challenging. It's nothing you can't manage. This guy is dark, sexy, and brilliant. You've got this."

Did Jill and Indi sip from the same optimistic cup?

"But I hate that I can't be straightforward in my approach. You know how I feel about honesty with my clients."

"It's not ideal," Jill said, nodding.

"That's an understatement. Not only do I have to come up with a kick-ass PR plan, I have to organize an undercover sting, too."

"You want to make the big bucks? With great power comes great responsibility."

"Isn't that a quote from Spider-Man?"

"It's still relevant."

She smiled, a feeling of competence ushering out her earlier negativity. The fact that she had the support of such wonderful people, like Indi, Jill, and even Mrs. Stowe, was a soothing balm to her self-doubt. She'd become the youngest executive manager ever through hard work and dedication. Her bosses had given her this assignment because they had faith in her abilities. She'd never let anything stand in the way of achieving her goals and she wouldn't start now.

"Thank you," Chelsea said. "You've had my back since my first day at Beecher & Stowe, and I couldn't do what I do without your support. Let's get to work on those files right away."

Jill clasped her hands together. "Whatever you need. I'm counting on you to get us to the top floor where your office suite awaits and I'll graduate to a space where walls go from the floor to the ceiling."

Chelsea didn't try to repress her grin. "You're ready to vacate your cubicle, aren't you?"

"You have no idea." Jill stood and moved to the door. "Do you want me to email the client files before or after I pull together a packet on Adam Bennett?"

As much as she valued her assistant, this task was too important to trust to anyone else.

"You take care of the client files. I'll handle Mr. Bennett personally."

Chapter Three

WHO IS YOUR *celebrity crush?*

Which shows do you DVR?

What is your favorite video game?

What is your favorite pizza topping?

Boxers or briefs?

These were the questions they wanted him to answer?

Adam Bennett scowled and thrust his fingers through his hair. His company's promotions liaison had been emailing him all week, requesting he answer five questions for a brief spotlight in a magazine. When he'd finally opened the message today, he'd expected the usual rote of queries from magazines like *CODE*, *Macro User Daily*, or *Engineering Today*, the only magazines that mattered in his field.

Instead, he'd gotten five questions from CGR, a magazine he'd thought discontinued years ago. A couple of keystrokes later, he'd learned CGR didn't stand for

Computer Graphics Review as he'd originally thought. It stood for *Celebrity Gossip Rave*, and their home page was a dizzying collage of bright colors, objectively aesthetic people, and headlines that touted "Cutest Baby Bump," "Sexiest Couple," and "Stars: They Do What We Do!" Thus, the absurd questions weren't that surprising.

He pressed a button on his keyboard and his central monitor blacked out. Five seconds later, a woman's image appeared. The petite redhead smiled, revealing the piercing beneath her bottom lip.

That had to be aggravating.

"Hey, Mr. Bennett."

"Anya, hay is for horses." He pointed to the forty-six-inch monitor on his right. "Now, what does any of this have to do with the HPC's product launch?"

"Any of what, sir?"

He sighed. "The questions you sent me. For *CGR* magazine."

There weren't enough hours in the day for all he needed to accomplish. Therefore, what time he had was valuable and he despised wasting it. He crossed his arms.

Anya's gaze dropped and her jaw sagged slightly. She licked her lip and the metal stud jiggled.

After three seconds he cleared his throat, impatient for her response.

"Oh." She jerked and lifted her gaze back to his face, a blush spreading across her cheeks. "The interview. It's about getting your face out there."

"Getting my face out where? It's fine where it is."

She shook her head. "Promotions. The more oppor-

tunities people have to see your face and name, the more
we increase your social quotient, which will increase consumers' perceptions about your authority."

"Oh." He considered her response. "Are you telling
me that my inclusion in a checkout line gossip rag will
compel people into believing my credentials as a computer scientist, engineer, and chief technology officer,
founder, and CEO of Computronix?"

Her smile was slightly askew. "That's the plan."

"That's not my plan. This strategy was unsuccessful
the last time and I refuse to participate again. I will not
whore myself out to the lowest common denominator. I
will be judged by my work, not for answering inane questions."

Her eyes widened. "Okaaay. Speaking of questions,
I've scheduled a podcast interview with—"

"I can't spare the time."

Anya rubbed the back of her neck. "Mr. Bennett, I'm
trying to do my job."

So was he. "Try harder."

He disconnected the video and scrubbed a hand over
his face.

He was a genius. He had an IQ of 176. He'd graduated
from Stanford University with a BS in Computer Science,
an MS in Hardware Design and Software Theory, and an
MBA. He wrote his first program at the age of fourteen,
started his first company when he was twenty, and made
his first million two years later. Some of his papers had
been presented at conferences, and he'd even advised the
President of the United States.

But when navigating daily, basic social interactions with people, he was reduced to a condition with which he wasn't familiar.

Confusion.

If only dealing with people was as simple as dealing with computers. Computers were logical, methodical, and unambiguous. You input a prompt, it delivered a response. You request a function, it carried out your command. No judgment. No miscommunication.

People were walking, organic structures of judgment. The way he spoke. What he neglected to do. Who he failed to be. They took it all in and judged him as different. And no one wanted different. No one stayed for different. No one loved different.

His mother had taught him that.

Which was why he dealt with them—people—as infrequently as possible.

It had taken him a long time to find a circle of people he could trust. People who accepted him, who said what they meant and didn't couch every word in nuance and double-talk. People who were reliable. He'd made mistakes along the way. Most recent and notably, Birgitta. She'd cost him a year's worth of work, but had reiterated his mother's infinitely more valuable lesson. One he'd almost been lulled into forgetting. Personal involvement with anyone, particularly women, had to be limited. He had no difficulties with casual encounters. Indeed, they were very beneficial. They sated his active libido while boosting his immune system and easing stress. But he'd never again risk another emotionally intimate relationship with a woman.

Enough introspection. He needed to fix the glitch in the search function and hand it off to his senior level programmers by the end of the week. His stomach grumbled and he frowned, glancing at the clock in the top right-hand corner of his center screen. Coding had kept him occupied for hours and he'd missed lunch. Again. Rolling back from his workstation, he stood, stretched, and headed to the kitchen to assuage his hunger.

He glanced through the glass-fronted door of his freezer and counted the white boxes. Only eight more meals. It was time to order another month's supply of food. When he was working on a project, he blocked out everything around him and got lost in the process. Having prepared meals on hand ensured that he had nutritious food he could consume in as little time as possible. The fare was also delicious, thanks to a hefty investment in his friend's popular San Francisco restaurant. He chose the meal he wanted and popped it into the microwave.

As the smells of asiago chicken and pasta filled the air, his cell phone rang. He checked the caller ID and answered the call.

"Mike," he said, speaking to his chief operating officer and one of the few people in his trusted inner circle.

"Adam, you've got to stop terrorizing the staff."

He rested his hip against the island's concrete countertop. "I didn't threaten or intimidate any member of the staff."

Where had Mike gotten that erroneous information?

"Anya from promotions said you refused to cooperate with her regarding a magazine interview."

"Declining to participate in an interview is all that's necessary to label someone as a terrorist in a post–9/11 America?"

"So I exaggerated a little."

"And that exaggeration cost us valuable seconds as we strove for clarity."

The microwave beeped. Setting the phone on the countertop and placing it in speaker mode, he retrieved his meal and a fork and stood looking out the large windows that usually afforded him a stunning view of the Santa Cruz Mountains. Currently, the thick sheet of rain that had doused the mountains for the past eight days obscured his view.

"Dammit, Adam—"

"Is this about those pointless questions?" He cut Mike off, needing to get to the reason behind his call.

"We discussed this," Mike said. "Your invention won't just change the computer industry, it's going to change the world. Everyone, in every walk of life, will be using your device, even the readers of that gossip magazine. You need to cooperate. Please. You know I hate getting these calls."

He took another bite and wondered, for the seventy-third time, why he hadn't kept his invention to himself. He didn't need the money. Most people used the hardware and operating systems his company had created on a daily basis. He'd made more than enough money to keep a small country running for the next fifty years.

But the technology industry was unforgiving. It had no patience for people who rested on their laurels, and even less for those who'd made a mistake. Those who wanted to stay at the top had to stay one step ahead of the competition, which was no longer confined to other computing firms. It had grown to include the possibility of every kid gifted with his or her first computer. The HPC would advance him several miles. The device he'd created would change personal computing the same way the iPod changed the way people listened to music. With it, he'd regain his reputation and his spot among the elite of Silicon Valley. He'd lost his foothold once. Never again.

"I don't understand the necessity of my inclusion in this launch, since I've never participated before."

"Times have changed since our last rollout. Like it or not, creators are the new celebrities. Jeff Bezos and Amazon, Mark Zuckerberg and Facebook, Adam Bennett and the HPC." Silence. "You wouldn't have to worry about this if you'd let me hire a PR firm to handle the product launch," Mike said.

Adam's body went rigid and his response was immediate. "No."

"It would free up your time. They'd take care of the interviews and promotions leading up to the launch and you could finish getting the device ready."

"No."

"You need help. Everything is riding on the launch and at your last press conference, you managed to alienate most of the people in attendance."

"So you recall the last time we utilized a PR agency? It was a failure. That publicist wanted acclaim for getting me in *People Magazine*, not based on my work, but on my physical features. And the press conference? I would consider that a living nightmare." He took another bite of his food and swallowed. "Besides, that wasn't an actual press conference. Those reporters—and I use the term sardonically—cover celebrities and entertainment. They were not the real press."

"They are for our purposes. A large portion of our advertising involves celebrities using our devices and television shows and movies spotlighting them front and center. The same people who were at that press conference, and more, will be at the launch."

Adam walked back to the kitchen area and set his container on the counter, his appetite deserting him. He'd promised Mike he'd do the launch, but he'd do it on his own and without the assistance of a person who was paid to convince people of a product's benefit, whether it was true or not.

"I will not deal with people who lie for a living."

"Fuck, Adam! It's not just about you. The company's resources are involved. This is the right thing to do. I need you to trust me."

The expletive, increased volume of Mike's voice, and the velocity of his words indicated he was upset. Adam knew he and his friend were under a similar amount of stress. But he wouldn't place Mike's welfare above his own concern for what was best for the HPC.

"I won't work with a PR firm, but I'll do my best to help the promotions team. That's all I'll promise."

Mike mumbled something he couldn't hear. Then, "Your best is better than ninety-nine percent of the world's."

"True. How's production coming on the other devices we're unveiling?" Adam asked.

He listened to Mike's response and watched the rain fall from the sky. The clouds and trees blocked any light, and the tableau from his window was gloomy and overcast. To the right he noticed a break in the murkiness and turned to see headlights coming up his drive. Squinting, he moved closer to the window.

What the hell?

He wasn't expecting anyone. Who would be foolish enough to traverse this far up the mountain in this type of weather?

He interrupted Mike mid-sentence. "Did you send someone to my house?"

"Of course not. I'm not heartless enough to strand any of our employees up there with you. Why? Is someone there?"

Adam ignored the question and continued staring as a light-colored Mercedes-Benz SUV crested his circular driveway, careened wildly, then skidded to a stop. From his vantage point he couldn't see the driver of the car, but he waited, hoping the new arrival would realize their mistake, turn around, and head back down the mountain.

The rain was thicker now, a veil of gunmetal gray, obstructing his view of any fine details. All he could discern was the flickering glow of the headlights and the rhythmic motion of the windshield wipers. The car didn't move. Suddenly, thunder boomed from above and the sky was lit in glorious streaks of silver and gold.

"Holy shit, that's loud." Mike's voice shouted from the phone. "All we've got is rain."

The car door opened. Adam placed a palm flat against the window and watched the tan canopied figure race from the car toward his front door. And out of his view.

No, no, no.

He moved away from the window and grabbed his phone, hurrying to the staircase that led down to his foyer. "I've got to go."

"But we haven't settled the issue of the inter—"

Adam hung up and slid the phone into the back pocket of his jeans as the chimes of his doorbell pealed. He bounded down the steps and pulled open the heavy iron door. "You can't—"

The drenched figure on his doorstep raised the coat covering her head. Before an impression of her could be imprinted on his brain, the sky ignited with light and another boom of thunder echoed in the air. The woman squeaked and ran into his house, pushing past him in her haste to seek shelter.

Dread rolled through his stomach. This wasn't happening. She must be lost. The last thing he needed was to waste time on a directionally challenged trespasser. He would direct her to the turn she overshot and send her on her way. He closed the door and turned to find her back to him as she shook out the coat that had served as flimsy protection from the torrential rains. Drops of water fell to his cork tile floors and he idly wondered if the moisture would damage them.

Then all he saw were curls.

A thick mass of corkscrew curls flowed down her back. A back that dipped into a narrow waist that flared into curvy hips and a lush, round ass. Long legs were covered in black stretchy pants and black leather boots that rose above her knees. Heat inundated his body and his hands tingled, fingers to palm. He was beset by a sudden urge to pull her back against him, wrap his fist in her hair, and bury his nose in those soft-looking spirals.

When she finally twisted to face him, his breath fled the prison of his being, leaving him light-headed, similar to his plight after Thomas Brown punched him in the stomach in the eighth grade. Her skin was the color of creamy milk chocolate, her eyes were dark and her long, thick lashes were spiky from the rain.

"I'm sorry for intruding," she said, "but I was trying to reach the Anderson house."

Her melodic and cadenced voice stroked him, eliciting visions of heavy breathing, tangled sheets and back-arching orgasms. He frowned. The haste and strength of his attraction unbalanced him, a state of being he despised.

He cleared his throat. "The Andersons moved."

The video game software developer had married an actress and relocated closer to LA, leaving his house empty most of the year. Every once in a while the developer rented it out to a writer or artist or anyone else seeking the isolation of being situated near the summit of the mountain. The area was too remote for the casual visitor.

Which was why Adam liked it.

"I know. I'll be staying there for a while."

She was his new neighbor? Dammit. He bemoaned the circumstances that didn't allow him adequate time to persuade her into his bed. If only he weren't busy with the HPC launch.

Maybe afterward . . .

"You passed the turnoff to his house two miles ago. It's difficult to spot if you don't know where you're going. Especially in this weather." He motioned to the steps. "If you want to come up, I'll draw you a map that will get you there in six minutes."

What was he doing? He hated visitors, especially uninvited ones. The interactions began pleasantly, but it wasn't long before misunderstanding, confusion, and awkward silences rendered the encounter uncomfortable. Still, he could be forgiven his change in policy. He'd never had an uninvited guest who looked like her. Hell, her body alone was enough to warrant a respite. But it would be a brief one, all in service to dispatch her and her distracting body.

Her appealingly symmetrical eyes surveyed the space where they stood, sweeping over the high ceilings, cool tones, and the windows that brought the outside in. She stretched on her toes and peered up the stairs before swinging her gaze back to him. She shivered slightly.

"I'm not a serial killer," he stated plainly. "Of course, if I were, I'd deny it in an effort to put you at ease before I struck. I have no way of proving what I say other than to tell you that I don't lie. But you don't know me. I could be lying now. If it will help you feel more comfortable, keep your phone close and stay a few feet away from me."

He stopped abruptly, annoyed by his own babbling. Unsure of what to do next, he started up the stairs, leaving her to decide whether to follow him or not. His phone rang, but he ignored it, grabbed paper off his desk, and began sketching a rudimentary map to lead her back to the Andersons' turnoff when he heard her audibly indrawn breath.

"That's an incredible setup. Are you a computer hacker?"

He glared at her. "No."

"It was a joke," she said in a low voice.

And so it begins. . .

He straightened and turned the sheet in her direction, demonstrating the route for her.

"Thank you so much. I really appreciate it." She held out a hand. "I'm Chelsea Grant."

Her mouth stretched into a bright smile that was a captivating contrast to her brown skin. She was a striking woman, all long limbs, sexy hair, and full, fuckable lips. He stared down at her fine-boned, outstretched hand before clasping it in his. Sensation shot up his arm.

"Adam." He nodded at their joined hands. "You're supposed to keep your distance. Aren't you afraid?"

"You don't seem dangerous to me." She dropped his hand and held up her phone. "But in case I'm wrong, I sent a text to my sister telling her where I am, so even if you kill me, you won't get away with it."

His lips twitched. He needed to get back to work, but he acknowledged an inclination to spend a few more minutes in this woman's company. When was the last time he'd chosen interaction with a woman over work?

Birgitta. The woman who'd lied to him and cheated on him. Because of his relationship with her, he'd lost his credibility in the technology industry.

And that was reason enough to send Chelsea Grant on her way.

He handed her the map. "Do you have any questions about the directions?"

"Not really. I think I saw the signpost you mentioned. I'll slow down and take my time." She laughed. "I hope no one comes up behind me as I'm driving five miles an hour."

He shook his head. "Not likely. I'm the last house up here. The Andersons' is next."

"Well, it was good to meet you. It's nice to know a neighbor in these parts."

Another crack split the air and the lights went out.

"Adam?" Her voice pitched an octave higher.

A moment later, he heard a click and the lights came back on. His cell phone rang.

Chelsea inhaled deeply and let it out, a tiny smile on her face. "I better hurry and get to the house before that happens again. And you'd better answer your phone."

Adam glanced out the window. Sporadic pockets of light dotted the mountainside. He looked up at the click of her boots scurrying across the floor.

"Wait! The power went out."

She raised her finely arched brows. "I know. I want to get my bags and supplies into the house before it happens again."

He shook his head. "You don't understand. You don't have any power."

She looked around. "You do."

"I have a generator. My work is important. I can't be without electricity." He motioned her over to the window and pointed to the lights. "Those people have generators. Not as powerful as mine, but sufficient for them to weather the storm." He pointed to the black void where the Anderson house was located. "That's where you're going. And I know for a fact he never put in a generator."

A loud buzzing sound emanated from his workstation and he shifted, focusing on the red-and-white letters that scrolled across the large computer monitor that occupied the left side of his desk.

"What's going on?" Chelsea asked. Her hands clutched the sleeve of his shirt.

His heart shifted in his chest. He stared at the convergence created by her touch, then up at her exquisite profile. "It's an alert from the county. Certain mountain roads are impassable due to fallen trees and mudslides. We've had a record amount of rain this week."

"Does that affect us?"

It sure as hell did.

He pointed to the screen. "The main road they mention where a large tree was downed? That's our road. It's one point two miles from here, down the mountain."

"It says due to the mudslides, crews can't get up the

mountain," she said, bending forward to peer at his monitor. "Good thing I brought some supplies with me. Looks like it might be a while before I can drive down into San Mateo."

"You don't have any power and—"

"You already said that." She clasped her hands together and pressed the knuckle of her index finger against her full lips. "Do you have a flashlight I can borrow? There must be candles at the house. I'll light a few to get me through the evening and in the morning, I can reassess my situation."

She had yet to fully comprehend their plight.

"The alert indicated the obstruction is approximately six miles from the peak of the mountain. My home is situated four point eight miles from the peak. I told you earlier the Anderson house is two miles from here."

"I'll be care—" Chelsea's mouth fell open. She rubbed her arms and stared out the window for a long moment. "So I can't get to the house?"

The beating of his heart was sluggish. "No."

"And I can't get back down the mountain?" she whispered.

He didn't bother to verbalize, just shook his head. His deductive reasoning was exemplary. He knew the only conclusion she could draw. He swallowed, trying to alleviate the ache in the back of his throat.

She turned her wide, beautiful eyes to him. "It looks like I'll need to impose upon your hospitality for a little while longer."

Chapter Four

THIS TURNED OUT better than Chelsea had anticipated. She'd planned to settle in for a couple of days and then drive to Adam Bennett's house for a quick introduction. She'd wanted him to see her face and know that she was staying at the Andersons'. She'd pulled a lot of strings to track down the owners and get their permission, believing lodging proximity would give her the means and opportunity to try to gain his trust.

But the whims of Mother Nature meant she didn't have to depend on the luxury of circumstance. She'd been unable to see much beyond her windshield, and the farther she'd gone, the worse the weather had gotten. Should she keep straight or turn around? Being unfamiliar with the road, she was afraid to do either. She'd been about to take her chances and head back to San Mateo when she'd spotted this gorgeous house built into the mountain. Turns out, it was occupied by the one man she wanted to see. And thanks to pouring rains, mudslides, and a downed tree, she was destined to be here for a while. She would make the most of the situation.

Thunder and lightning ripped through the sky, causing her to jump. For a brief moment, bolts of electricity illuminated the beauty of her remote surroundings. She frowned. It had taken over forty-five minutes to reach his house. What would possess a man to live miles up a mountain in isolation? The celestial light subsided and once again darkness shrouded the sky, turning the floor-to-ceiling windows into large mirrors that reflected her image and current accommodations.

And Adam.

She whirled around.

"Here," he said, his deep voice stilted. He set a thick stack of towels down on the counter. "To dry off. And for your hair. You're dripping water on the floor."

"Oh, sorry." She rearranged her face into a smile.

How about some manners? Yes, she'd intruded into his space, but she had no control over the weather or the power outage that stranded her in his house.

She looked at the towels and winced. They wouldn't work on her hair. Crap. Annoy him further or risk looking like a Chia Pet? Annoy him? Chia Pet?

"I hate to bother you, but do you have a cotton T-shirt I could use?"

His brows slammed together. "A T-shirt?"

"I know. You'd think a towel would work, but using it will turn my hair into a ball of frizz and it'll be—"

She broke off as he disappeared down a hallway on the far side of the room.

What the hell? Had no one taught him it was the height of rudeness to walk away in the middle of a conversation?

He returned almost immediately, carrying a white shirt that he handed to her.

She read the slogan on the front. " 'Talk Nerdy To Me'?"

He shrugged. "A gag gift. It's a garment I've never worn, so you can't ruin it."

He gave her another thorough once-over from his dark, intense eyes before heading back to his evil genius workstation on the other side of the large room.

Wow. It was just water. Did he think her color would rub off on his shirt and damage it? Cursing under her breath, she bent over at the waist and used the shirt to blot the moisture from her curls. She'd known this assignment wouldn't be easy. She now wondered if it would even be possible.

Maybe she'd been a bit unfair toward Peter Sonic, the blond PR agent who'd dealt with Adam during his press conference. She'd blamed a lot of Adam's behavior on poor preparation and lazy management. Now that she was up close and personal with the man, it was possible she'd been hasty in her condemnation.

Flipping her hair to reach the curls on the other side, she glanced at Adam from beneath her lashes. Holy cow, he was *not* what she'd been expecting. He stood with his arms braced in a wide V against his desk. The wheat-colored Henley clung to his broad shoulders, stretched across his wide, muscled back, and fell in folds to rest against a very nice ass covered in dark jeans. She swallowed the sudden moisture that flooded her mouth. If it were anyone else she'd assume he was a disciple of the "casually disheveled" trend, but she was certain Adam Bennett dressed for convenience, not fashion. Convenience or not, his body was . . . wow. The man was sexy as hell. Computer geeks were supposed to be reed thin, not built like elite athletes.

"Dammit!"

She jerked away from her musings, flustered to find her gaze still glued to his ass. She refocused farther up his body. One hand rubbed the back of his neck and the other was jammed on his hip. He radiated an intellectual intensity as staggering as the storm that raged outside. It stirred her, made her wonder what it would feel like to be the focus of that concentration. Did he bring that same fervor to every task he performed?

She shook her head, trying to erase her thoughts like a mental Etch A Sketch.

"Are you all right?" she asked, responding to the tension in his stance and the anger in his voice.

"What?" He stared at her over his shoulder, his brow furrowed, his lips parted. She had the feeling he'd dissolved into his work and had forgotten she was there.

She gestured in his direction. "Is everything okay?"

"No, I—" He sighed and pushed his hands through his hair.

She recognized the motion from the recording of the press conference. His hair was longer now, a little shaggy, and the dark strands slid through his fingers and settled in a thick glossy wave, the ends brushing the collar of his shirt. The action was done absentmindedly, but it had a deliberate effect on her, setting butterflies loose in her belly.

His cell phone rang again and he answered the call.

"Hello, Anya . . . Yes, I talked to Mike . . . No, I haven't completed the interview . . . Because it's ridiculous . . . Fine, it's your choice."

He tossed the phone on his desk, the expensive device sliding across the smooth surface and crashing onto the wood floor.

She cringed at the destructive sound even as adrenaline pumped through her at the words from his side of the conversation. He mentioned Mike—that had to be Mike Black from Computronix—and an interview.

Had she picked up a penny? Helped an old lady across the street? Cleared her aura with positive thinking? Chelsea didn't know what she'd done to warrant this sudden good luck, but she was incredibly thankful.

"Is that about work?" she asked, trying to disguise her excitement.

He turned and leaned back against his desk, crossing his arms over his chest. "Why would you reach that conclusion?"

She shrugged as if it didn't matter whether he answered her question or not . . . and as if she wasn't distracted by the material stretching over his biceps. "I heard you mention an interview and that's usually about work, so . . ."

She trailed off, hoping she hadn't jumped the gun

and ruined the advantage she'd managed to obtain. She needed this to work. She had three weeks. She wouldn't have time to regain any ground she'd lost.

He exhaled heavily and looked out the window. The sharp angles of his face stood out against the gray canvas of the thunderstorm.

"They want me to do an interview for a magazine, but the questions . . . They're asinine, juvenile, pointless." The volume of his voice increased with each word. Then his lips twisted and he shook his head. "I'm unsure how to proceed."

Those last words were issued haltingly, frustration at admitting a shortcoming staining every syllable. That sudden expression of his vulnerability caused an ache to lodge in the back of her throat and she wrestled with a moment of guilt.

Maybe she should approach him in a different way. She could send him an email offering her services or call him and request a meeting. Hell, she could try a little honesty and admit that Computronix hired her and trust that she could get him to understand the importance of the product launch, for him and his company.

Then she remembered what was at stake. Her partnership depended on a successful launch and her life's happiness depended on that partnership. Mike Black assured her that Adam wouldn't get through a presentation with the media, and after watching his last press conference, she knew they'd devour him alive. That wouldn't be good for him, Computronix, or her.

Even if she was slightly uncomfortable with the subterfuge, she needed to trust the opinion of the man who'd hired her. Mike Black knew Adam and seemed to believe a ruse was their only option. She'd follow the instructions of the man who had years of history with Adam versus her scant ten minutes. And when it was finally revealed, she was confident he'd understand they'd done what they thought was best.

Hoping she'd made the right decision, she said, "Maybe I can help you."

"How?"

"I can tell you how to answer the questions."

He narrowed his dark eyes. "Why would you assist me?"

"Because you're helping me. You're giving me a dry place to wait out the storm." She smiled. "And you haven't murdered me. Please. This is a way I can repay you."

She worked hard not to shift from one foot to the other while he stared at her. Why did he make her feel as if he could see straight through her? He didn't look at her—he studied her, like she was a frustrating puzzle he couldn't solve.

Finally, he nodded once and waved her over to his impressive workstation. She'd never seen anything like it in real life, only on TV or in the movies. His desk was shaped like a horseshoe, surrounded on all three sides with monitors the size of large televisions. Centered on a separate, higher back tier, were three smaller monitors like the ones that typically came with computers. She didn't see any system units, so she assumed those must be hidden behind the wooden cabinet doors beneath the desk.

Adam placed his hand on the leather chair and pulled it back. The coasters scraped against the floor. "Have a seat."

She did. The buttery soft material hugged her body, while the structure forced her spine to straighten and provided a supportive frame for her lower back.

She sighed in pleasure. "This is the most comfortable chair I've ever sat in."

"It's my design. There are days when I spend twenty hours in that chair."

"You designed your own chair?"

"I'm an engineer. I created the prototypes for most of Computronix's earliest products."

His scent enveloped her and she inhaled deeply, her lashes fluttering as she breathed him in. God, he smelled amazing. Clean, fresh, and with an earthiness that recalled the bracing air of the mountains. He leaned across her and his long, elegant fingers flew over the sleek, wireless keyboard, mastery showing in even this simple task.

When she turned her head, her eyes were level with his ear. Silky strands of dark hair feathered the ridge and drew her attention to the tiny dark mole on its shell. A hidden treasure one could only find if he let them into his personal space.

He turned toward her. "These are the quest—" He broke off abruptly.

Their faces were inches apart.

The air in the room stilled. Her glance lowered to his mouth. If she leaned forward, about four inches, their lips would touch. Chelsea looked up and her gaze slammed into his. She was surprised to see his eyes weren't black or brown, but a deep shade of midnight blue. For several blazingly hot seconds they bored into hers, demanding her confidences, holding on to his own, before his thick lashes swept down, both granting her a reprieve and prematurely ending her attempt to see what made him tick. He stood and moved several steps away from her. The air flowed again and she took a deep breath.

"The questions," he said, pointing to the screen. His tone was gruff, the words having survived the treacherous journey past his clenched, bearded jaw.

His obvious agitation gave her the push she needed to get back on track. Her job required her to get close to him, but not *that* close. In fact, an involvement with this man couldn't happen at a worse time. She was one project away from being made a partner and then everything she'd ever worked for would be within her grasp. As long as she kept her eyes on that goal—and off his ass—it would be a win-win for everyone.

She read the questions on the screen. "Celebrity crush? Favorite video game?"

"It has no bearing on understanding the HPC. Am I supposed to believe that my choice in undergarments will determine whether or not someone will purchase the device? 'Oh, he wears briefs, the HPC is not for me.'" He ended with a shockingly funny falsetto and she laughed.

He'd mentioned the HPC, and thanks to the file Mike provided she knew what it was. But a typical person who'd stumbled into this situation wouldn't have the first clue.

"What's an HPC?" she asked, tilting her head to the side.

Did she sound as fake as she felt?

He gave her another of those piercing, soul-searching looks, and again she felt like he could see all of her secrets—not just the ones related to him and this assignment, but the ones in her life, from her past.

"You ask a lot of questions about my work."

Her stomach churned. "You said something I didn't understand. I was asking for clarification." She whirled around in the chair and stood. "I didn't mean to pry. I only wanted to help."

She knew the question she'd asked was a valid one. *Not* asking would've been suspicious. But she'd made the wrong call.

Dammit.

He stood in front of her, halting her progress. "I shouldn't have mentioned the specifics of the device. That's classified information."

The tension in her belly unfurled. "No problem. Do you still want me to look at those questions for you?"

"Yes."

She sat back down in the chair, sighing once again when it curved to her body, and spun to face the monitor. She'd recognized the questions from a popular magazine's *Five Things I Like About You* section, which queried various celebrities. She understood why Adam thought the questions were irrelevant for scientists and engineers. But technology had gone mainstream. Every person used a computer and the HPC he'd designed would affect the way all computers were used in the future. His audience wasn't other engineers. His customer was every person who'd ever owned a computer.

"You're right. Your peers are probably not interested in learning your favorite pizza topping—"

"Exactly," he interrupted, triumph in his voice.

"But they won't be reading this article. You know who will? The everyday consumer who'll make you a success. It's the difference between the Linux operating system and the iPod. One used and respected by people in the industry, the other a pop-culture phenomenon that not only changed the way we listened to music, but changed the way we consumed music as a product.

"Now, I don't know what you've created," she hedged, when he subjected her to that laser-eyed stare again, "but if you're being asked to do this interview, it means the company is trying a mass market approach. And that means appealing to people outside of your usual sphere."

She was fascinated by the way he considered her opinion. She thought she could see the rotors and gears in his brain sifting through the options.

"How do you know who my peers are?"

Her breath caught. Damn, this was hard. "I don't. But anyone with this setup, and who talks the way you do, must work in an industry with intelligent people. And those people tend to read industry journals, not celebrity magazines." Hopefully, that appeased any suspicions he had . . .

Finally, he nodded. "No one, nothing, Unmapped, pepperoni and banana peppers, and combo."

Chelsea gaped at him. He'd delivered the information so smoothly that it took a moment to realize he'd responded to the questions. She glanced at the monitor and matched each answer he'd given to its proper mate.

"Okay, that's a start."

"Start? I'm done."

"Technically, you answered the questions, but your replies are basic and, well, boring. You've got to elaborate, spice it up."

"I told you, I don't lie, Chelsea."

Did she imagine the extra grimness in his voice? A tingle of apprehension skittered down her spine and she shook off the feeling.

"You're not lying. You're selling yourself to your future customers. Think of an apple. Apples are good for you. They're healthy. But that's not enough for people to buy them. We make them look appetizing. We emphasize the taste—tart or sweet—and the texture—soft or crisp—all to make the apple more appealing. And in the end, it's worth it because we've sold an apple and we know the person who bought it will be healthy."

"You're presuming it's not enough to tell people that apples are healthy. That's pessimistic."

"Not pessimistic. Realistic. I can help you with this. Let's take each question one at a time. You don't have a celebrity crush?"

"No."

"I find that hard to believe. Come on, who do you find attractive?"

"This isn't the appropriate time to answer that question."

His blazing stare gleamed down on her, causing her nipples to tighten against her bra.

It wasn't?

No! What was wrong with her? Had her body declared mutiny against her brain's rationality and decided to throw its lot in with the nearest source of testosterone? Sure, she hadn't been laid in a while—*In over eight months!* her body screamed—but she'd been around numerous men during that time and her body had never rebelled like an overprivileged teenager. Why was she reacting *this* way to *this* man?

She swallowed thickly and looked away from his heated gaze, crossing her arms over her chest. "We can come back to that one. What about question number two? You don't watch television?"

"Of course I do."

"You don't record shows?"

"I work extensively. I don't watch anything in real time."

"Then why did you answer 'none' to the question of which shows you DVR?"

"Because I don't use a digital video recorder. I can watch whatever I want online and on demand."

She drummed her fingers on the desk. "You don't have to be so specific. All they want to know is your favorite show on TV."

He shrugged. "Then that's the question they should ask."

"They did," she cried, throwing her hands in the air. They were on question number two. Two! Was he being difficult on purpose? She took a deep breath and exhaled. "Moving on, why do you like the video game 'Unmapped?' "

"The graphic set pieces are innovatively atmospheric and the game allows its players to make logical and reasoned decisions without penalizing the fun of the play."

"That's a great response," she said, pleased he could compose a compound answer. She checked the monitor. "What do you mean by 'combo?' "

"Boxer briefs."

Blood rushed to her cheeks, but she knew her complexion would hide the evidence of her embarrassment. This was ridiculous. She was a grown woman. She'd seen her share of men in their undies and less, but something about imagining Adam in the sexy form-fitting underwear, the rippled plane of his muscled abs, the fabric molded to his ass and thighs, the waistband teasing the package beneath . . .

She needed to chill out or she'd never make it through the questionnaire without her pelvic region bursting into flames.

Ten minutes later, Chelsea sat back in the chair, relieved that her body had settled down and pleased with the progress they'd made. She'd helped him craft solid responses to the other four questions and he returned the interview to the person who'd requested it. Despite their shaky start, the end result was well done. Their answers were intelligent, insightful, and funny. Maybe this *could* work out.

"What is your profession?"

His question snapped her out of her reverie. "Excuse me?"

"Your use of the terms 'consumer' and 'mass market approach' sound like words marketing strategists use. Are you in that field?"

What should she do? Admit her professional knowledge or play it off?

"I work in the entertainment field."

Which was the truth, just not the entire truth. If she had to prevaricate, the safest course of action was to stick as close to the truth as possible. She waited, not sure if he would buy her explanation or detect her evasion and call her and Mike on what they'd tried to do.

"You're not an actress, are you?"

She laughed. "God, no."

Those gears in his brain commenced rotating, but were interrupted by the ringing of his cell phone. He picked it up off the floor, wiped the screen against his jean-clad thigh, and answered it.

"Yes, Anya . . . I know . . . You're pleased with the outcome? Good."

He disconnected the call. "That was the media liaison. She's never sounded that . . . content while talking to me on the phone. You must be good at your job."

He smiled and the gesture knocked the wind out of her body. With his keen intellect and devastating good looks, he was already hard to resist, but add that satisfied grin, and it was a lethal combination. The elation didn't lessen his sexiness; it made him approachable. Which made him exceedingly more attractive. It suddenly occurred to her that Adam Bennett could be detrimental to her emotional well-being.

She *was* good at her job and she deserved that promotion. She'd do whatever it took to complete this assignment and claim her partnership and the better life it represented. With that bolster to her resolve, she was able to ignore the part of her that screamed she should overlook the storm, get in her car, and haul ass back down the mountain and away from the provocative genius.

Chapter Five

WHAT HAD HE been thinking?

That question summed up his dilemma. His brain hadn't been able to perform its primary function because a portion of his blood had been diverted to another area. He'd awakened in the middle of the night, with a raging hard-on, aware that his house seemed different. Though two thousand square feet separated their bedrooms, his body hummed and burned as if Chelsea were lying next to him. Under him. On top of him.

There was another person sharing his space. And not just any person. A gorgeous woman with curves he wanted to analyze and curls he wanted to explore. How would she look sprawled across his bed? Would her skin feel as dewy soft as it looked? Would he relish the flavor of her on his tongue? His mind zipped through the endless possibilities that began with him stripping her naked and ended with him buried deep inside of her.

He'd been delusional to assume her proximity wouldn't disrupt his life, but what other options were available? The storm knocked down a tree one mile from his house. The probability of her reaching the Andersons' was nonexistent. He hadn't wanted her to stay, but forcing her to leave would be morally reprehensible.

This morning, standing under the cold water that failed to calm his roused cock, he wondered if he hadn't made a terrible mistake. Yesterday, when he'd shown her the magazine questions on the screen and turned to find her tantalizingly close, he'd yearned to ignore caution and crush his mouth against her kissable, plump lips. But he refrained, and rightfully so. He rued the strength of this sudden attraction, knew the level of distraction it could be. He didn't have the luxury of getting involved in a physically intimate relationship, not when the launch required his undiluted focus. He would never again allow his business to suffer because of poor decisions made due to the woman he was screwing.

Resolved, he dressed and left his room. Stroking a finger over his mouse pad, he activated his computer and sought to ascertain the current status of the storm cleanup. A few keystrokes and clicks later, he learned crews had been working throughout the night and the road should be cleared in a few hours.

He raked his fingers through his hair and let his head fall back as he exhaled with relief. He hadn't shared his living space with another person since his first year of college. His heart thudded in his chest as he pictured Chelsea strutting around his house, her jeans-clad long legs and shapely ass rendering his hormones unruly. Thank God he'd be spared that torture.

Maybe she'd render his worrying useless and sleep late. Perhaps she'd lounge in bed and read a book. He rolled his eyes. Not the best imagery to soothe his desire. He could offer her the opportunity to watch a movie, or let her use a laptop if she'd like to be online. Anything to keep her busy and out of his space until the road was cleared and he could send her on to the Andersons'. And out of his orbit.

Satisfied with his formulated plan, he brought up the schematics of another product they were launching—it was the first item he'd need to check when he began working—then strolled into the kitchen. He grabbed the blender and the ingredients to make his breakfast. The whir of the blades settled him as his body went through the motions of his morning routine.

He'd always craved structure. As a boy, he'd established the ideal morning procedure: wake up, timed plank and push-ups, floss and brush teeth, shower and get dressed. He performed it daily, in the same manner, never deviating. He used to advocate it to others in his life and was bewildered when they failed to recognize his routine's many benefits. Through time and his friendship with Mike and Jonathan, he learned to accept that others might choose different options, even when those options were senseless and inefficient.

He took a deep breath. This day was no different from any other. He'd gotten riled up over nothing.

"Good morning."

He stiffened and looked up to see Chelsea standing in the entrance to the hallway that led to the other set of bedrooms in his house. He swallowed, his mouth suddenly brimming with moisture. He hadn't gotten worked up over nothing. He'd gotten worked up over her. Clearing his throat, he nodded and returned his attention to the machine blending his smoothie.

She moved to the windows, where clouds still blocked the sun, although the storm had ended. "Where's my car?"

Against that backdrop she cut a stunning figure, wearing dark, fitted jeans—just as he predicted—and a creamy long-sleeved shirt that looked lush against her dark skin. In comparison, she probably found his ripped jeans and T-shirt slovenly. He clenched his jaw. Too damn bad. He wouldn't let her presence cause him to curate his behavior. His clothing was appropriate for working by himself, which he would be.

Shortly.

"I parked it in the garage next to mine."

Her chin grazed her shoulder as she gazed back at him. "Thanks again for bringing in my bags and supplies."

"They would do no one any good sitting in your car."

"Right." She pressed her hands together and sighed. "It's finally stopped raining. That's a good sign."

"The crews have been working all night clearing away debris from the storm," he said. "You should be able to leave in a few hours."

"Great," she said. Was there a slight tremor in her voice?

With the smoothie reaching his desired consistency, he turned the machine off, leaving a sudden and conspicuous silence. She turned to face him and slid her hands into the back pockets of her jeans. Her breasts pushed against her shirt and his hands clenched into fists on the kitchen counter. He was a rational, intelligent adult male. He was more than capable of corralling his hormones, despite certain physical indices determined to prove him wrong.

"I slept well," she said. "The bedroom was quite comfortable."

A shiver of awareness slid through him. The image of her tangled in his sheets flashed in his mind.

"Mike convinced me to use one of the three extra bedrooms for its intended purpose. I use the others for a workshop and for storage."

"Is Mike your roommate?"

He narrowed his eyes. "I'm a grown man and I'm gainfully employed. I don't need a roommate. No, Mike is my business partner and best friend."

He poured half the smoothie into a tall glass and grabbed a straw.

"Sorry. I didn't mean to offend you. Uh, do you have any coffee?"

He frowned. "I don't drink coffee."

"That's okay, I usually bring my own. There's this incredible coffee shop around the corner from my office and they import their coffee beans from eastern Africa. I'm totally addicted to it but I can't find it anywhere else. So I stock up on it and take it with me whenever I travel."

She crossed to his kitchen and stared at his uncluttered counters. "If you tell me where your coffeemaker is, I can take care of everything else."

"I told you, I don't drink coffee."

"I got that," she said slowly, opening a cabinet. "I don't need coffee, just the maker."

"If I don't drink coffee, why would I own a coffee-maker?"

She turned bulging eyes in his direction. "Because sixty-one percent of American adults drink coffee. What do you do when you have visitors?"

"That statistic isn't as staggering as you may have intended," he said, amusement at her aggrieved tone curving his lips. "On the very rare occasions I have guests, I offer them what I have. If they don't want what I offer, they remain thirsty."

She blinked. Her mouth opened, closed, and opened again.

His smile expired. Not the proper response? Social niceties didn't come naturally to him, as they did to everyone else, and it had taken years to figure out what people expected in various situations. Eventually, he'd culled together a resource of acceptable responses to certain social interactions. A protocol for politeness. Unfortunately for her, he'd been alone on the mountain for a long time. It had been a while since he'd had to refer to it and he was out of practice. Without a word, he turned on his heel and stalked over to his computer workstation.

"Do you have anything I can eat for breakfast?"

He couldn't be blamed for this. He hadn't expected

guests. Why would he stock his house with ingredients he didn't consume? It wasn't logical. He pointed to the blender on the counter.

She sighed. "May I have some?"

He nodded.

She poured the remaining green smoothie into a glass and took a sip. Her head tipped to the left and her expression . . . brightened? "This is really good."

He warmed with pleasure.

"How long have you been up?" she asked.

He shifted, his semi-erect member refueling. No, not that. She probably meant the time he'd awakened. "Six and a half hours."

"Seriously? It's only 9 a.m."

"The closer I get to the product launch, the less I sleep."

"What are you working on today?" she asked, after taking another sip from the glass.

"From now until the launch, the majority of my focus will be last-minute preparations for Computronix's presentation."

"You work for Computronix?"

"No. I own the company."

She laughed. "I own your phone. Are you unveiling the latest model or some other gadgets?"

Gadgets? He didn't deal in can openers or video watches.

"We'll roll out a line of *devices*"—he added emphasis to the word to correct her error—"in our business and entertainment arenas, but the HPC will be the featured product."

She trailed her fingers along the back of a bar stool. "The HPC? You mentioned that yesterday. What is it?"

"I told you that was classified information."

She rolled her eyes and drank more of the smoothie. The schematics on the screen in front of him may as well have been a toddler's picture book for the effect it had on his attention, namely an inability to hold it. Chelsea's presence was kryptonite to his concentration, leaving him powerless to focus on anything except her nearness.

His pulse pummeled in his throat and he cast a side-long glance in her direction. After placing her empty glass in the sink, she'd settled on his couch with her back against the armrest, her profile a temptation. Her curls were gathered precariously on the top of her head and stray spirals teased her brows, ears, and nape. Thankfully this would be a short-term problem. Once the road reopened, she'd be free to leave and he'd have a much-needed respite from her and this unprecedented attraction.

Perhaps he'd call and volunteer his assistance to the county if it would make the cleanup occur faster.

"Is this all you do?"

His focus widened, shifting from the curl bouncing near the corner of her eye to her entire face. "What?"

She draped an arm over the back of the sofa. "Is this all you do?"

"I don't understand your question."

She waved a fluid hand, indicating his workstation. "This. You spend a lot of time working. Do you do anything else?"

"No."

Why would he do "anything else"? The theoretical study and application of computer science was his calling. It helped him to discover order in a world he often found chaotic. Additionally, it was an avenue for acceptance. In the scope of his work, he was embraced, not judged, for his differences.

"Do you have family?" she asked.

His chest tightened and the back of his throat burned. "Yes."

He heard her embellished sigh. "Does your family live here in California? Are you close to them?"

He abhorred discussing his family, often burdened with twin sentiments of guilt and responsibility. "My parents are divorced. I'm the youngest of three, the only son. My father and sisters still live in Colorado."

She tilted her head to the side, creating an acute angle with her shoulder. She did that often. "Friends?"

"Mike and Jonathan."

"Is that it?"

A deceptively simple query.

Did he have friends other than Mike and Jonathan? People attached to him by feelings of affection or personal regard, not by economic necessity, greed, or sexual desire? He'd been involved with Birgitta, but had he ever considered her his friend? How could he when he'd never invited her here, into his sanctuary?

"I have work to complete. If you require entertainment, you'll have better luck with the TV. The remote is on the table."

He forced himself to study the latest HPC income projections, but he couldn't block out the evidence of her presence. His ears pricked at the pulpous sound of her body sinking into the cushions on his sofa, the heavy thud of the remote landing on the table, the varied voices erupting from the powered-on television. Approving the rollout of his company's newest device was failing in comparison to his growing fascination with Chelsea Grant.

"I love this movie."

Do not turn around. Do not turn around.

He swung around to see two women standing in the hallway of a government building or courthouse. Unable to stop himself, he left his desk and perched on the other sofa arm. He frowned, watching one woman wildly gesticulate in her effort to advise her blonde friend. "I've never seen this one."

Chelsea sat up and smiled. The effect caused an unusual tingling sensation beneath his skin. "You're joking, right? It came out a few years ago and made a boatload at the box office. This woman meets this guy one morning and they end up spending an amazing day together. The next morning, she vanishes without a trace. He goes to the place she said she worked and finds out the superficial stuff she told him—her name, where she works—was a lie. He spends the rest of the movie searching for her, using clues from their brief encounter. Turns out, she was an accountant and was turning state's evidence against the company she worked for, a front for organized crime. He finally finds her and helps her evade the mob."

Sounded like the typical insipid, dewy-eyed schmaltz consistently fed to the masses. He crossed his arms. "I don't enjoy that type of movie."

"What type of movie?"

"Movies like that. It's ridiculous. She lied to him and abandoned him yet he wastes valuable time searching for her."

"He's in love with her."

"She lied to him. He doesn't *know* her."

The corners of her mouth turned down. "It was for a good reason. She was trying to protect him."

"That's irrelevant."

"Things aren't that simplistic."

"Yes, Chelsea, they are. A morally right outcome doesn't justify the immoral means used to achieve it."

"Just like that?"

"Just like that."

She shifted away from him. "It must be nice to be clear on everything. To never be worried about ethics or morality."

"Ethics shouldn't be an issue. If people spoke their minds, instead of hedging and engaging in double-talk, humanity would benefit."

"Unfortunately, that's not the world we live in. Sometimes people do what they do because they don't have a choice."

"You always have a choice, even if the options are unpleasant."

She stared at him and an expression crossed her face he couldn't decipher. Then she laughed. "How did we get on to such a heavy topic anyway? It's just a movie." She grabbed the remote and sank back into the cushions, changing the channel to another program. "We need to chill out. Relax."

He shrugged and headed back to his desk. He had too much to do to even consider relaxing. Although there were numerous ways he could unwind with Chelsea.

Sex was the top five entries on that list.

He prided himself on his discipline, so it wasn't long before the data on his computer quelled the distraction of Chelsea's movements and he lost himself in the challenge of his work. This launch was the most important one of his career. The HPC was a product with global ramifications. Once it premiered, everyone would forgive his company's previous disastrous rollout. Maybe then, he would, too.

A small rectangle flashed across the top of his central monitor, capturing his attention and breaking his concentration. It was an email from Anya. He hated being pulled from his work, but this close to the presentation he couldn't afford to ignore any messages from the company. Countless small problems could derail their launch, and he and Mike needed to stem any issues to prevent them from becoming obstacles.

Accessing his email program, he scanned the message from Anya. The success of the *CGR* interview led her to determine he could handle several others. She was informing him that more would be forthcoming.

Shit! He pinched the bridge of his nose and closed his eyes. This was why he didn't deal well with people. He'd assumed his answers to the interview meant Anya would cease bothering him about promotions. He'd done what she'd asked, and rather well, so she should require nothing further from him. Instead, she'd seen his achievement as a reason to give him more. And just as egregious was the lack of specificity. What did she consider several? Four? Five? Ten? It made a difference!

The peal of his doorbell dragged him from his mental debate.

Chelsea sat up and swung her legs off the sofa. "Are you expecting anyone?"

"No."

He definitely hadn't been expecting her.

He stood and walked over to the window. A white county work truck, with black rails and piles of orange construction cones, sat in the driveway.

His chest tightened and he rubbed the spot with the heel of his hand. They'd cleared the road. No reason remained for her to stay. She would leave and he'd find himself alone again. Achingly so. He shook his head and pushed the traitorous feelings away. This was the best outcome. Chelsea's presence extracted attention he couldn't spare. Too much was riding on the success of the launch.

He descended the steps into the foyer and opened the front door. A young man, wearing the typical county work crew garb of baggy fluorescent-yellow overalls and thick black boots, stood waiting.

"Road's clear," the worker said, jerking his thumb over his shoulder.

Before Adam could respond, the guy tromped over to

the truck. He'd barely shut the passenger door before the truck took off, heading back down the mountain. Adam trudged back to the great room to find Chelsea gathering her belongings.

"They've cleared the tree away," he told her, shoving his hands into his pockets.

"I heard."

So this was it. Would he see her again? When the launch presentation was over and he had more time, would she still be here?

"How long are you staying at the Andersons'?"

"A month. Maybe two."

Tension eased from his shoulders and they lowered. He nodded, trying to stifle any further outward manifestations of his inner turmoil. "Maybe we'll run into each other."

"Do you mind giving me your number?" she asked. "In case I need help or something."

He retrieved his phone from his desk, engaged the appropriate app, and sent her his information. When she received the data, she looked up from her screen and smiled.

His pulse strummed. "The garage is down the stairs and through the door on the right. Your keys are in the ignition."

"Thanks. For the car and for your hospitality."

He nodded and held out his hand. She hesitated before sliding her palm against his. As his fingers closed around hers, his heart hammered against his chest, and he was engulfed with a feeling he couldn't describe. She stared into his eyes for a long moment before squeezing his hand and turning away.

Then she was gone.

That feeling swept over him again, similar to the sensation he experienced when he finished an invention, but different. Less satisfaction, more melancholy. He rubbed his hand against his chest. Whatever it was, he was confident it would soon pass.

Chapter Six

FIVE HOURS AFTER Adam said goodbye to the distraction personified by Chelsea Grant, his mind finally cooperated with his will and turned its full attention to the work he had yet to complete. He needed to be alone and focused. The launch was three weeks away. If he buckled down, and avoided any other interruptions, he could still meet his deadline.

When his doorbell rang, he almost succumbed to a roar of frustration. What now? He pushed away from his computer and glowered out the window.

A steel-gray Jaguar XJ was parked in his driveway.

Fuck.

Adam considered ignoring his guest, but immediately dismissed the notion as futile. Mike was strategic, determined, and persistent. The same traits that made him one of the best COOs in the industry also meant he wouldn't leave until he'd achieved the outcome he wanted.

Adam took his time descending the steps to his foyer. Opening the door, he found Mike standing on his doorstep, dressed more informally than usual, in khakis, a white collared shirt and a navy half-zip pullover. A partial smile creased the blond man's countenance while his gaze bounced between Adam's face and the vestibule.

When a car door slammed shut, Adam's frown deepened.

What the hell?

He angled his head, glancing beyond Mike's shoulder. Jonathan, in his familiar uniform of jeans and a T-shirt, strode up the walkway, a large box in his arms.

Adam straightened, rubbed the back of his neck and inhaled deeply through the tightness in his chest. "Is this your way of solving my reclusive tendencies?"

"Is that even possible?" Mike countered, then shrugged. "I'm due for a visit."

Adam nodded toward Jonathan. "And you thought reinforcements were necessary?"

"The more, the merrier."

"In whose estimation? Not mine. I'm the recluse, remember?"

"Don't worry, I'm not offended," Jonathan said, coming up behind Mike, smiling widely as he used the box to muscle them aside. The other man always appeared to be smiling, even if his lips weren't curved upward. "I know this warm greeting is your way of saying you're happy to see us."

He winked, shifted the box in his arms, and jogged up the stairs.

"You know I hate sarcasm," Adam called after him. "And if I were happy to see you, I'd say so."

"I know," Mike said, clapping Adam on the shoulder as he, too, entered the house and followed Jonathan up into the great room.

Adam closed the door and leaned his forehead against its cool, smooth surface. A visit from his two best friends three weeks before a crucial product launch? This wasn't an arbitrary social call. They were here because of his last conversation with Mike but, mentally reviewing the discussion, he could discern no detail that would cause the other man to rush up the mountain, with Jonathan in tow. He didn't have the time or inclination for this inquest. He concluded his best course of action was to ascertain what they wanted, solve the problem, and send them on their way. Then he could get back to his work.

Climbing the staircase, he found Mike positioned next to his workstation and Jonathan in his kitchen removing supplies and ingredients from the box he'd brought with him.

Jonathan looked up, a wedge of cheese in his hand. "You doing okay?"

Adam shoved his hands into the front pockets of his jeans. "I'm trying to figure out what I've done to deserve the influx of visitors to my secluded mountain home."

"That's just it," Mike said, turning from the desk. "The last time we talked you asked if I'd sent someone here, then abruptly hung up. I called back several times but when I couldn't get through, I was worried. With us being this close to the launch—"

"You wanted to check on your investment," Adam finished.

"That's not fair and you know it."

Adam met Mike's gaze, lifting his chin to emphasize his point. His statement may have been harsh, but it wasn't inaccurate. Computronix was doing well. Their shares had rebounded from the debacle of their last big launch and neither he, nor Mike, wanted to become complacent. The HPC would be a game changer, and, as Mike emphasized yesterday, the growth of the company was dependent upon its success. Adam didn't doubt Mike's concern, but he was certain interests other than their friendship had brought the other man to his home.

"So, *was* someone here?" Mike asked.

"It appears I've got a new neighbor," he said.

"How would you know?" Jonathan interrupted. "You're not the 'homemade goodies basket, welcome to the neighborhood' type."

Adam recoiled. Just the thought sent cold shivers slithering down his spine.

"I met her during the storm."

"Her?" Mike's blond brows shot up into his hairline.

"Yes, her. As in, a member of the female sex."

Mike turned his head slightly. "Are you making a funny?"

"It's been known to happen on rare occasions," Adam said, deadpan.

"She must be attractive if you thought her worthy of mentioning," Jonathan said.

Was she . . . ? "She's agreeable."

Mike shook his head. "If it were anyone else, I'd assume 'agreeable' was a nice way to say 'unattractive,' but with you, it could mean anyone from a plain Jane to Angelina Jolie."

The sound of heavy steel hitting concrete grabbed Adam's attention. Jonathan littered his counter with an assortment of tomatoes, a loaf of crusty bread, cream, onions, and several herbs. And the cause of the initial noise?

"Is that a panini maker?"

"Yup," Jonathan said, shifting the groceries around.

"What are you making?"

"What does it look like?"

Adam leaned against the bar and assessed the ingredients. "Grilled cheese and tomato soup?"

Jonathan nodded. "Your favorite meal."

"In college. Although you didn't need all of this"—he indicated the mess with a nod of his head—"back then."

"I told you he wouldn't like it," Mike said.

Jonathan paused, a sharp knife in his hand. "I was twenty-two and working twelve-hour shifts as a line cook in a college town. This is the version we have on our brunch menu. I guarantee you'll love it." He grabbed a tomato and swiftly chopped off the end.

"There was nothing wrong with the way you used to do it," Adam said.

"No. But I've changed in the past ten years. I own and operate a three Michelin-starred restaurant. I can't open a can of soup and slap some cheese between two slices of bread."

Adam frowned. Change. Everyone appeared to be happy with the concept, but it was hard to view it beneficially when you were the one people always wanted to change.

"Have you given a thought to what's next?" Mike asked.

"You invaded my space. I'm clueless about your plans."

Mike shook his head. "Not now. I meant, after the presentation." When Adam opened his mouth to respond, Mike interrupted. "Theoretically, not practically. The future. Your next step."

Oh. That clarification altered his reply. "I have several ideas about our next project. Once the launch has passed, I'll come into the office."

"You're moving back to the city?"

Adam's scalp prickled and the muscles in his shoulders tensed. When he'd mentioned going into the office, he'd meant for meetings with Mike and their senior level staff. Two days, a week at the most. This mountain had become his sanctuary from censure and judgment.

He'd never considered moving back to Palo Alto.

He rolled his shoulders, attempting to loosen up. "No."

Mike pinched the bridge of his nose. "Dude, it was okay when you retreated up here to put your considerable focus into the device. But once it drops, we're going to need you back at the office."

"We've made this arrangement work for the past eighteen months. Why couldn't that continue?"

Mike and Jonathan exchanged a long look.

"What?" Adam asked, through clenched teeth. "Even I can tell you have something you want to say to me. What is it you say, Jonathan? 'Speak your piece'?"

Jonathan set his knife down. "Even after everything that happened, you can't hide away from—"

"I'm not hiding," he said, instinctively reacting to that word.

"The HPC is almost done." Mike took over the argument. "After the launch you're going to be even more famous than you are now. Your presence will satisfy stockholders. You are Computronix. Confidence in you is confidence in the company."

Mike made a valid point and yet Adam still believed the problem could be solved without his permanent relocation.

"Fine. I'll increase the frequency and duration of my visits to the campus."

"Is this about Birgitta?"

"Mike . . ." Jonathan's tone contained a clear warning.

Adam's face heated. "No."

And it wasn't, not in the way Mike meant. Adam's anger wasn't misplaced grief about their breakup. It stemmed from his failure to prevent his experience with her from affecting his work and his company.

"I'm just saying, you're better off without her."

"Speaking of women we're involved with," Jonathan loudly declared, "Mike's been spending a lot of time with Skylar Thompson."

Mike blew out a noisy breath and shook his head.

Adam turned to Jonathan. "Who?"

"Skylar Thompson. Daughter of Franklin Thompson, the media mogul." Jonathan's knife rhythmically struck his cutting board. "How'd you hook up with her?"

"We met at a charity fundraiser."

"Saw pictures of you both at the opening of the San Francisco Ballet. You looked like the classic golden couple. Is it getting serious?"

Mike shrugged. "Maybe. I've surpassed every goal I set in my ten-year plan. The company is doing well, I'm financially able to provide for someone else—."

"That's an understatement," Jonathan muttered.

Mike glared at him but continued. "It may be time to think about settling down and starting a family. By the time my dad was my age, he and Mom were already married and pregnant with me."

That reasoning sounded faulty to Adam. "You honestly believe that you're bound to the same choices your father made?"

Jonathan nodded. "You do have a tendency to treat your father's life and words as gospel."

Adam settled onto a bar stool, his leg bouncing slightly, interested to see if Mike enjoyed having his wounds dissected and discussed.

Mike blinked. "There's nothing wrong with following in my father's footsteps. He's a great man."

"What worked for your father may not work for you. Men become great when they forge their own path," Adam argued.

Mike pointed a finger at him, his nostrils flaring. "Fuck you. I could've gone to work for my father, but I started Computronix with you." His cell phone rang and he pulled it from his pocket, stalking over to the windows and grumbling, "Gonna talk to me about forging my own path."

Jonathan raised both brows and extended his fist for a bump. "That was Machiavellian."

Adam shook his head. "My behavior wasn't dishonest. Nothing I said was a lie. If he wants to examine me, he should be prepared for it to be reciprocated."

"He's worried about you."

"I don't require his concern. Not in that way. I'm not the kid he rescued back at Stanford."

"Of course not," Jonathan said, his face devoid of emotion. "You're one of *People*'s Sexiest Men Alive."

The laugh started low in Adam's belly. He laughed so hard his cheeks hurt. He pressed a fist to his lips and attempted to catch his breath. "Will you ever let that go?"

"Not as long as there's air in my lungs."

"If I get you running a couple of these mountain trails, we can take care of that." Adam shifted on the stool and let his arm fall behind its back. "What are you doing here?"

"I believe Mike already explained that," Jonathan said, chopping tomatoes with a surgical precision Adam couldn't help but admire.

"Not here in my house. Here in California?" Adam reached in and deftly grabbed one of the chopped tomato pieces, popping it into his mouth. "You said you were researching opening a new restaurant in DC. I thought you were heading out there."

Jonathan was originally from a Virginia suburb just outside of the nation's capital and he'd always wanted to open a restaurant in the District.

"I am. But I don't need to be there until next month. I'll leave after your launch."

"That's not why you're staying, is it?"

Jonathan stopped chopping, but he didn't meet Adam's gaze. "My brother is moving back to DC."

As long as he'd known Jonathan, his friend didn't get along with his brother. Which was strange. He couldn't imagine anyone not getting along with the outgoing and talented chef.

"How long has it been since you've seen Timothy?"

"Oh, we've seen each other. We play nice for my parents when necessary, but . . ." He shrugged. "My mother said he's met someone and they're going to settle down near the family."

Opening a restaurant in DC should be exciting for Jonathan, but he didn't look or sound enthusiastic. Adam wanted to know more, but struggled to determine what he should ask. After years of friendship, he knew Jonathan. His personality was even-tempered, as opposed to Mike's more reserved nature. If Jonathan wanted to share more with him, he would. Wouldn't he? Or was this a situation where Adam needed to show he cared by inquiring further?

It was enough to induce a stress headache. If it were any other people, he wouldn't bother to make the effort.

"What's this?"

The question interrupted him before he'd made a decision on how to proceed with Jonathan. Glancing over his shoulder, he spied Mike sitting in his chair, facing the powered-up computer screen. His breath caught in the back of his throat and he hurried over.

"You know I hate when people meddle with my things."

"I haven't touched anything."

"The monitor is on."

"Okay, I touched the track pad. I wanted to see what you were working on."

"I'm tweaking code for the HPC." Adam scowled, remembering . . . "But I may not finish if Anya continues to bother me with pointless tasks."

"Give the kid a break."

"Kid is an accurate descriptor. I checked her personnel file. She's only twenty-four. Why is she working on the most important launch of our company? In the history of personal computing?"

"Never an issue with self-confidence, eh, Adam?" Jonathan called out.

Adam narrowed his eyes. "When it comes to my work, no. I don't have that same confidence in our neophyte promotional liaison."

"Anya's great at her job. She has an uncanny knowledge of digital marketing, of using new and cutting edge social media to promote the HPC. She knows what she's doing. She finds innovative ways to do what needs to be done."

"If you don't rein her in, she's going to find herself unemployed."

"She's just doing her job," Mike said, leaning back in the chair.

"Her job is beginning to infringe on mine."

"Speaking of jobs, hiring and firing staff fall under mine."

"Which is why I'm giving you the courtesy of a warning," Adam said, rubbing at the stiffness in his jaw.

Mike reached out and picked up a pen, spinning it between his fingers. "Why are you fighting us on this? Anya was raving about your responses to the *CGR* interview, calling them informative, concise, and entertaining. She said if it weren't for the content of your answers, she'd never believe they came from you."

"My abilities were never in question, only my desire." For some reason, his words evoked an image of Chelsea. His pulse picked up the pace and he squeezed his eyes shut.

"She wants you to do more."

Heat rushed through him on a downward trajectory. He wanted to do more, too. He'd start with that mouth.

"She thinks you can handle it and I tend to agree."

His dick stiffened and he wondered how much *she* could hand— Wait, what?

His eyes popped open and he frowned. "What are we discussing?"

Mike's head flinched back. "Anya and more media interviews. What else would we be talking about?"

After only one day, Chelsea was invading his thoughts like an insidious computer virus, and that was disturbing. It was a well-documented field of study that the mind was capable of multitasking. Unfortunately, that was the rare function his brain had difficulty accomplishing. He tended to put the considerable power of his mental resources toward a sole focus. Right now, that focus needed to be his work and not the enticing stranger who'd swept in with the storm. Getting her out of his house and physically away had been in his best interest. And with her physical distance, it was only logical that her mental hold on him would diminish. As for more interviews . . .

"I can continue prepping for the launch or I can spend my time answering questions about my favorite comic book. I can't do both."

"Why not? As you're fond of telling me, you're the genius."

Adam scowled and gritted his teeth at his friend's easy smile.

Mike's grin faded. He leaned forward, resting his elbows on his desk. "You'd rather stay behind the scenes and let the HPC speak for itself. But in this new environment, the creator is as much a part of the story as the device. We need you."

So? That didn't automatically mean he should do the interviews. What if he said the wrong thing?

"We've been friends since we were eighteen years old," Adam said. "You know I have no problem cataloguing my strengths and weaknesses. Being charming and engaging with the press falls into the latter category."

"Those skills can be learned."

He elevated a brow. "In three weeks?"

"Yes. You just have to—"

"Change." The word of the day. "I can't. I am who I am."

"That's not what I was going to say. I know opening up to people is difficult for you. But in the same way you came up with your politeness protocol, you can come up with a way to deal with the promotions and publicity aspects of the presentation."

As if that resource had been created in a moment of whimsy. It had taken years of rejections, jeers, and ridicule before he'd determined which responses were appropriate and which would get him labeled as weird. Even if he had the time to do the same for publicity—which he didn't—he didn't have the access to the press that would be required.

"Dinner is served," Jonathan announced.

The three men settled onto the bar stools and Adam noted they'd unconsciously situated themselves the way they had in college, him in the middle, Mike on his right, Jonathan on his left.

He inhaled, the aroma rising from the meal in front of him. "Do you stand by your guarantee?"

Jonathan leaned his head back and smiled. "I do."

Adam took a tentative sip of the soup and sighed in pleasure as the flavors burst on his palate. The various herbs and spices blended harmoniously and the creamy texture coated his tongue.

"This is really good," Mike said, his spoon quickly descending back into his bowl.

"Thanks, man."

Adam bit into his sandwich. "Can you add this to my food delivery rotation?"

Jonathan dropped his spoon and sat back. "I'm actually steps ahead of the genius!" He bumped Adam's arm. "Soup is already in the freezer, and since I was coming up, I bought several more meals for you. Oh, before I forget . . ."

Jonathan stood on the rungs of the stool, reached into the box still on the counter and pulled out a glass bottle filled with dark amber liquid.

Adam's eyes widened. He grabbed the small elegant bottle from Jonathan's hands. "Is this Jefferson's Presidential Select Seventeen?"

Jonathan nodded. "I managed to get my hand on a case."

"Now *that's* what I'm talking about." Mike grinned and held out his glass.

"Unless you'd rather have . . ." Jonathan reached into the box again and pulled out another bottle.

The sight of the distinctive white label with its red-and-gold ribbon and wax-sealed letter B caused Adam's stomach to roil and triggered his gag reflex.

Mike pressed the back of his hand to his lips. "Are you trying to make us sick?"

"Good." Jonathan dropped the offending drink back inside the box. "Just holding the bottle brings back bad memories."

Adam laughed. "Remember when we went to the movies to see *Borat*, and you drank half the bottle and passed out in the theater? We had to carry you all the way back to the dorm."

Mike chimed in. "And when we got there, a naked girl was lying on your bed."

Jonathan winced. "I don't even remember her name."

Adam and Mike shared a glance. "Heather Wallace-Webb," they both said.

"You remember that?"

"I have excellent recall. I'm going to remember the name of the fourth girl I saw naked in person. Especially a girl who'd pierced her clitoris."

"Dude!" Jonathan punched his shoulder.

"That's what it's called."

They finished dinner and settled in the great room, laughing and sipping bourbon for the rest of the night. Adam felt himself relax in a way he hadn't since his failed engagement. He'd missed this, spending time with his friends, people who loved and accepted him.

A little after 10 p.m., Jonathan stood and stretched. "We gotta get on the road."

"I have plenty of room if either of you need to stay," Adam said.

"I appreciate it, but I want to check on the restaurant." Jonathan headed into the kitchen.

"And I can drive," Mike said, standing and brushing invisible lint from the front of his pants. "I switched to water earlier."

After collecting his supplies, Jonathan placed the box on the arm of the sofa, shook Adam's hand and pulled him in for a brief hug. "It was good to see you, man. Let's not wait another year before we do this again."

"How about three weeks?" Adam asked. "I'll need a drink after the presentation."

"No doubt."

They bumped fists and Jonathan headed down the stairs.

"We're good?"

Adam hated when Mike slipped into colloquial language. It made deciphering his meaning more time-consuming. It took a moment, but when he understood Mike's question he nodded and answered, "We're good."

"After the mini game console, you said you'd do anything to put Computronix back on top."

Adam's vision clouded as he recalled the disaster of the console's launch. Though the HPC was eons ahead in terms of tech and readiness, he couldn't deny the stench from that failure lingered.

"I meant it."

"Then we're going to need your best for the HPC launch. It's an extraordinary device and I want to give it every chance to succeed. Whatever you called upon to answer the *CGR* questions, put it on speed dial for the presentation."

Adam sighed. He hadn't consulted a higher power to answer those questions. His turnaround had been due entirely to Chelsea. It was only after he'd accepted her help that Anya had been happy with his responses.

After saying goodbye to his friends, he headed back up to his workstation. There were numerous reasons why no further contact with Chelsea was best for his work, but there was one reason for association that trumped them all: he needed her help to make his launch of the HPC a success.

And should her nearness begin to tempt him, he'd

remind himself of his genius. That he only needed to learn a lesson once before he imprinted, then implemented it into his life. His mother *and* Birgitta had taught him that allowing a woman too close was a mistake. Once there, they'd see he was different and then they'd leave. They always did. He couldn't afford to let that happen this time. Not when the success of the HPC was riding on maintaining a strong professional relationship with Chelsea.

Personally, he'd keep his distance.

Even if it killed him.

Chapter Seven

WHAT WAS SHE supposed to do now?

Chelsea strode over to the window in the Andersons' great room. While not as big as Adam's, it still offered a charming view of the mountainside. A view she'd have to appreciate another day.

She pulled her hair back, lifted the mass off her neck, and let the curls flow through her fingers. She needed to find a way to get back on track. She'd exhausted the good luck she'd acquired two days before. Why couldn't the road have stayed closed longer? If she'd had more time, she would've found a way to broach the subject of his work again and parlayed that into another opportunity to offer her assistance and gain his trust. It'd been harder than she'd originally imagined. Most of the clients she worked with loved talking about themselves. Not Adam. He didn't answer questions. He uttered monosyllabic grunts.

If that didn't make her job difficult enough, the man was too damn sexy. She trembled remembering his fierce gaze when she'd left his house. Was she a glutton for punishment? Maybe she was crazy? The fact that she found him so compelling made her question her own sanity. Hadn't she matured past the folly of youth when the only attribute that mattered was a guy's looks and not his personality? If not, how was she supposed to focus on the job at hand when any contact with him made her toggle between wanting to hit him or kiss him?

Her phone beeped. She slid it from her back pocket and checked the screen. A text message from Howard.

Progress?

Crap.

Chelsea stared at the phone and massaged her forehead with her available hand. Could there be a worse time to have to report to her boss? She dialed Howard's number and waited for him to answer.

"You got my text?" Howard asked, his voice a pleasing, smooth timbre, with no hint of his geographic origin. Or personality.

"Yes. I was just with him."

"You've already established contact? That's impressive."

"I don't have a lot of time. The launch is in three weeks."

"Is it doable? Please, tell me things aren't as dire as Mr. Black insinuated?"

Oh, they were. But her motivation was stronger than anything in her path. She wasn't ready to admit defeat. She straightened her shoulders. "It's challenging, but I'll get it done."

"Good." His satisfaction purred across the line. "I knew you were the best choice for this assignment. Keep me posted."

She disconnected the call and sank onto the over-sized sofa. She had to do something . . . and fast. She had less than a month to get Adam ready for the launch, and based on what she'd seen, she'd need every single minute of that time. She thumped her fist against her forehead. *Think, Chelsea, think.*

How could she get close to him in a way that would give her time to catalogue his personality and figure out how to present him in the best light possible?

But getting closer to him, spending more time with him, was a double-edged sword. When she was near him, he gave off this magnetism that made thinking akin to trying to walk through knee-high mud pits in four-inch stiletto heels. She couldn't explain it. God knows it's not like he was blessed with a charming personality. But his intelligence . . . his intensity . . . his eyes . . . that body . . . Lord, he affected her more than any other man she'd ever met. He threw her off her game and made her lose her equilibrium—which was crazy considering she was re-nowned throughout the company for her composure.

Her phone vibrated against her hand and she jumped. She looked at the caller ID, expecting it to be Howard again and seriously considering ignoring it. She was sur-prised to see Adam's name flash on the screen. Speak of the devil.

"Hello?"

"Just wanted to make sure you're okay." His deep, serious voice slid over her, causing goose bumps to rise on her arms and warmth to throb between her thighs.

"I am."

"You have power?"

"Yes, thankfully."

"Good."

Heavy silence blanketed the airways between them. She frowned. Who was she, a young girl talking to her high school crush? *Get your head out of the clouds and concentrate on this job.* She needed a reason to keep him talking, or at least to get an invitation back to his house.

"Did they send you any other—"

"So, you're in entertainment—"

They both broke off. What did he want to know about her work?

"I'm sorry. You go," she said.

"Being in the entertainment field, you must have direct contact with the media. Have you acquired tips on how to deal with them?"

"Of course."

"Though I appreciate your help with those questions yesterday, I'm now faced with a dilemma. They want me to do more. I wondered if you would be available for further assistance?"

Adrenaline rushed through her like a fashionista at a couture sample sale. She executed a couple of dance moves. "No problem," she said, careful that her voice did not betray her excitement.

He paused. "There are other tasks with which I'm having difficulty. Would you consider helping me prepare for the launch I mentioned? I'd be willing to pay you for your time."

She gasped. It was the dream outcome. He'd invited her to do the job Computronix had hired her to perform. Short of telling him the truth from the beginning, there was no better scenario.

"I'd be happy to help you," she said, visions of corner offices, six-figure bonuses, and social respectability dancing in her head.

As for her burgeoning fascination, she needn't worry. She never mixed business with pleasure. She'd worked with a lot of handsome men and to many of them, flirting was as natural as breathing. She'd resisted them; she'd resist Adam. Her attraction might make her task difficult, but it wouldn't make it impossible.

"WHAT ARE YOU doing here?" Adam asked when he found Chelsea on his doorstep late Thursday afternoon. This was the fourth time visitors had shown up without notice, and while a part of him acknowledged his annoyance at his inability to no longer control who visited his home, he couldn't deny the jolt of excitement he experienced at her appearance.

"I thought that would be obvious," she said, smiling.

That jolt was quickly squashed by another swell of annoyance.

Obvious? Not to him. She stood in his doorway, a black bag slung over her shoulder, looking crisply professional in tan trousers, a white shirt, and an orange sweater.

Once again, his white T-shirt, running pants, and bare feet would be found lacking when compared to her.

"Guess not," she muttered, the smile morphing into a frown when he didn't immediately respond. "May I come in?"

He stepped back and opened the door farther, allowing her to enter his residence. When she passed, a tremor of awareness shook him. His body clamored to press against hers, magnet to metal. He'd experienced that feeling before, the night of the storm. What did they call that phenomenon? Déjà vu. That could explain his physical reaction.

If one believed in that nonsense.

Which he didn't.

He shook his head, irritated by the rare, fanciful thoughts invading his way-too-busy mind, and closed the door. This was the danger of having her in his space. She abducted his attention from his work and placed it squarely onto her curves. But he'd already decided to assume the risk. He needed her for the HPC and nothing was more urgent.

He hoped.

"I wasn't expecting you until at least Friday."

She blinked. "Why Friday? I never specified what day I'd stop by."

"You said you'd see me in a 'few' days. Few usually denotes three or four and since I last saw you on Tuesday, I didn't foresee your arrival before Friday."

She tilted her head to the side. "Are you always so literal?"

"Not always. Mostly. I'm improving."

She stared at him, her lips pursed, then burst out laughing. The sound swirled around him, bubbly and light. She tossed her hair and nudged back curls that, in her merriment, had flown in her face. He allowed a brief smile, unexpectedly pleased that she'd gotten his joke.

Her eyes widened slightly, then fell to his lips. He stiffened in surprise. He knew that look, had come to recognize it as it traversed the faces of many women and some men in the years since he'd grown into his body. Chelsea wanted him. Though he knew it was scientifically impossible, the air molecules around them seemed to expand and vibrate from the heat between them. Her tongue darted out, leaving a tempting sheen behind on her lips and causing his thumb to tingle. He wanted to reach out and sweep his thumb across her bottom lip before leaning forward and pulling it between his teeth. He tightened his hands into fists at his side.

It was difficult enough to restrain himself when he believed the attraction was one-sided, but knowing she wouldn't spurn his advances . . .

Just when he felt himself swaying toward her as he lost the battle for control—God help them both—she glanced away and cleared her throat. "I spent the past two days settling in," she said, her gaze skipping around his foyer, before alighting back on his. "I drove down to San Mateo and thought I'd come by before heading home to see if you needed my help today or to get a timetable for when you'd like to begin work."

Work. Right. That's why she was here. That's why he

allowed it. He waved her over to the staircase. "Come on up."

In the great room, Chelsea hung her bag from one of his mid-back bar stools. Needing a moment to seek and settle into composure, he walked over to his desk and took a long drink of water from his glass. Self-possessed once again, he set it down and turned to face her. "Do you recall my mentioning that Computronix is unveiling a new line?"

"Yes."

"We're doing a presentation and for the first time, I'm participating. I'm not an in-front-of-the-camera person." An understatement. "I need help with my demonstration before the media, in addition to drafting answers when I receive new interview questions."

"That's feasible." She tapped a finger against her lips. "Can you tell me about the devices you're unveiling? Would that include the HPC you've mentioned?"

"Before that, you'll need to sign this contract." He handed her the written pledge he'd prepared the day he'd called her.

This time her laugh rang brittle and coarse. "Good Lord, what is it with you people and contracts? You'd think we were discussing issues of national security."

Her words gave him pause. He rubbed his beard. "Have you signed another contract recently?"

She stilled and her eyes widened. "Uh . . . no. Why?"

He leaned his hip against the counter. "You said 'you people.' That implies more than one person."

"I meant it in the general sense, like businesspeople," she said.

He nodded. That seemed logical. She'd told him she worked in entertainment and because of business Computronix did with a studio four years ago, he knew how secretive movie executives could be when it came to the properties they had in the pipeline. His misgivings eased. "We can't proceed if you don't sign the paper."

Chelsea reached beneath the flap of her bag and pulled out a pen. With an excessive sweep of her hand, she signed the contract.

"There." She slid it down the smooth surface of his counter and he caught it before it floated to the floor. "Now, what is the HPC?"

He confirmed her signature at the bottom of the page, and then deposited it on his desk. He opened the top drawer and pulled out the small black box. Excitement sparked to life in his body as he handed it to her. "Open it."

The corner of her mouth tilted up.

Those lips. . .

"Isn't this a little sudden?" she asked.

What had he missed? "Excuse me?"

"Little black box, like an engagement ring . . ." She shook her head. "Never mind."

"Oh. As if I were proposing." He didn't find her quip amusing. He would never get married.

She lifted the top and plucked out the device, holding it between her thumb and forefinger. "What's this?"

"The HPC."

Her eyes widened, giving her an owlish demeanor. "I'm signing secret blood oath documents for something that looks like a Bluetooth headset with a slide antenna attached to its end?"

"Documents?" he asked, placing emphasis on the *s*. "I gave you one sheet of paper."

She lowered her gaze briefly, and then smiled. "There you go, being literal again. Don't change the subject. What is this?"

She wasn't the first person to comment on his literal-mindedness and she wouldn't be the last. He'd been told it was one of his more frustrating traits, but since his move back up the mountain, he hadn't concerned himself with others' opinions of him. He beckoned to her and she dropped it in the palm of his hand. "This is the prototype for the HPC, or the Holographic Personal Computer."

"This little thing is your next product?"

"It's going to change the world. I'll show you."

He moved behind her, his eyes level with the curls on the top of her head. Unable to resist, he inhaled deeply and the rich, alluring fragrance ripped through his body, stirring the hair on his arms and on the nape of his neck. This woman affected him in a manner he found discon-certing. It was neither neat nor tidy.

Why? What was it about her? And how did he stop it?

He placed a hand on her shoulder and slid the HPC behind her ear. It sat snugly, similar to a hearing aid. She shivered beneath his fingers.

"This side piece extends," he said, his voice gruff. He

pulled on the stem until it locked into place with a click, the clear tip protruding 3.2 inches beside her left temple.

"Now, with a touch . . ." He pressed the button and the small computer transmitted the home page of a popular social networking site onto the air in front of her.

She jumped, bumping back into him. He grasped her upper arms to steady her.

"Oh. My. God."

"Indeed," he said, squeezing her shoulders in response to the reverence decreasing the volume of her voice.

"Is— What— Is that—?"

"Yes, it is."

"Yes? But . . . where is the computer screen?"

"It doesn't require one."

"How is that possible? What is it projected on?"

"The air."

"The air? How do you—?"

Her hair was fascinating. What harm could come from touching one curl? He succumbed to temptation, watching it stretch from a coil to a spiral before springing back into shape.

He pulled another one. "This conversation will continue more expeditiously if you refrain from repeating my answer to your preceding question before asking the next question."

She turned her head to the side, attempting to glance at him over her shoulder. The HPC projected the image of the website on to his kitchen cabinets. "How does it work?"

"A broad question. Can you be more specific?"

She planted her hands on her hips, though she didn't turn to face him. "Seriously?"

"I'm trying to ascertain what you want to know. There are many facets to the HPC and I could talk about them for hours. But what if I start with an area that doesn't interest you and spend the next twenty minutes discussing the use of lasers to excite oxygen and nitrogen atoms, never broaching the subject you actually want—"

"Ugh!" she groaned in a theatrical manner. "Fine! How do I post my status?"

He blinked. Her frustration with him was clear, yet she recognized his point and altered her initial query. No hysterics, no name-calling, no judgmental pronouncements.

His pulse escalated. Interesting.

"Do you see the small keyboard icon in the bottom right corner?"

She nodded and the image bobbed.

"Move your right hand in that general location and motion as if to grab it."

She paused and he understood her hesitation. He'd found it odd the first time he'd executed the motion. He slid his hand down her arm and moved her hand toward the icon. She curled her fingers and the image glowed.

"Propel it upward."

"What?"

He thought for a second then said, "Throw it in front of you."

She did and gasped when a foot-long illuminated keyboard appeared before the projection of the website.

"Did you see that?"

"Of course. I'm standing behind you."

She reached out and touched the image. A letter appeared in the air. She snatched her hand back as if burned.

"It's okay. Type."

"Are you sure?"

"I wouldn't tell you to do so if I wasn't."

Her fingers flew over the keyboard.

"Adam! I had no idea. I mean, this is incredible. You invented this?"

He nodded, his chest expanding with pride.

"You're a genius!"

"I know."

He tapped the power button on the HPC and the screen dissipated. He took the device off her ear and placed it back in the box on his desk.

Chelsea faced him, her eyes bright, her lips stretched into a wide grin. "This launch has to be perfect. The HPC deserves nothing less."

"Exactly. I'm glad you understand." He squeezed her hand. "I'll assemble the information you'll need to compose the speech."

This was great. He headed for the storage room where he kept work-related files. His previous worries had been absurd. He'd get her the specs and she could start drafting—

She tugged on his sleeve, halting his progress. "Wait. I'm not writing your speech."

He frowned. "You said you would help me. That's the help I need."

She shook her head. "I think there's been some confusion."

He crossed his arms over his chest. "Not on my part. I recall our conversation accurately."

She shifted her stance, one hip jutting laterally. "I don't care what you recall. I'm not writing your speech. What I will do is help you make the HPC stand out among all the other products Computronix will launch."

He clenched his jaw. "The HPC doesn't need an ostentatious reveal. You've seen its capabilities. It will succeed based on the merits of its performance."

"Your naiveté is amazing considering your intelligence. You will be the face of this product. It'll be your passion, your words that will link you to it. You reading my words will be fake."

"Fraudulence will be the least of my problems if I fuck up the presentation, in which case that same focus on me will hurt the HPC."

She exhaled slowly and shook her head, her lips compressing to create divots in her chin.

A swarm of anger heated him. He was well acquainted with versions of that expression, had seen it on the faces of countless family members, acquaintances, and dates. When his mother begged him to be like the other boys in his playgroup. In the eleventh grade when Annette Connors told him it didn't matter how cute he was, no girl would suffer through twenty minutes of why the latest video game was more nuanced and mature than 99 percent of Hollywood horror movies. When his first college roommate asked to be reassigned because "this weirdo gets up at 6 a.m. every day to do push-ups. Even when he doesn't have class!" It was the look that usually preceded a remark used to remind him he was different, odd. But seeing it eclipse her features . . . He clenched his jaw so tightly his back teeth clicked.

He'd accept a spectrum of emotions from her, but he'd be damned if he'd endure her exasperated pity.

"Perhaps I overestimated your abilities. You assisted me with a few pop culture questions, a talent on par with a teenage girl and her Twitter account, but hardly worthy enough to entrust with the HPC."

She flinched. "You're an asshole. Good luck. You're going to need it," she said, snatching her bag from the bar stool and stalking to the stairs.

Just like that, his anger subsided. Dread clogged in his chest and his feet moved of their own accord, carting him after her. "You can't leave. You promised to help me."

Her heels stomping down the steps was her reply.

He closed his eyes and dropped his chin to his chest. *Epic fail, Bennett.* He should go after her. He needed her help with the launch, but his unparalleled attraction to her disturbed him. A classic example of the lesser of two evils: risk that the HPC presentation would fail without her guidance, or risk spending more time with a woman who made him question the wisdom of keeping her at a distance.

"I Googled you."

His head shot up. She hadn't left?

Chelsea stood there, shoulders thrown back, head held high. "You've presented papers at tech conferences all over the world. Why is this different?"

He shrugged. "When I present a paper, the audience attends for the information. All that's required is for me to read the paper aloud. No one is there to judge me, only my work. And my work is stellar."

She laughed. "Wow. Ego much?"

First Jonathan commented on his conceit and now Chelsea. Was it really an issue?

"That's not ego, it's fact. If I were presenting a paper about the development of the HPC for an audience of my peers, I'd excel without a qualm. But Mike informed me the mainstream press would be covering the event. Like the magazine that sent me those questions. They'll be looking for a story to titillate their readers and sell issues."

"Like the *People Magazine* press conference?"

His shoulders stiffened. "You know about that?"

"Funny thing about Google. You put in a question and it gives you pages upon pages of search results."

"Right." He stared down at his feet, unsettled knowing she'd seen that catastrophe. "The press conference heightened an already intolerable situation. That's why I need your assistance. I can't ruin this opportunity. At the moment, no one else has this technology. Once it's launched, other companies will reverse engineer it, but by the time they come to market, Computronix will be synonymous with the HPC. My company will be years ahead of our competitors."

She set her bag down on the rough-hewn side table and moved to stand in front of him.

"I'll help you, but we need to come to an understanding. I'm not your speechwriter. It's going to take more than a pithy speech or reading an excellent paper for this presentation to be a success. I need you to trust me and cooperate."

She had amazing eyes. "Are you certain this is how you want to spend your vacation?"

"I hate being idle. This will give me something to do. Besides, I have some issues I need to think about."

Issues? He inched closer to her, heeding an internal urge to share her space. "Do they involve a man?"

He told himself his concern was business-based only. He needed her focused on his task, not on personal problems.

Her lashes fluttered. "Why would you think that?"

"With someone like you, there has to be a man involved."

"Someone like me?"

"Warm. Social." He gave in and caressed her cheek with his index finger. "Beautiful."

They stared at one another and those molecules began to kindle.

"No, it's not a man," she whispered.

God grant him the strength to keep his attention on his work and his hands off of her.

He tugged on a curl. "Then I agree to your terms."

Chapter Eight

CHELSEA STEPPED INTO Adam's walk-in closet and gasped. It was sleek and polished with enough space to house the wardrobe of ten regular people.

Or two celebrities.

After their argument yesterday, Chelsea knew she had her work cut out for her. Considering the transformation needed, she decided to start with the easiest task: his wardrobe. Gorgeous though he may be, Adam Bennett didn't strike her as the type of man who slid easily into change.

More like wrestling into skinny, stiff leather pants in the summertime.

The wall on her left was glass, providing a picturesque view of the mountains. *He must really like windows,* she thought, recalling the same breathtaking architectural feature from the great room and her guest room. The remaining walls held an intricate ebony-hued shelving unit with cream-colored linen baskets, like those showcased on the covers of design magazines.

Despite the grandiose dimensions, Adam's clothes took up one small section of the shelving unit, close to the door, as if that was all the space the closet could bear to spare. Jeans and sweatpants were folded and neatly arranged in appropriate cubbies, and an assortment of T-shirts, flannel shirts, and sweatshirts hung from the rod. God, she hadn't seen the cohabitation of this much flannel and denim since MTV reality shows in the nineties. All items were white, black, gray, navy blue, or in the case of the flannels, a checkered combination of the four. Somewhere, fashion icons shivered as Adam stomped all over their sartorial graves.

She wrinkled her nose and flicked a gray-and-white T-shirt, watching it sway on the hanger. "Don't you own a suit?"

"No."

When he didn't elaborate, she prodded, "Why?"

Adam scratched his cheek. "I never needed one."

"Never? You've never had an occasion to wear a suit?"

His eyes slid upward and he pursed his lips. After a moment, he shook his head. "No."

"Weddings? Funerals? Graduations?"

He continued to look at her without responding, and though she had only known him for a few days, she guessed it was because his answer hadn't changed.

"You've taken meetings with people dressed like that?" she asked, motioning to his clothes.

Adam glanced down at his faded jeans and navy T-shirt.

"What's wrong with this? It's functional, clean, and good quality. It would be impractical to wear a suit when I'm either sitting at the computer all day or creating prototypes."

Chelsea let her gaze drift down his body, pausing to admire the way his cotton tee hugged his broad shoulders, and marveling at how the well-washed jeans sat low on his hips and emphasized his long, muscled legs. Heat darted through her body and she resisted the urge to fan herself. As a woman, she had to admit there was nothing wrong with what he was wearing. Her eyes met his and the corner of his mouth lifted. He knew. He'd seen her checking him out. Crap.

And that was part of the problem. She was here as a PR professional, not as a woman. And while those two things weren't mutually exclusive, her reactions to this man meant they needed to be. She wanted to focus on getting the job done, not waste time reminding her pulse to settle down. She wanted to determine whether he needed a haircut, not notice his damp hair, still wet from his shower, which sent her mind in all sorts of steamy directions. Being attracted to this man was a nuisance she had to endure. Acting on that attraction would be professional suicide.

And it would be foolish to immolate herself for a man she didn't even like most of the time.

Satisfied with her inner pep talk, she took another look at the clothes hanging in his closet, managing— almost—to see past the body they covered. She raised incredulous brows. He was right. They were quality garments and carried the labels of top department stores and designers. She turned and noticed vivid colors dancing at the corner of her periphery.

"Do you agree?" he asked.

From this angle she could see the bottom of the closet normally hidden behind the open door. Row upon row of sneakers in assorted colors lined the floor.

"With what?"

"With the suitability of a computer programmer's wardrobe."

Bending down, she picked up a shoe and her mouth fell open at the famous basketball player's logo on the sole. She lifted shoe after shoe and found the same insignia. Adam was a sneakerhead? She smiled, oddly charmed by the discovery. It was like finding out the Queen of England could do the Electric Slide.

She straightened and turned back to him. "Where do you shop?"

"I don't. I engage the services of a personal shopper. I tell her what I need and"—he frowned, reached into his pocket, and pulled out his phone—"what sizes I wear and have the items delivered."

Now, *that* made sense.

"The shoes, too?"

His head shot up and his glare could have vaporized her. "Of course not. Buying sneakers is a personal experience. I purchase those myself."

She ignored the somersault in her belly. "Can I have your shopper's name and number? Since she's already worked with you, talking to her would save me some time."

"Give me a minute." His voice thinned in distraction as his fingers flew over the phone's touch screen. "Are we done here? I need to resolve an issue that has—"

Chelsea reached over and snatched the phone out of his hand.

"Hey!"

Her victory was short-lived as he grabbed it back with startlingly quick reflexes and shifted his body, holding the phone out of her reach.

"You can't take my phone." His brows were mashed together in a thunderous formation.

"Cooperation," she said, overexaggerating the multi-syllabic word. "You promised."

She lunged for the phone but he held up an arm to block her attempt to retrieve it. Said arm landed squarely against her breast.

They both froze, a provocative statuary. Oh. My. God. How did she continue to find herself in these situations with him?

Her breath caught in her throat. The corded muscles in his forearm seared through the thin material of her silk top and her nipples responded, pebbling against the delicious friction. His eyes shot to hers and the heated lust she saw in their depths floored her. Like he was two seconds away from pushing her back against the wall and covering her body with his own. She staggered back and he dropped his arm like he'd just been informed she had a contagious disease. So she wasn't the only one affected. She didn't know if that made her feel better or worse? The muscle in his cheek ticked and he slid his phone back into his pocket. Her heart pounded mercilessly as she opened her mouth, then closed it, unsure of what to say.

Just pretend it never happened.

"This is important," she said, her voice a strangled mess. She cleared her throat, trying to get back on track. "You said you wanted my help."

He hesitated for only a second. "I do. I only asked for a minute to respond to a text."

"You were getting ready to blow me off."

She winced as her last three words echoed between them. He lifted a brow.

She cleared her throat. "I meant, you were going to abandon me for your work."

"I asked if we were done to figure out the approximate time of our completion. I wanted to inform the engineers when I would be able to answer their questions." A tentative smile teased the corner of his lips. "I had no intention of blowing you off."

Her stomach tumbled over the cliff. His smile could sell a million HPCs before he uttered one word.

"Besides, this can't take too much longer, right? Just tell me what deficiencies you detect in my wardrobe and I'll order the appropriate replacements. So, fifteen minutes?"

And like a pendulum, her feelings swung back toward mild irritation.

"No. Not fifteen minutes." She crossed her arms. "Clothes are more than fabric used to cover your body. They also serve as your greeters to the world. People see you and make a split-second decision about who you are based on what you wear. Whether you're rich or poor, conservative or more liberal. Whether you like punk or country, if you're shy or outgoing. And if image is relevant to your occupation, you become a walking advertisement."

Which was why Chelsea never ventured into public without her stylish armor intact, believing it didn't matter how you felt inside, you should always look like a winner. Especially now that she had a choice. Growing up, the idea of dressing well hadn't been within her grasp, although it was often in her dreams. Now, her business depended upon it. No one would trust a slovenly public relations professional, believing she'd be as messy and careless with his or her reputation as she was with her appearance. These days there was no excuse for anyone not to understand the importance of projecting the right image.

"And that's a good thing?"

She laughed. "It's the way things are."

He curled his lip. "That's absurd. The only assumption anyone should make about me, based on my clothing, is that I can afford to keep myself warm. To discern my personality or any of my beliefs or values by the type of clothes I wear is a waste of time."

"Really? Would you get a haircut from someone whose own hair was chopped all to pieces? Would you go to a dentist whose own teeth were rotted and falling out?"

"You're making two different arguments. The barber's and dentist's appearances have to do with their skill level, not the clothes they're wearing. If the dentist's teeth were rotten, I would question the quality of his work. And that wouldn't change, whether he was wearing sweatpants or a ten-thousand-dollar suit."

It was an effort to speak through her clenched teeth. "You're missing my point."

"No, I'm waiting for you to make a cogent one."

"Arrrgh!" she yelled, stomping away from him and counting to ten.

No one could be this difficult. It was the second time he'd caused her to lose her composure. She never lost her composure. It was their first lesson and he was giving her grief over something as basic as wearing clothes appropriate to the situation. She was filled with a rush of sympathy for his mother. He'd probably been born breech.

She inhaled deeply and blew the air out of her mouth. She took another cleansing breath, then walked back to where Adam stood, typing into his phone.

"Adam?"

He looked up.

"Think of it this way. Certain professions require their employees to dress in a particular manner. You're right that a suit can't be the basis by which a bank manager's competence is judged, but the customs of his profession require him to wear it. The custom of a launch of this magnitude would require you to wear something other than jeans and a T-shirt. Does that work for you?"

He stood there staring at her and she realized he was thinking about her question. Finally, he gave a curt nod. "Okay."

Thank God.

"We need to go shopping," she said. She started out of the closet, then turned back and motioned toward his phone. "You can tell your engineers that we'll be done in a fe—three hours."

She hardened herself against the gratitude that made his beautiful eyes glow as he held her gaze.

"The shopping mall is thirty minutes away," he informed her.

Thirty minutes in a tight, inescapable space?

In an ordinary situation, she'd use that time to discover more information about her client. Strengths. Weaknesses. Interests. Causes. But there was nothing ordinary about this situation, Adam, or her reaction to him. And she despised being out of her comfort zone.

Decision made, she said, "We'll take separate cars."

CHELSEA LOVED THE look of upscale department stores, and this one was no different. Warm recessed lighting shone on dark wooden tables draped in colorful wheels of men's dress shirts and coordinating ties and hand-kerchiefs. The familiar tableau calmed her, reminded her of the reason she was there. Adam was just another client in need of a new wardrobe. The atmosphere had become strained back at his house—for a few reasons—and she was willing to blame some of that on the intimacy of their isolation. Being in public would bring a welcome dose of reality and hopefully dissipate some of the lingering tension.

A young man approached them. "May I help you?"

"Yes," Chelsea said, all business once again. "We have an appointment with Monique."

"One moment."

He headed over to a sleek phone mounted on the wall, his sport coat and trousers nicely tailored for his slim build. Chelsea sensed a teachable moment.

"Based on his attire, wouldn't you trust him to help you buy a suit?" she asked Adam.

He stood next to a grouping of athletically attired mannequins, his hands shoved in the front pocket of his jeans, his expression impassive. It was the first time she'd spoken to him directly since they left his house. She was relieved to note that she could finally do so without reliving the exquisite pressure of his arm against her breasts.

"Once people witness the HPC in action, they will want to buy it. The clothing I wear as I sell it will be irrelevant," Adam said in a matter-of-fact tone.

She narrowed her eyes. He had to be putting her on. If it were anyone else she'd think he was secretly enjoying his attempts to annoy her.

"Miss Grant?" a cool voice inquired.

Remembering the place and her purpose, Chelsea composed her face into calm lines and turned to see a petite woman walking over to them, her dark hair styled into a sleek bob.

Chelsea held out her hand. "Hello. I'm here with—"

"Mr. Bennett," Monique said, her eyes widening. She defrosted her demeanor and it flowed thick and sweet.

Like taffy. "I didn't know this appointment was for you. It's lovely to see you again. It's been a while."

Chelsea frowned and let her slighted hand fall back to her side.

"Eight months, two weeks, five days," Adam responded, giving her a crisp nod and taking a step back.

Monique laughed and the sound grated on Chelsea's nerves. "Counting down the days? You're always so . . . precise." She laid a hand on his arm. "Did you need to place another order?"

"Chelsea believes I do."

"Oh." Monique finally spared her a glance. "And she is . . . ?"

Give the woman a pole and tackle box; she was fishing for information.

The cold shoulder wasn't a new occurrence. Chelsea had been in numerous situations where people fawned over her client while ignoring her. She knew enough to ascribe it to the offender's lack of manners and keep her professionalism intact. But this was the first time she imagined telling someone to remove their hand or she'd do it for them. She wanted to slide *her* hand into Adam's and let Fisherwoman Monique know he wasn't available. But she couldn't. While it would be satisfying, it wouldn't be professional.

Plus, Mr. Tell the Truth wouldn't back her up.

Monique's hand flexed against his sleeve and Chelsea clenched her teeth. Maybe he *was* available. He wasn't moving away from her touch.

"*She* is in need of your assistance." Chelsea smiled and Monique straightened her shoulders. "We'll need to see some pieces different from what you've previously sent him." She ticked the items off on her fingers. "Casual slacks and shirts, mix-and-match business casual pieces, and a couple of suits. You offer custom tailoring?"

Monique's nostrils flared. "We do."

"Excellent. We'll need him fitted for one custom suit and we'll tailor another one off the rack." She turned to Adam and explained, "There isn't enough time for the custom suit to be ready for the launch."

Monique gazed at Adam before motioning with her hand. "Of course. Please, follow me."

She led them through an unmarked door that opened into a private dressing area. A high-backed, tufted dark leather sofa sat in front of a large rectangular platform surrounded by mirrors.

"Can I get you anything to drink?" Monique asked Adam.

He turned to Chelsea. "What would you like?"

The small gesture of tenderness, of caring about her comfort, was noted with appreciation. She stared into his warm eyes. "I'm fine."

"Yes, you are," he murmured, returning her stare. Monique cleared her throat and he looked away. "Nothing for us."

Adam indicated she should precede him to the sofa, but before he could follow he stilled, frowned, then reached into his pocket and pulled out his phone. Chelsea thought *she* had an unhealthy attachment to her cell. His was surgically linked to his brain. Maybe that's how he'd come up with the HPC.

"Mr. Bennett, do you want to try on the clothes or see them on someone first?" Monique asked, trying once again to claim some of his attention.

When he didn't respond, Chelsea reached over and took the phone from him. Having learned her lesson from earlier, she immediately slid it into the front pocket of her slacks and smirked when his hand halted mid-grab.

"Look, I know you do important work, but this is important, too. You can give me a few hours of your time. Afterward, I won't bother you for the rest of the day."

His attention bounced between her face and the pocket where she stashed the phone.

"I'll turn it off," he said, relenting. He held his hand out, palm up.

She patted her hip. "I'll hold on to it for you. Now, do you want to try on the clothes or see them first?"

"See them." He sank down onto the sofa.

"He'll see them first," she repeated to Monique. The other woman stared at them, a frown marring her attractive features, before she spun on her heel and hurried off.

Adam sat on the edge of the sofa with his elbows resting on his thighs and his head bowed.

She sat next to him. "What's wrong? Are you really upset because I took your phone?"

"I asked for your help to prepare me for the product launch," he said, his voice hollow.

"That's what I'm doing."

He twisted his head to look at her and the misery that stained his face tightened her chest. "No, you're co-opting my life."

"Not your entire life. Just the parts of it that have to do with other people."

He didn't smile as she'd intended. "I don't need help dealing with other people and I don't need new outfits. Only one. For the launch." He shook his head. "You're trying to change me and it won't work."

With that gorgeous face and his tall, muscled body, no woman in her right mind would want to change him. But this wasn't about what she might personally prefer in a man. It was about what Computronix preferred for the face of the HPC.

"You can't fake your way through a product launch. It's not a fifteen-minute press conference where you can stand to the side and pray no one will notice you. This is a sixty-minute interactive presentation between you, Mike, and the reporters."

He narrowed his eyes and angled his body away from her. "You know a lot about product launches."

Damn. She'd have to be more careful. She couldn't make many more mistakes like that if she expected to keep him in the dark about her true motives. Guilt arrowed through her and made her voice sharper than she intended.

"Research, remember? Like you said, I'm good at my job. Once you hired me, I even watched several of Computronix's previous launches to get an idea of what would be required of you. If you thought you'd sail through it with a new outfit and some previously written quips, the question is, did you do *your* research?"

Before he could respond, the door opened and Monique rushed back in. "I have Jordan pulling some items for you."

"Thank you," Chelsea said.

Her phone rang and she dug into her bag and checked the caller ID.

Shit.

It was Howard. She'd just talked to him a few days ago. Why was he calling her again? She was tempted to let it roll to voice mail, but what if he had information that impacted the account, something she needed to know? Why else would he call? If it was a standard work issue, he would've informed her assistant or sent her an email. "I've got to take this."

He scowled. "I thought the use of our cell phones was prohibited during this outing?"

"I'm not the one who needs help," she said, slipping out of the private dressing room and accepting the call. "Hello?"

Adam's solemn "That's a matter for great debate" followed her through the door and collided with Howard's terse "Status report."

"This is two times in one week. I haven't needed to call in for a status report in years." It was true. Once she was given an assignment, she assembled her own team who reported to her. She didn't report back to Howard until the project's conclusion. She pursed her lips and mentally questioned the sudden hands-on management.

"Do I need to remind you how important this account is? We're all answerable to someone on this one."

His anxiety pacified her growing ire. She wasn't the only one feeling the pressure. "You're right, I'm sorry."

"Will Bennett be ready?" Howard asked.

"I believe so."

A pause. "I don't think I've ever heard doubt in your voice. It makes me nervous. Is there a reason to believe he *won't* be ready for the launch?" he asked.

How about the fact that every time Adam stared at her from those intense blue eyes, her lungs drew a reviving breath and her heart pounded in her chest? What about the way he caressed her face and fondled her curls made her yearn for his touch in other, more sensitive places? Or maybe the fact that he often had her emotionally careening between annoyance and desire?

She had so little time to prepare him for the presentation, and they'd wasted a percentage of it as they navigated from professional to personal and then back again. If it were any other client, she wouldn't hesitate to pass him off to another colleague. But in this case that wasn't an option. Her partnership was on the line. She'd just have to try harder to keep them settled on business terra firma.

"No," she said, relieved her boss couldn't see her facial expression. "He'll be ready."

"A successful outcome on this project is imperative to the firm . . . and to your future."

She didn't need Howard to echo the warning. Again.

"Every person with a social media presence thinks

they can do their own PR," he said, settling into his rant. "To continue to thrive, we have to stay relevant. Being connected to the tech event of the decade will bolster our reputation and solidify your place with Beecher & Stowe. Remember, firm-first mind-set."

Chelsea glanced over her shoulder at the closed door that led to the dressing room. No one had passed her carrying a rack of clothes. Was there another entrance to the room? If not, she'd left Adam alone with Monique. Her stomach tightened. "I've got to go, Howard. He's waiting for me."

When she stepped inside the room her concerns were validated. Monique stood next to Adam, her head tilted back, her lips curved in invitation. "—happy with the service we've been providing, Mr. Bennett. You didn't have to come down here. I would've been thrilled to personally deliver your order to you." She dropped her voice. "Like last time."

What the hell?

Adam smiled. The son of a bitch smiled! Okay, so it wasn't his sell-a-million-HPCs smile, but his lips did quirk. When they parted, Chelsea knew she didn't want to hear his response.

"I'm back," she said, waving her cell phone in the air. Monique stiffened and Adam lifted his head. Chelsea made a show of peering around the room. "Where are the clothes?"

Monique's frustration was obvious, as was the glower she catapulted in Chelsea's direction. She exhaled loudly. "I'll see what's keeping Jordan."

Possibly your instructions for him to stay away while you seduced my client.

Conflicting emotions swirled in her gut. As soon as the door clicked shut behind Monique, Chelsea marched over to Adam. "Did you sleep with her?"

He blinked, his dark blue gaze steady. If he was startled by her verbal assault, his expression didn't reveal it. "No."

It was none of her business. She had no right judging Monique's professionalism when she was down in the trenches with her. And yet none of those considerations could stop her from asking, "Do you want to?"

She held her breath and his intense inspection stole it from her meddlesome clutches. He tilted his head. "Why do you care?"

"I don't," she said, feigning interest in an imaginary loose thread on her silk tunic. "Not really. But she's acting as if you did."

He shrugged, still not releasing her from his visual hold. "I can't control her behavior, only my response to it."

"You might want to review your response," she said, thinking of Monique's hand on Adam's arm when they first arrived and the scene she'd just interrupted. "Because I guarantee she thinks there's something between the two of you."

"You don't know what my response would've been. You interrupted me."

Well, if he needed to point fingers . . .

The door opened and Monique entered, carrying

a stack of folded sweaters, followed by the young man who'd approached them when they'd arrived at the men's department, pushing a wheeled clothing rack teeming with apparel.

"If you'll start looking through these selections," Monique said briskly, gesturing to the garments, "I have another rack I can—"

"Monique, can I speak with you? Privately." Adam's voice was firm.

"Of course, Mr. Bennett," Monique said, a contented feline grin spreading across her mouth.

Chelsea turned her back to them and began considering each garment. She had a job to do. She wasn't here to get caught up in Adam's personal life, especially as it had no bearing on the launch. Her skin heated. Okay, get caught up *any further* in his personal life. If he wanted to partake of what the other woman was offering, then it was none of Chelsea's business.

Maybe if you tell yourself it's not your business one more time and *click your heels, it might actually become true.*

Chelsea tried to focus on the clothes in front of her, even as she strained to hear the conversation taking place on the other side of the room. She couldn't decipher any of the words, just Adam's low, measured tone.

"Fine." The other woman finally said, her voice tight.

Chelsea glanced at Monique from beneath her lashes and saw two red splotches materialize on her pale cheeks. Her thin, scarlet lips were pressed into a firm line. Jerkily, like a badly handled marionette, Monique walked over to Jordan and pulled him from the room without a backward glance.

"What did you say to her?" Chelsea asked Adam when he joined her at the racks, his hands shoved in his pockets.

"I told her I wasn't interested in pursuing a personal relationship with her."

Pleasure bloomed in her chest, but she couldn't look at him, afraid her relief would be blanketed across her face. Instead, she chose to continue perusing the clothes. "There's a good lesson in this. It's always wise to be clear about your intentions."

"Chelsea."

He cupped her shoulders in his large, strong hands and turned her to face him. Her body was becoming accustomed to his touch, already leaning into him, awaiting his attention. He tugged on one of her curls and she felt an answering tug in the pit of her stomach. The strength of her attraction to him terrified her. Especially considering the stakes involved. She stood in a hypnotic trance as his fingers glided down her arm and entwined with hers, shivers of sensation following in their path.

His heated stare bored into hers as if trying to imprint his message on her brain. "I may prefer the company of computers to most people, but I have no problems being understood when I'm interested in a woman."

She exhaled. Holy hell.

He pressed a kiss to her neck as his fingers trailed along her waist, slipping beneath her blouse to sweep against her bare skin. She trembled as bolts of sensation tap-danced up and down her body. Was this his way of telling her he was interested in her? Did she want to listen? What happened to the solid ground of business? She tried to concentrate. God, he had wicked lips and skilled fingers. Too late, she realized his intentions. His fingers dipped into her pocket and rescued his phone. One corner of his mouth ascended in a sensually satisfied smile.

Would that same smile grace his lips after sex?

She pulled away from him, dragging in deep breaths of air, hoping it would clear her lust-addled head. Denying the chemistry between them had been foolish. Maybe it was better to acknowledge its presence and avoid placing herself in provocative situations. The launch. That was all that could be between them. The sound of a throat clearing caused her to whirl around.

Jordan stood in the doorway. "Monique has turned your account over to me. May I be of service?"

Adam looked up from his prized possession. "Does that service include pursuing a physical relationship with me?"

Chelsea gasped, certain the younger man would be offended. Adam's seductive words had lulled her into forgetting why this man needed her help. Headlines proclaiming the sexy genius's penchant for salesmen floated before her vision. She'd let her personal feelings distract her from the task at hand. Again. Forget the promotion. She deserved to lose her job.

But Jordan surprised her by laughing. "No."

Adam nodded and shot her a look, a slight twinkle in his eye. "Then we'd be grateful for your assistance."

Chapter Nine

CHELSEA'S LEG ROCKED while she waited for Adam to return. He'd let her into the house, but a phone call had claimed him immediately. Now she stared, unseeing, out the window, her arms crossed over her chest. They'd had a moment three days ago. Standing there in the private viewing room of the department store, she'd lost herself in the storm of his dark blue eyes.

I have no problems being understood when I'm interested in a woman.

Those words had meandered through her mind every night since, like a playlist on repeat. What had he meant? He could be so literal. Was he saying he would tell a woman if he was interested in her and since he hadn't said anything, he wasn't? Or, as she'd been foolish enough to dare to hope, had he meant the exact opposite?

And even as that hope stirred to life, she squashed it down. Nothing could happen between the two of them.

How many times did she have to repeat it to herself before she believed it?

As many times as it took.

He was her client, her ticket to the promotion she'd wanted her entire life. Nothing was more important. Not even a tall, gorgeous, brilliant man who managed to look inside her soul and pull at emotions she hadn't anticipated.

"What's that?"

Chelsea jumped. Adam stood watching her. Her heart raced. He was a visual guilty pleasure. His dark hair was damp and swept back from his face. A sleeveless dark gray T-shirt hugged his broad shoulders, and a pair of loose athletic pants hung from his hips. He looked strong, healthy, and powerful. Yet she knew, no matter how capable he looked physically, the most dangerous muscle in his body was his brain.

And she found that sexy as hell.

"What's that?" he repeated again, pointing at the object in the middle of the room.

Chelsea wiped her hands down the sides of her pants. *Relax and breathe.* The irony of the self-directive wasn't lost on her. When she'd initially planned this course of action, she'd imagined bringing someone in to perform this exercise. But his insistence on not inviting anyone else to his home, plus his unavailability all weekend, left her with little time and even fewer options. She'd considered deleting the activity from her agenda, but a stubborn part of her refused to believe she couldn't get through the lesson with her professionalism intact.

"A massage table," she managed, proud when she sounded lucid instead of flustered.

He walked over to it. "Who's getting a massage?"

"You."

His fingers trailed against the navy blue terry cloth and the muscles in his bicep ticked.

She swallowed. "Maybe."

She needed to pull herself together. How was she supposed to teach him to relax when she was a jittery wreck?

He shot her another of his patented, probing looks. "You always travel with one of these?"

"No." She forced a laugh. "There were two of these at the Andersons' house. I grabbed one because I thought it would help us with today's lesson."

"Which is?"

"Relaxation."

His brow creased. "When will your lessons involve concrete tasks I can complete?"

"Concrete?"

"Yes, concrete. Pertaining to or concerned with reality rather than abstractions."

She didn't try to contain her laugh. "Everything we're working on will have tangible effects on your presentation. That includes relaxation. It's important that you stay calm and focused during the presentation. If you project confidence, your audience will lean into the experience."

"That's touchy-feely nonsense. This presentation is the most significant occurrence of my career. I'll be worried about my clothes, interacting with Mike, and engaging with the press. There is nothing relaxing about that scenario."

He had a point, but . . . "That's exactly why you'll have to do it. The press can be like a pack of rabid dogs. They'll take their mood cues from you. They'll be coming to the presentation having watched your last press conference and expecting you to behave in a similar manner. In fact, most of them will already have that meltdown as the lead for their story. They won't care about the launch of the new device. They'll want to release another story about how you deal with the press. Let's not do their work for them. We want them excited about the HPC so they have no other option but to write about the device."

"You make a persuasive, compelling argument."

A major compliment, coming from him. "I can get you through this launch successfully. Do you trust me?"

She tried and failed to ignore the burn in her throat when she said "trust me." He stared at her for a long moment. The thick lashes of his eyes, the only softness on his face, were too beautiful for a man. One could be forgiven for believing a man with the planes and edges of his bone structure would be callous. But no one who possessed those lush lashes could be heartless. Finally, his lips curved upward.

"Yes, I trust you."

The implied vow echoed through his words. They'd crossed a milestone. And her stomach plummeted with the knowledge of the lie she carried.

"Great." She exhaled and pasted on another smile. At this point, she'd be lucky if her face didn't crack by the end of the day. "You mentioned spending most of your time at your computer. Are you doing any stretching? Yoga? Pilates?"

He laughed, the sound a bark of masculine amusement. "Yoga?"

"Don't knock it. Yes, yoga is known for its relaxing properties, but certain versions of it can provide a very strenuous workout."

"If you say so," he said, his condescension as high as his ego.

"So, you don't do yoga. Any type of stretching at all?"

"For exercise? No."

She scanned his body and her heart threatened to burst from her chest. "You're obviously in very good shape. You don't get that body"—she waved her hand in his direction, not meeting his gaze—"by sitting in front of your computer sixteen hours a day."

"I run."

She blinked. "You have a treadmill here?"

"No, outside."

"You have a treadmill outside?"

"I run outside," he said with exaggerated enunciation.

She craned her head to peer around him and through the large windows. All she saw were trees and the rooftops of houses down the mountain. "Is there a track or something around here?"

He laughed again, the action brightening his eyes and producing appealing crinkles at the corners. The flash of white teeth against the darkness of his beard sent her pulse soaring.

"There are trails throughout the mountains. I run those."

She thought of the steep, curving road she'd been driving this last week. There were very few flat stretches on the public road. Most of his run on the trails had to stretch uphill. His legs were probably like rods of steel.

"Does that relax you?" she asked, feeling anything but relaxed, as she attempted to stay on task.

"I've never considered the relaxation component. I do it consistently and experience the known endorphin rush, so my body finds it beneficial. As for my mind, if I'm working through a problem, going for a run usually helps."

She nodded. "It sounds like, even though it might not be relaxing in the way I was thinking, it does work for you. I would suggest you go for a run the morning of the presentation. A nice, long, steady run to prepare your mind for what you're about to do."

"I can do that."

"Good." She clasped her hands together in front of her chest. "Can you take a seat on the table?"

He did, and she moved to stand in front of him. His head was level with hers and the heat from his body darted out and singed her. She took several steps back.

"I want to show you some simple deep breathing exercises that will help you calm down and focus in the moments before you take the stage. Are you willing to try them?"

"Yes."

No arguments, questions, or conditions? He really *did* trust her.

"These are also beneficial if you need a moment during the Q & A to gather your thoughts or choose the right words after an antagonistic question. Now, close your eyes."

His lashes swept down, casting a silky shadow on his cheekbones.

"Inhale slowly and hold it, one . . . two . . . three . . . four. Now, exhale, slowly, one . . . two . . . three . . . four. That's it. Again."

He drew in a breath and contained it to her tally, then released it and repeated the process.

"Your mind shouldn't wander. Concentrate on the numbers and count to yourself as you inhale and exhale. Good, one more time."

His chest rose and fell and her gaze slipped to his mouth as his lips parted to let the breath escape. God, he was unbearably attractive. His face had lost some of the tension it normally held, something she hadn't realized until this moment, when she saw his forehead smooth and his jaw relaxed. Her fingers itched to trace his features, find out if the scruff on his face was soft or coarse, and slide her fingers through his long, dark hair.

"When was your last haircut?"

She slapped a hand over her mouth. That's not what she meant to ask.

His eyes opened. "January."

Three months ago. That would explain its length. She

wondered if he always went several months between hair-cuts or if something special happened in January.

His look probed into her soul and she resisted the part of herself that wanted to let him in. She shook her head and tried to remember what she'd actually meant to ask him.

"Have you ever received a professional massage?"

"No."

"A massage is an effective way to help you relax. They can ease pain, manage anxiety, and stimulate your mind. I'm going to give you a basic one, so you'd know what to expect."

"Are you a licensed therapist?"

"No. I've picked up a few moves over the years. Part of my job is to know a little bit about a lot of things."

"I can see how that would be useful."

"You might like it enough to schedule one for your-self. They're especially good at the end of a long day in front of the computer."

"I'm aware of ergonomics. It's the reason my work-station is set so my monitors are all at the optimal distance and angle and my chair is custom-designed for proper spine and hip alignment."

The memory of sitting in that chair almost produced a moan. And speaking of sounds of pleasure . . . How was she going to do this?

"Take off your shirt."

He grasped the hem of his shirt, and in one smooth motion ripped it over and off his head, tossing it on the floor.

Her mouth went dry. His chest was spectacular. Golden skin stretched over solid muscle but not so many that he looked unreal. A smattering of dark hair covered his chest and trailed down over the ridges of his abs, to disappear beneath his waistband. She groaned inwardly. What would he do if she reached out and let her fingers follow the path?

"Lie down on your back." The words squeezed their way from her throat.

The corner of his mouth twitched but he swung his legs onto the table and did her bidding. His muscles rippled with the movement, said abs contracting and releasing as he flattened.

"While you relax, think about what you're going to say at the presentation."

She moved until she stood at the head of the table. Before her, the windows of his great room showcased the amazing view, but it was no competition for the vision of his long, lean body stretched out on the massage table. She dropped her chin and flinched, startled to find him staring up at her. She wanted to look away, but his gaze held hers captive, like he was searching for the answer to some elusive equation that could only be found in their depths.

Inhaling, she sank her fingers into his hair and the crisp strands tickled her fingers. She stroked her fingertips along his scalp and down either side of his head to his nape, then shifted her hands until her palms cupped his head and her fingers channeled back up to his forehead. She repeated the process several times, enjoying the feel of his hair against her skin. His eyes fluttered shut and his chest rose and fell evenly.

What was she doing? She'd never thought of herself as a daredevil, but how else to explain this reckless compulsion to brush the fire and risk getting burned? She let her thumbs trace a path across his thick brows, down his temples, around his ears, and to the back of his neck, her fingers like experimental teenagers disobeying her brain's command to stop. On the next pass, she gently squeezed his earlobes. Over and over her fingers worked until she'd smoothed the creases from his countenance.

She lifted his head, the weight of it warm in her hands, and turned it first to the left, then to the right. She placed it gently back down on the bench and closed her eyes. This was supposed to be relaxing, but she was panting, trying to draw air into her deficient lungs. She felt lightheaded and overheated. Praying that Adam was reaping the benefits, she glanced down at him and froze. If the impressive ridge growing in his sweatpants was any indication, she was failing on that score, too.

"Turn over," she whispered, her usual crisp tones softened into husky, mushy notes. When he reached down to adjust himself before turning over, her belly dipped.

She could do this. Stopping now would be an admission that she couldn't handle it.

She reached for her bottle of body oil and poured some in her palm. Moving back to the head of the table, she rubbed her hands together, then placed her palms on the wide expanse of his upper back, her fingertips pointed toward his hips.

"Is that oil?" he asked, gruffly.

"Yes, why?"

"Grab a towel. Oil stains."

She stiffened and her desire dissipated like fog with the rising sun. She flashed back to the night they'd met. First his T-shirt, and now his floors? Seriously, she found his obsessive need to keep his possessions in pristine order unflattering. Heaven forbid a little oil dripped on the floor.

"What?"

Had she said that aloud?

He lifted his head. "What did you say, Chelsea?"

Damn. She had. "Nothing."

"You think I care about the floor?" His tone implied only an idiot could believe the statement was true.

Annoyance flared through her. "I'm trying to help you!" She removed her hands and held them in front of her. "A little rain, some oil. I'd hope you'd consider the big picture and conclude a spot on your floor or the ruination of your precious 'talk nerdy' T-shirt would be worth it."

The muscles bunched in his shoulders as he turned over and rested on one elbow. His stare immobilized her. "I don't care about the floor. You're wearing a beautiful outfit and I was concerned the oil would stain your clothes."

She glanced down at her garnet-red slacks and black sweater.

Oh.

Wait, what? He thought she looked beautiful?

"And I didn't give a damn about that T-shirt. I told you I didn't wear it, so you could do whatever you needed to for you hair not to end up looking like a 'ball of frizz.' Your words, not mine."

She opened her mouth to speak, then closed it. What could she say? Oops, my bad? Could she really be blamed for thinking what she did based on what he'd said?

Who was Adam Bennett? Was he the cold and distant computer genius she'd seen on the video of his press conference, or was he actually thoughtful and considerate, as his recent admission seemed to suggest? It bothered her that she couldn't get a grasp on him. She prided herself on quickly sizing up people and situations, yet this man refused to be defined.

Not knowing how to respond, she placed a palm on his shoulder and pushed, indicating he should resume lying flat. He resisted briefly, the muscles in his back flexing, before submitting. Once again, she was treated to the view of his broad, powerful back. She shifted her weight onto her hands and leaned forward, slowly gliding her palms down his skin in one long stroke. Each time she touched his strong, well-built body, a heady flush of power tingled through her. She repeated the motion several times more and a moan of pleasure rumbled from him.

She stilled. Should she stop? No. He was benefiting from the massage, and recalling this feeling of relaxation on the day of the launch would be valuable. So she had to continue . . . and attempt to ignore the deafening cacophony of her pounding heart.

Her fingers danced over his skin, sliding down his lower back and then up the sides of his rib cage and back to the base of his neck. She massaged, in broad circular strokes, from his hip joint to the base of his spine, up along his spinal column, and to the base of his neck. His back was a series of mounds and valleys that ended at a firm ass that teased her from the waistband of his pants. Over and over, she kneaded, rubbed, and smoothed his glorious body. She alternated the pressure of each stroke and by the time her hands fell from his hips, her touch had lost the firmness of a massage and was more of a light caress.

"We're done." She was breathing heavily and her body trembled with need. She moved away from him, grabbing a nearby towel and wiping her hands. This wasn't what she'd intended when she'd begun this exercise.

"Chelsea?" She turned and found him sitting up on the table, his legs over the side. His eyes burned into hers and he held out his hand. "Come here."

Her nostrils flared and, unable to refuse, she took his hand, letting him pull her into the space between his thighs. She was so close she could see the streaks of black that radiated out from his irises. The heat from his body warmed hers. Still, she couldn't help the shiver that rocked her body from his nearness.

"I'm not relaxed."

She knew it, could tell from the muscle ticking in his cheek, the flush on his cheekbones, the feverish glow in his eyes. His hand released hers and settled against her hips, his fingers flexing into her skin and pulling her forward. Her body melted, reacting to the desire that flowed off him in waves.

"Social interaction can be difficult for me." His voice was low and her gaze dropped to stare at his lips as they formed the words. "Facial expressions and tones of voice act as a second language, one in which I'm conversant but not fluent."

"Okay," she responded, unsure of his intention.

His finger dipped an inch beneath the waistband of her pants and trailed back and forth against her skin. She trembled.

"If one isn't careful, one can act on flawed knowledge."

"Uh-huh," she said, with all the coherence she could manage.

He licked his bottom lip. "The last thing I want is another misunderstanding similar to the oil and T-shirt situations."

She nodded, her body as tight as a flexed bow.

"So let me be clear," he whispered. "I want to kiss you."

She swallowed.

"Not only am I informing you of what I want, it also serves as notice of my intent. I'm going to kiss you."

It was the sexiest notice she'd ever received.

"If you don't want that to happen, tell me to stop or move away."

His hands continually grabbed and released her hips. Moisture pooled between her thighs, her body sensitive to his touch and the images his words were forming in her mind. Her nipples hardened against her thin sweater and his flaring nostrils told her he'd noticed her reaction.

"Time's up."

His mouth covered hers and he kissed her with a mastery that left her breathless. His lips were firm and her knees went weak when his tongue swept inside and tangled with hers. She held on to him, stunned by the strength of her reaction. God, he was an excellent kisser. He was passionate and commanding, nothing like she expected. And he smelled so good . . . like soap and fresh laundry, mixed with her body oil and . . . him. Adam. His kiss, his scent, his touch—the combination made her dizzy and she leaned into him. He held her tightly to his chest and the hardness pressed against her breasts, abrading her aching tips. She wasn't sure how long they kissed, but she needed more.

She shifted her weight onto the table and turned, forcing him to lie back on it. She straddled his hips and pressed her aching femininity against the rock hardness of his cock. She cradled it, rubbing her body against it. She wanted this man at this minute more than she'd wanted anyone. Ever.

He massaged her breasts, his thumb and forefinger plucking her nipples, sending arrows of pleasure straight to her core. She moaned and arched into his palm. Their breathing was harsh as they groaned and writhed against each other. She felt him at the button of her pants and she lifted her hips to make his access easier.

His fingers slid in and then under the waistband of her panties to twirl in the crispness of her hair. She shivered as his lips left her mouth and trailed down her jaw to her neck, licking and nibbling at the pulse there. The softness of his beard swept against her sensitive spot and she moaned again, holding his head to her, not feeling that it was possible to get close enough. She was on fire, sensation flowing through her blood. Her brain had shut down, leaving her body in charge, and it wanted to feel.

In this moment, she didn't care that her goal of partnership might be in jeopardy, that she found him demanding, or that she was lying to him. She just wanted to keep kissing him.

She shifted and the table almost collapsed.

Adam's shoulders tensed beneath her fingers and they broke apart, breathing heavily. He clasped an arm around her hips and, shaken, she looked over the side of the table. She clutched hold tighter and when she looked back at him, their gazes locked. She could see the haze of lust that clouded his normally clear gaze. Unable to help herself, she brushed her lips against his. Once, twice. Their lips clung. She couldn't stop kissing him.

The table shifted again and common sense intruded. Reluctantly, she inched off him, untwisting their arms and legs and climbing backward off the table. Adam sat up and swung his legs over the side of the table. Reaching down to adjust the thick evidence of his arousal, he reached out a hand to her, his intent clear in the direct heat of his eyes.

She wanted to go to him. She wanted to take his hand and let him draw her into his embrace again. She pressed the heels of her palms against her closed eyes and mentally pressed the Rewind arrow on the cosmic DVR remote. She pictured the table re-steadying itself, Adam lying back down, and her climbing back on top of him, re-twining their limbs. Then she'd press Play and lose herself in his frenzied embrace.

She exhaled and dropped her hands. She couldn't. Dammit. Life wasn't a movie she could direct. And even if it were, becoming sexually involved with Adam would be a mistake. She wanted to be a partner. She'd worked her entire adult life toward that one goal. It wasn't about the money. She already made a great living. It was what the job represented. It meant that she, Chelsea Grant, was not like her mother. She would never be poor, used, and disgraced. That she couldn't be defined by the circumstances of her birth. She wasn't on the outside. She was the ultimate insider. People needed *her* to make *them* acceptable. And making partner meant she was one of the best at it.

Then there was the lie that hovered between them. It had seemed harmless in the beginning. It hadn't mattered who'd hired her—him or Computronix. The job was the same: get the client ready for the launch. Now, knowing the absolutist position he held on any falsehood, hiding the truth from him was beginning to bother her, a sliver of censure beneath the surface of her skin.

All of these conflicting emotions swirling around in her head were enough to tamp down the desire that had torn through her body, leaving a guilty conscience in the cold light of day.

He stared into her eyes, the passion from a minute ago still blazing bright in his. He captured her hand, but when he tried to pull her to him, she resisted, standing her ground. He was more than strong enough to pull her to him, but he hesitated, his eyes waiting to see what she'd decided.

"I can't. I'm sorry."

He nodded. "Me, too."

Knowing that he accepted her decision and wouldn't push her, she moved closer to him and leaned her forehead against his. "It's too much. As good as you feel, as good as this feels"—she stroked her hands up and down his arms—"you're my client now, and I've always believed it was a bad idea to mix those relationships."

"Then you're fired."

She pulled back and stared at him, her stomach contorting into knots, only to straighten and calm down when she saw his lips quirk at the corners.

"Another joke, Mr. Bennett? You can't fire me, I'm having an effect on you."

"You most definitely are," he said, his voice smooth as warm maple syrup. "Want to feel?"

Not about to take that bait, she leaned in and gave him one final kiss before grabbing her purse and rushing out. She couldn't risk allowing that wonderful feeling of lethargy to steal her common sense and convince her to change her mind.

Chapter Ten

LETTING HER GO without pressing the issue was one of the hardest things he'd ever done.

Even now, hours after she'd left, he stared unseeingly at his computer screen, recalling in minute detail every sigh, every moan, every caress. Before her, every other kiss had been a waste of breath. It seemed God had been on a sabbatical when he'd asked for the strength to keep his focus on his work and his hands off of Chelsea. Anytime he was in her presence, he was touching her.

In his closet.

At the store.

Here, in his great room.

Though he couldn't be blamed for today. No man could've resisted after thirty minutes of her hands roaming all over his body. Or of deciding between the twin tortures of glancing up and seeing her breasts suspended over him, so close he could flick her fabric-covered nipples with his tongue, or closing his eyes and drowning in the heightened sensation of her touch. In fact, if *she* hadn't resisted, he would've carried her to his room and fucked her until they both passed out from exhaustion.

But then what? Once he'd taken the edge off his hunger for her, he'd still need her help with the presentation, and she'd told him she preferred not to mix business with pleasure. Even if he'd managed to leap that hurdle, he'd find himself in a situation where he was spending a lot of time with a woman, both in his bed and out of it, thereby granting her an intimacy he vowed to never again offer. Awareness and familiarity followed intimacy, and it wouldn't be long before she left.

Like everyone else.

So he should keep his distance, sexually, at least until the presentation was over. Sounded easy, except he recognized his burgeoning fascination and knew he'd have a difficult time staying away from her.

He sat up and rolled closer to his desk. Clicking on the appropriate icon, he pushed several keys on his computer. The center monitor blacked out and five seconds later, Mike's image filled the screen.

"How's it going?" Mike asked, his voice low and raspy. Several Starbucks cups littered his desk and he'd removed his jacket and tie.

"Good. The video testimonials from the beta testers of the new phone look phenomenal. A/V did an exceptional job."

"That's what I like to hear. I'll make a note to pass

along your praise." He tapped on his iPad. "And the pre-sentation?"

Adam sighed. "You know this launch is important to me. If you believe my being involved in the presentation is the HPC's best shot, then I'll do what's necessary."

Even try to stay away from the one woman he wanted more than anyone else.

Mike pushed back from his desk, waving his arms wildly. "I can't believe it. This isn't the Adam I know. What happened to you?"

I met a tall, gorgeous woman with smooth, dark skin and the softest curls I've ever touched.

Mike didn't wait for his response. "You won't regret doing this." He consulted his iPad. "I have the perfect person to help you—"

"No. I'll do it on my own."

He would not be dealing with another PR firm after the last one. The overly cheerful, too familiar representa-tive had made his skin crawl. Besides, he had Chelsea.

Mike frowned. "Come on, Adam. There are people who specialize in public relations and we can get them to help you."

"Don't push me on this."

"Fine. But you have to do a better job than the press conference. We're all depending on you."

Adam was aware of his obligations. The company was depending on him. People whose salaries they paid, their benefits and retirement. All were betting on the HPC being the success Adam knew it would be. He owed it to them to focus his considerable intellect on the presentation and not the lovely woman who had been dominating his thoughts.

That's why he was surprised when he heard himself say, "Remember my neighbor?"

"What?"

"My neighbor. The one I met during the storm last week?"

"Right. The 'agreeable' one," Mike said, laughing.

"She works in entertainment."

Mike cocked his head to the side. "You've spent time with her?"

"Some." Not enough.

"In the middle of prepping for the launch? That's . . . unprecedented."

"I can't seem to stop thinking about her."

Mike frowned. "We don't have time for you to think about her."

"I'm well aware of our timetable, Mike. How can I forget when you bring it up every fucking day?" He shoved his hand through his hair.

"Sorry," his friend said softly, rubbing the back of his neck. "Have you told her?"

He didn't attempt to feign ignorance. "That I have Asperger's? No."

He wasn't sure if he ever planned to tell her.

"In the time you've spent together, she hasn't noticed your literalness, your difficulty deciphering social cues, and your rigid adherence to routines?"

"They've manifested, but she attributes them to my being an asshole."

Mike laughed. "The two aren't mutually exclusive."

"Neither is being a charming bastard," he said, confident enough in his friendship with Mike to engage in this conversation.

They'd met in college, when Mike worked at the local video game store. It took several visits and quite a few stilted conversations, where they learned they were both attending Stanford, before they'd managed to become friends. The bonds of that tentative friendship were strengthened during an awkward Christmas dinner with Mike's family when Adam finally had to explain his behavior. Adam knew that being his friend wasn't easy, but over the years Mike had proven his trustworthiness and his loyalty.

And speaking of trustworthiness and loyalty . . .

"Telling Birgitta was the beginning of the end of our relationship," he said.

"Relationship? I thought you'd just met. Now you're talking a relationship?"

"There's something about her. She gets me, and gets to me, in a way I've never experienced."

"So this is more than a 'hit it and quit it' scenario?" Mike asked, using Jonathan's term of choice for a one-night stand.

"It's a strong possibility."

Mike thumbed his ear. "Maybe you should wait until the launch is over. Not just for Computronix's benefit, but for yours. You'll have more time to weigh the pros and cons of getting involved with her."

"That's what I decided, except—"

"That other wonderful Aspie trait of yours, single-minded fixation. Fuck, man, your timing couldn't be worse."

"Again, something I already know."

"This could backfire against you. Big-time."

"Don't worry. I won't let anything distract me from the product launch."

"Suddenly, it's not the launch I'm worried about."

ADAM OPENED HIS front door and came face to back with Chelsea's enticing rear. She spun around and her curls tumbled over her shoulder.

"It's about time. We have to . . ." Her gaze wandered from the base of his neck to his bare feet. "I've seen your closet, and this ensemble," she said, gesturing to his sweatpants and faded Stanford University T-shirt, "would be considered too scruffy even for your wardrobe."

She brushed past him and her scent tickled his nose. He smiled and closed the door in her wake.

This was going to be fun.

Chelsea stood before him in a white button-down shirt, brown pants that molded to her legs, and high-heeled ankle boots that created the optical illusion of unbelievable length. She looked glamorous, professional, untouchable. Gone was the woman with soft, parted lips, who'd gazed deeply into his eyes and trembled in his arms.

But that's the Chelsea he wanted.

And that's the Chelsea he'd have.

It had come to him during the night, when he should've been working. His attraction to Chelsea had been quick and intense, unlike anything he'd ever experienced. And when that happened, didn't he owe it to himself to figure out what was going on? It's possible it could have been exacerbated by the storm and the intimacy of their surroundings, but he wouldn't be able to focus on his presentation until he knew the answer. Achieving his goal wouldn't be easy, but he'd never allowed a problem's level of difficulty to prevent his attempts to solve it. She'd expressed her reluctance to combine work and play. In order to test his theory, he needed her to see that playing with him could be pleasurable *and* not affect their work. Then he could determine if what they were responding to was based in the isolation of their circumstances or on an actual connection.

"Hello? Adam?" She waved her hand, palm side out, in a vertical motion. "You can't stay in your own world, you have a guest. That's what we're working on today. Lesson Three, engagement."

He narrowed his eyes. Did she believe they could return to the status quo of two days ago? Before they'd kissed? Before he'd jerked off to the remembered sounds of her moaning in his arms? That was no longer a viable option for him. He grabbed her wrist. "I'm well aware of your presence, Chelsea. And I'm prepared."

Her glossed lips parted and her pulse fluttered against his hand. He smiled. Further evidence the desire that soared through him was reciprocated.

"Then why are you dressed like this?" she asked, pulling from his grasp. "We're supposed to head down into the city. What should I infer from this outfit?"

"That I have no plans to leave the house. It's hump day and I'm playing hooky."

"You can't play hooky. You have to prepare for the launch."

"I managed to complete a great deal during your two-day absence. I'm due for a break."

She looked away from him and shoved her hands in her back pockets. "I wish you would've told me that before I came over. I wouldn't have disturbed you."

"You aren't disturbing me. I've been waiting for you. I have something planned for us."

She leaned away from him. "We talked about this. I can't get involved with you."

"I wasn't referring to sex, although I'm not averse to it." He smiled. "I'm talking about enjoyable, non-sexual fun."

He headed up the stairs and his tension dissipated at the click of her heels when she followed him. He retrieved the bag from the counter and held it out to her.

"What's that?"

"A gift for you. I couldn't expect you to participate if I didn't provide you with the proper gear."

She held up her hands, palms facing out. "This isn't a good idea."

He cupped her cheek with his left hand and stared into her eyes. Her curls brushed softly against his finger-tips. "I'm not asking you to engage in an afternoon orgy. Trust me."

Her agreement didn't come instantaneously. She pulled in a deep breath and released it in a long, steady stream. Pressing her lips together, she snatched the bag from him and closed the guest bedroom door behind her.

He put his hands on his hips and lifted his gaze skyward. He'd been correct—this wouldn't be easy. But it'd be worth it.

He'd placed the cooler on the floor next to the coffee table when the bedroom door opened. Chelsea stood in the doorway, twisting the thin gold-and-garnet ring on her right hand, refusing to make eye contact. He couldn't catch his breath, a sensation similar to the one he felt after an eight-mile mountain trail run. She was so appealing in the sweatpants and T-shirt that it required every ounce of patience he had to remain where he was and not rush over to her and crush those soft, full lips beneath his own.

"Hi," he said, stunned to find his hands trembling. He crossed his arms over his chest.

"Hi." She bit that plump bottom lip and he noticed the gloss was gone. He considered her face.

"You removed your makeup?"

She applied it sparingly, unlike Birgitta, who'd never appeared in his presence without it, and always managed to get the heavily caked cosmetics all over his clothes and hers. Now he could see that Chelsea didn't need an abundance of artifice. Her creamy complexion was smooth and clear, her brown eyes wide and bright.

She shrugged and pulled at the hem of her white "Girl Gone Gamer" T-shirt. He thought she'd appreciate it, given her response to his "Talk Nerdy . . ." shirt the night of her arrival.

"Where did you get the clothes?" she asked. "I don't remember these in your closet, either."

"I drove down to San Mateo and bought them yesterday."

"But . . . you've been busy with the presentation."

He *should've* been busy with the presentation. "It was important."

Her lips quirked. "They fit perfectly . . . almost like you knew my size."

The memory of his close contact with her curves sent blood rushing to his dick. "A couple of days ago I had the opportunity to survey your body thoroughly. I interpreted what I felt to figure out your approximate size."

She dipped her head, but glanced up at him through her lashes.

"Come here," he requested, holding out his hand. When they touched, sensation trailed up his arm. She twined her fingers with his and followed him to the couch in front of the television.

"What's all this?" She gestured to the coffee table.

"An assortment of apples, grapes, fresh pineapple, chips, various beverages, two game controllers, and a PlayStation 4 system."

She laughed. "Yes, I know what each item is. They're some of my favorites. Why are they here?"

"They were in your supplies the night of the storm."

"Let me try again. What are we doing with them?"

Wasn't it obvious? "We're going to play video games."

"Seriously? Sweet." She rubbed her hands together. "I kick ass at Wii Sports."

He snorted. "Laudable for a teenage boy who depends on his parents for gaming gear. We're playing a third-person shooter."

She frowned, taking a couple of steps back. "A shooter game? I don't play those."

"It's not hard. You can learn."

"I don't want to learn. And speaking of learning"— she smoothed her hand down the side of her pants—"we really don't have time for this. You still have lessons for your presentation."

He studied her, noticing the tense set of her shoulders and the downward turn of her lips. "There's no shame in trying something you may not excel at."

"Easy for you to say, Genius George. But for us mere mortals, there's nothing fun about looking stupid."

"In the week since we've met you've asked me to do things that have made me uncomfortable. I've done them, which required a level of trust. I'm asking for that same level of trust in return. Playing video games is how I relax and have fun and I'd like to share that experience with you. If you don't enjoy yourself, you can leave and we can resume our lessons tomorrow."

A dent appeared between her brows and her gaze bounced away from his. An evasive maneuver. Fuck! Was she going to decline his invitation? A week ago he'd denounced déjà vu as fanciful nonsense. What he wouldn't give in that moment to be a mind reader, to know her candid and unfiltered thoughts. He waited, his breath caught in the back of his throat, hoping she'd decide to stay. Finally, the corner of her mouth tugged upward and she walked around to the front of the sofa and sat down.

"So, what game are we playing?"

Lightness spread throughout his chest, and he resisted the urge to pump his fist in triumph. Instead he settled next to her and picked up a controller. Pressing a few buttons, the television sparked alive in a burst of color.

"UnMapped 2."

"UnMapped. Isn't that your favorite game?"

She remembered. "Yes," he said, trying not to sound too pleased at this revelation.

"Is this a new version? You didn't mention a series when you answered *CGR*'s questions."

"The designers sent a beta to select players for feedback before its release early next year."

"How did you manage to get on that list?"

He smiled. "I may not be much in the entertainment field, but in the computer world, I'm a big deal."

She slid him a sidelong glance. "I hate to tell you this, Mr. Bennett, but you're a hotshot in anyone's world."

The words were innocuous enough, but he thought he detected a warmth in her tone and a sparkle in her eye. It could be an illusion of the light, still . . . His dick twitched in his pants.

"It's great for all gamer levels. It's a third-person POV shooter that hard-core gamers love, but there's a storyline with romance and extended cut scenes that I think newcomers will enjoy as well."

"I'll be the judge of that." She laughed and clapped her hands together. "I've always wanted to say that. So this is what you do for fun?"

"Yes." He brought up the game's menu. "It's also beneficial for my work. If I encounter a problem and the solution eludes me, playing for an hour often yields an answer. A release of dopamine, combined with a relaxed state of mind and a distracting activity, can lead to a burst of creativity."

"And you said you needed help. That type of endorsement should be splashed all over the packaging."

He laughed and reached over to hand her the other remote. "I took the chance you'd agree to play and set up your avatar."

Her digital character, complete with mocha skin, big brown eyes, and a riotous mound of black curls, appeared on screen.

"I'm not much of a gamer," she said, narrowing her eyes, "but even I can tell that avatar is pretty specific."

In prepping their game session, he'd been surprised at the limited choices of avatar options for women of color. And none of what was available came close to capturing the richness of Chelsea's skin tone. So he installed a mod file organizer and uploaded his own modifications until he was satisfied with the end product.

"The choices were narrow-minded and shortsighted. So I modded details about your character's face and body."

She said nothing for several seconds and he frowned. Had he done something wrong? Maybe she would've preferred a generic avatar and was annoyed that he'd made the choice for her. When he looked at her, she had a hand pressed against her chest. "That's . . . amazing. Thank you."

Warmth dispersed throughout his body. "It was my pleasure. It makes the experience more enjoyable. My feedback will contain a recommendation for more ethnically diverse options in creating game characters."

A nanosecond after her sweet fragrance provoked his senses, her hand landed on his thigh and she kissed his cheek. Her luminous eyes pinioned his for a long moment before she released him and returned her attention to the screen.

He reached up and swept his fingers over the sensitized skin on his face. The warmth in her eyes, the kiss on his cheek felt more intimate than anything they'd done days before. This was exceeding his expectations. He cleared his throat and refocused on the controller in his hand. Pressing more buttons, he used his thumb to move the joystick. His avatar, created from the stock selection, popped up on the screen next to Chelsea's.

"Is that your character?" she asked. "He's hot."

He winked at her. "A cyber imitation of the original."

Hoping he could deliver on all he'd promised, he started the game.

"The graphics are incredible," she said. "I feel like I'm watching a movie."

"These sequences are called cut scenes. They're used between game play to give backstory, show conversations between characters, and as rewards if you reach a certain level. This scene informs us of our character's motivation and sets up the adventure." He pointed to the screen. "We need to get to that ship. Are you ready?"

She flexed her fingers around the remote. "Yeah, I think so." The corners of her lips inclined upward. "I can't believe I let you talk me into playing video games when we should be working."

"You can't work all of the time." Mike and Jonathan would never believe that *he* was the one championing a respite.

"I have to if I want to be successful."

"And being successful is important to you?"

She narrowed her eyes and lifted her chin. "It's everything."

Later, he'd consider what she'd revealed, but now he activated the characters and led his avatar to the ship, where he took fire from the enemy. He ducked behind a cargo crate and looked for Chelsea's avatar. She was several feet away, engaging in a bizarre choreography of moves. She paced left and right, jumped up and down, crouched, then straightened, pulled out a gun and knife, then re-sheathed them. She was shielded from enemy fire by the broken-down pickup truck near the pier's entrance.

"What are you doing?" he asked, mesmerized by her avatar's frenetic gestures.

"I've got to learn the controls. I can't look down at my hands the entire game."

He stared at her, captivated by her logical thought process. Two minutes later, she scurried across the pier toward the shipwrecked boat. She didn't draw her weapon, appearing to value stealth over confrontation and brawn. Seeing that she didn't intend to protect herself, he became her muscle, shooting anyone who even looked in her direction, as she made it to the ship. When his avatar joined hers, the scene froze and wording on the screen indicated they'd successfully completed the level.

"That was so much fun," she said, edging forward on the couch. "Now, somewhere on this ship is a treasure map, right?"

"Yes, but the money isn't our endgame. There's an ancient artifact he believes will cure his sister. The money is for the scouts who'll guide them through the jungle to the sacred temple. To get the artifact, we'll need to locate the map."

She firmed her lips and nodded. For the next hour he marveled at her complete dedication to searching for that map and interviewing guides for their expedition.

"This is crazy. He can't believe they're going to live up to their promise. They're the bad guys," she yelled at the screen, when a cut scene showed their characters interacting with a group of mercenaries who were seeking the map for different reasons.

She surprised him with the questions she asked, more invested in the game than he'd anticipated.

"Why did you make that move?"

"What would've happened if we'd declined their deal and explored on our own?"

"If we think we've made the wrong decision, can we

go back and change it? Will that error affect the game's outcome?"

And through it all, he was cognizant of her next to him, her scent a subtle tease to his senses. Even as he pushed the correct combination of buttons to take out his prey, he was aware of when she reached for a drink, scratched her neck, or shifted on the sofa.

Thirty minutes later, they'd crossed the first threshold in their game mission.

"That was really good," she said. "It was better than I expected."

Unclenching his fingers from the controller, he stood and stretched. "Better than Wii Sports?"

She laughed. "Yes! You know, it reminded me of those books I used to read when I was a kid. The *Choose Your Own Adventure* books. This was like an interactive movie where you could decide how you wanted it to play out."

He grabbed two bottled waters from the cooler and handed one to her. He plucked a grape from the bowl of fruit on the table in front of them.

"Not your typical gamer fare."

"It's not," he agreed. "But I spend a lot of time in front of a computer screen. Programming can be a sedentary lifestyle." He patted his stomach. "I don't want to get fat."

Her eyes swept down his body and a rush of desire made him light-headed. When their gazes met, hers was feverish. "I don't think you'll have any problem with that."

He sat down slowly and shifted on the sofa until their knees were touching. He assuaged the aching in his fingers by reaching out to lightly stroke a curl. His body tightened as the spiral encircled his digit in a gesture he yearned for their bodies to mimic. Her lips parted, then she blinked, exhaled, and moved away.

He smarted from the severed connection. Shaking his head, he took a drink of water from the bottle and swallowed. He picked up the other controller and offered it to her. "You ready for the next level?"

He expected her to demur, to decide that she didn't want to continue. Instead, she straightened her shoulders and lifted her chin. "Bring it on," she said, and he placed the controller in her palm.

He smiled and pressed the buttons needed to begin the next level. She had no idea what was coming. She'd completed a few levels and believed herself experienced.

"Holy hell! Where did they come from?"

The pirates he'd been expecting swarmed their characters on the screen. She leaned forward, her eyes narrowed as her fingers moved over the controller, depressing buttons in different combinations.

"Stop staring at me and get your ass in gear. I can't hold them off by myself!"

He grinned and settled back against the sofa. For the first time in years, he was content.

Chapter Eleven

FIVE HOURS LATER, her fingers cramped and almost numb, Chelsea dropped the controller on the coffee table. She didn't try to repress her giddiness.

"That was incredible!" Outside, the sun had set, the orange glow bathing the mountains in a warm light. "I can't believe we played all afternoon! It feels like we sat down ten minutes ago."

Next to her, Adam set down his controller. "Only if one of us were capable of traveling at the speed of light."

He stood and stretched, the movement lifting his white T-shirt and treating her to another glimpse of his golden, muscled skin. Her mouth watered at the sight, and she had to swallow to avoid an embarrassing drooling incident. Her response to him no longer surprised her. She glanced up and their eyes met. The air between them thickened. Without breaking the visual contact, he lowered his arms and his tongue darted out to moisten his bottom lip. Her nipples tightened and tingled, blood rushing to all parts of her body.

Dammit. It's like the time she spent lecturing herself hadn't happened. It would be so easy to give in to it, in to him. Especially now that she'd had a taste of him. Knew how intoxicating his kiss could be. Knew how strong he was, how being held in his arms made her feel sexy and desired. But it couldn't happen again, and the fact that she was still obsessing over it made her question her once-dependable sanity. She had a job to do. And as much as she'd come to like him, she'd been working toward this partnership for a long time. Once this was over, she would go back to her job and never see Adam again.

She ignored the twinge that thought engendered. It didn't matter how she felt or how she'd enjoyed the day or how much she reveled in his kisses. She needed to keep her goal in mind. She was here to get him ready for the project launch.

And they'd lost an entire day because she'd let him distract her from her goal.

"Well, that was fun, but I'm starving. I'm going to head back to my house and grab something to eat. Good night."

"Wait."

He reached out and grabbed her hand as she started to walk away. Jolts of electricity tingled up and down her arm at the contact. She looked at their joined hands, at his strong fingers gripping hers, before peering up into his face.

His eyes were dark and intense as they stared at her. He was so gorgeous; she could look at his face forever. She wondered whimsically if this was some sort of trial. Was the universe testing her to see if she really wanted this promotion? Was he the pond's reflection and she Narcissus? Would she spend all of her time looking at him as things around her changed and died, like her career focus and goals?

She flexed her fingers and he dropped her hand. Her body wept at the loss of contact.

"Our day isn't over," he said, his voice thick and husky.

"I think I've played enough video games for a while." She held up her hand and wiggled her fingers. "These babies need a rest."

He laughed, as she'd intended, the thickness of tension easing in the room.

"No more games today, I promise. We're having dinner in San Francisco. Quartet," he said, naming a popular restaurant beloved by some of her clients.

She'd always wanted to eat there. Swallowing hard, she shook her head. "I'm sorry, I can't."

"You said you were starving. I'm offering a practical solution."

"Adam." Her self-preservation alarms went off as she stepped closer to him. She could dance around this, but that wasn't really her style. "We shouldn't do this. Not if you still want me to help."

She moved away, heeding her inner warnings.

His gaze was steady. "More than want. I need your help."

She nodded and turned away.

"But I also need to understand what's happening between us."

His words stopped her, an invisible verbal leash.

"You shouldn't be concerned about us. The Computronix launch is in a week."

"You think I've forgotten?" He closed in on her, his tone urgent. "This presentation means more to me than you could possibly comprehend. But when I spend as much time recalling the feel of your lips pressed against mine as I do rechecking code, there's a problem."

Oh. She locked her knees to keep from sinking to the floor.

His eyes blazed, their intensity hypnotic, refusing to allow her to look away. "I know what I should be doing, but until I can figure out what's between us, I'll continue to be distracted. Are we reacting to something real, or are we victims of circumstance?" He lowered his voice. "If you can't be altruistic, be selfish. The sooner I can focus on my work again, the sooner we can get back to your lessons."

She wrapped an arm around her waist and rested the opposite elbow on it, tapping her fist against her mouth. None of this should be happening. How had she ended up here? It was ridiculous to even consider getting involved with this man. Her client. Someone she was lying to.

Then why was she contemplating saying yes?

"It's only dinner," he said, tilting his head.

"I shouldn't." *Stay strong, Chelsea. Do the right thing.*

He breached her personal space. "Do you want to?"

He smelled incredible. So much for fortitude. She leaned her forehead against his chest. "I need some time."

"How about two hours? Our reservation is for eight thirty."

She shouldn't entertain this notion. But she was. What was happening to her? Why was she willing to risk everything she'd worked for on a genius with the fate of the technological world on his broad shoulders?

As SOON AS she closed the front door of the Andersons' home behind her, Chelsea brought up the favorites screen on her cell and pressed the first contact listed.

"Were your ears tingling?" India asked. "I was just bragging to a couple of coworkers how I know someone who's friends with Ellis York. I contend it makes me a friend by association."

Love and warmth flooded her at the sound of her foster sister's voice. She dropped her purse on the table in the foyer. "I told you, we're not friends. I worked with her a couple of years ago."

"She's in that new big-budget drama movie and that wouldn't have happened if you hadn't thinned out her entourage and polished up her image. She should be begging you to be her bestie."

Chelsea laughed. "I'm pretty sure you're the only one who holds that opinion. How's work going? Have you gotten to the beach yet? The water is probably too cold for swimming, but you can wade in to your ankles."

"I know there are lakes nearby, but Nashville isn't known for their beaches. I'll have to check them out."

"Wait, Nashville? I thought you were working at that resort in Charleston?"

"I was, until they reassigned me to their nursery. You know I don't do kids and I wasn't about to spend hours watching other people's children when they're either too lazy or too selfish to do it themselves."

The words were harsh but Chelsea knew they originated from pain. She'd been fortunate that her stint in the foster care system had only been eight months. For Indi, it'd been twelve years . . .

"What made you choose Nashville? You're not into country music."

"I didn't plan on staying here. One of the girls from the resort is an aspiring singer and she'd saved up enough money to make a go of it. When she announced she was driving to Nashville, I caught a ride. I figured I'd hang out for a day or two and make my way down to Key West."

"That's not an efficient travel route."

Indi continued as if Chelsea hadn't spoken. "But one thing led to another and—"

"You've set up short term residence in the fifty-ninth city in the past eight years."

"Stop exaggerating. It hasn't been that many."

"Close to it."

"What can I say, I'm a citizen of the world. I'm not meant to be tied down."

Chelsea had called Indi seeking advice, but was filled

with second thoughts hearing her so blithe and carefree. She spruced up her frustration with gaiety. "And my sympathy to the person who tries."

"You know me too well." Indi paused. "As I know you. You sound odd. What's up?"

"I'm fine."

"No, you're not. You called me and your voice *does* sound weird. What's going on?"

Chelsea kicked off her shoes and strode over to the window in the great room. Taking a deep breath, she pressed the fingertips of her left hand to the cool glass and blurted out, "I've met someone."

Indi uttered a soft curse. "Is that all?" A rush of expelled air and then, "That's nothing new. You're always meeting someone. Who is he?"

"It's Adam Bennett."

"That name sounds familiar."

Chelsea rolled her eyes heavenward. "*People*'s Sexiest Man Alive last year."

Indi shrieked and Chelsea pulled the phone away from her ear.

"*That* Adam Bennett? He's hot. You can see his intelligence and passion vibrating off of him. And those eyes." She sighed. "Wait, wasn't he involved with Birgitta?"

"Yes." Chelsea pictured the mono-monikered leggy Scandinavian model with her trademark ice-blond pixie cut and pale blue eyes. Another reason not to get involved with Adam. Who wanted to follow her?

"How did you meet him?"

"He's the important client my promotion hinges on."

"Oh." That one word carried weighty significance, and Chelsea knew Indi understood her dilemma.

"I can't get involved with him. It wouldn't be professional."

"Oh, please. You've never let anything get in the way of your career. You're one of the most professional people I've ever met. Jump his bones."

"Why am I not surprised? Not everyone believes in free love and living in the moment."

"They should. They'd be a hell of a lot happier. Besides, I've seen that man. He looks like a dark sex god. And you have the opportunity to be with him?"

"I do."

"Then what's the issue? Go for it. You're not talking forever, right? Just a little fun?"

"He made me an avatar."

"What?"

"An avatar. Like in a video game."

"I know what avatars are. I'm surprised that you do."

"I know about video games."

"Dance Dance Revolution doesn't count," Indi said, snidely.

"Very funny." She left the window and settled into an oak rocking chair. She pulled one leg beneath her and used the other to set the rocker in motion. "He wanted me to play this game with him. One of those adventure games where you go on missions. He didn't like the selection of avatars available, called it 'narrow-minded.' So he hijacked it and made one that looked like me. Curly hair, skin tone, everything."

Silence hummed on the phone between them.

"That has to be one of the most romantic things I've ever heard," Indi finally said.

"I know, right?"

"So, you're saying this might be more than just a little fun?"

"Maybe."

"Where are you?"

"In the mountains of Northern California."

"And you're with him?"

"For the most part."

"How long?"

"A few weeks."

"Is he pressuring you?" she asked.

"No. He's not pressuring me. It's the situation. I don't have a lot of time to work with him, and he says he can't focus until he knows what's going on between us. He said I'm a distraction."

Indi whistled, then laughed. "That's a line if I ever heard one."

Chelsea nodded, even though Indi couldn't see her. "Normally I'd agree. But not with Adam. He means it. He doesn't lie."

"Everyone lies."

Chelsea shifted in the chair, uneasily aware of her own deception. "I know it sounds naïve, but he doesn't. He's direct, sometimes to the point of rudeness."

"Since when are we attracted to men who are rude?"

"This from the woman who took up with the French soccer player who abandoned her in Denmark?"

"Well played, sir. But in my defense, he was sexy as hell." Indi's laugh trailed off and her tone took on a mantle of seriousness. "It's been difficult for me to let people into my life. You've been the rare exception. And when I was being a special kind of brat, you told me we only get one life and we needed to live it with purpose and to the fullest. Now, while you probably intended for that advice to steer me toward law school, it changed my life. Be smart enough to heed your own counsel."

Tears burned Chelsea's eyes. "I hear you."

"Good." Indi cleared her throat. "You know your purple and light blue silk scarf? The one you wore to dinner the night I got to LA this last time? The one I really liked?"

The one Chelsea suddenly realized she couldn't remember finding when she packed.

"Yesss," she said, dragging the word out, confident she wasn't going to be pleased by what Indi said next.

"Yeah, well I borrowed it and I . . . uh, kind of forgot it when I left Charleston."

"Indi!"

"I know, I know and I'm so sorry. I'll replace it, I promise. Nashville has some awesome boutiques."

"Unless you want to avail yourself of some of LA's hostel accommodations the next time you visit, you'd better."

Chelsea ended the call, but she continued to rock. Adam asked her to dinner. As a way to find out if there was actually something between them or if the events that brought them together was enhancing the effect. Despite the time crunch, it was a logical request. Especially if it turned out to be the latter. Then he could get back to work, she could get back to their lessons, and in a week she'd leave with everything she always wanted.

But what if it was the former? What if there was something between them? How would they handle that knowledge? On a date? And with the fire heating his eyes, there was a chance the night might end with more than a handshake at the door, despite what he said. Was she ready for that? Once they took that step, there was no taking it back. And it would affect what she was here to do.

But it was more than their working relationship. She was lying to him. If they acknowledged something was between them, did she have the strength to still push him away, not wanting to sleep with him under false pretenses? Questions tumbled around, like a mental lottery ball machine, making her head hurt from the numerous possibilities. It was so much for her to think about and she'd been thinking for so long. Calculating every move to get where she wanted to be. Where she needed to be. Suddenly, she wanted to let go of everything that tethered her in this world and follow him into his.

She accessed her favorites screen again and pressed a contact listing.

"Chelsea?"

"Yes, Adam. I'd love to have dinner with you."

Chapter Twelve

CHELSEA'S PROFESSIONAL AREAS of expertise were the entertainment and sports industries. She routinely found herself in meetings with men who were paid to look good and keep their bodies in peak condition.

Considering that, the Adam Bennett that stood before her was the best-looking man she'd ever seen. Sleek and powerful in a dark suit and royal blue crew neck sweater that she recognized from their shopping spree. His gleaming hair was swept back from his forehead and—she gasped—his jaw was clean-shaven. Leaning against a late model black Range Rover, he stole her breath.

She started down the steps of the house. "I see they delivered the clothes."

He pushed away from his car. "This morning, before you first arrived."

"And you picked this outfit yourself?"

"I did."

When she reached the bottom she stopped, her clutch held tightly in her grasp. "I had hoped, but I have to admit, I wasn't sure you'd do it." At his blank stare, she clarified, "Wear any of the clothes outside of the presentation."

"I never cared about my attire before. Now I do."

"Why?"

His stare scorched her. "Because you do."

Sparks of pleasure tingled in her chest, lending her buoyancy.

He opened the passenger door for her. When she reached him he said, "You're beautiful."

His low, smooth tone wound itself around her heart and squeezed. She smiled and stroked his smooth jaw before sinking into the butter-soft leather seat. He closed the door and headed around the front of the car to get behind the wheel.

Who was this man? She thought she'd had a handle on him and what she needed to do for her job. But she'd only scratched the surface. As tech savvy and nerdy as Adam had been when they'd first met, this Adam was assured, sexy, dangerous.

On the dark mountain roads, he handled the car with an ease she found incredibly sensuous. His strong hands caressed the dark wood grain and leather steering wheel, his long, elegant fingers gripping the wheel as he skillfully executed the turns. The smell of his aftershave and the dark interior of the car shrouded them in a cocoon of intimacy. The silence was comfortable and she went with it, leaning back into the headrest and watching the scenery out of the panoramic roof window.

It was only dinner. Accepting his invitation didn't mean she was accepting that they would sleep together. It meant they could continue spending time together in an effort to get him back on track.

Right.

"We're here."

Chelsea frowned at the large stone and glass building fronted by tall, skinny poles at spaced intervals. "This doesn't look like a restaurant. Where are we?"

"The California Academy of Sciences."

"I thought we were going to dinner."

"We are."

"Then why are we stopping here? Aren't they closed?"

"To the public. Not to me. Come on."

Intrigued, she took his outstretched hand and followed him around the side of the building to a nondescript opening. He knocked twice and a young woman, dressed in black business attire, opened the door.

"Good evening, Mr. Bennett," she said, waving them inside. "My name is Katie and I'm your maître d' for tonight. We have everything prepared to your specifications."

"Thank you," he said. With a hand at Chelsea's back, he guided her inside the building. His touch flared through her dress, a tempting brush of warmth against her skin.

"Our maître d'?" she mouthed, brows raised.

She'd assumed he was taking her to the restaurant, but it appeared he'd rented out an entire museum for their dinner. She was no stranger to extravagance, considering the fame and wealth of her clients. She'd visited athletes in their multimillion-dollar mansions, had even flown on a private plane to visit a well-known actor filming on location. But being the recipient of such luxury? Having someone make such a big deal for her?

Her decision to accept Adam's invitation hadn't really been a decision. It hadn't even been another instance of following her instincts. She'd succumbed to a moment of passivity after years of resistance, thinking what were the odds that this spark of attraction would flourish when subjected to the light? Despite what she'd hoped, she hadn't expected him to show such care and consideration. She glided beside him, anticipation blooming to life in her belly.

They followed Katie down a long hallway that opened into a room bathed in soothing, flickering tones of blue. When they turned the corner, Chelsea's eyes widened. They stood in the entryway of an aquarium tunnel, surrounded by an underwater wonderland.

Schools of fish, sharks, and all manner of sea life swam around them. She walked a little farther and gasped. A bloom of jellyfish floated by, their pink umbrella-shaped caps and silky ribbon tentacles glowing with an otherworldly light.

Katie stood at a small table with a bottle of champagne chilling in an ice bucket. "I'm going to let the staff know you've arrived. Enjoy the exhibit and I'll be back in about twenty minutes."

Chelsea looked at Adam in wonder. "This is amazing!"

The muscle in his cheek jumped. "And it still doesn't compare to you."

She looked away. How should she respond? She honestly didn't know. She knew the smart thing to do. Act as if the attraction wasn't real. She could claim they'd given it a shot, it hadn't worked out, and they could settle into a normal business arrangement for the next week. That's what she should do.

But the feelings he aroused in her were addictive. His presence was so consuming. It made her yearn to be away from him so she could breathe. And yet when they were apart, she wanted to be with him, to interact with him, even if he was driving her crazy with his intractable nature.

Since she was unsure of her response, she decided to say nothing, choosing instead to take in her surroundings. She imagined during the day the place was filled with visitors, their voices echoing off their surroundings in a raucous babble. With just the two of them, and the low music playing in the background, it was quiet, tranquil. Intimate.

It was too much, too soon. They'd just gotten here. She couldn't let herself be carried away by the romance of it. She reached for the nearest flute. "How about a glass of champagne?"

They strolled along the corridor where she saw a living, colorful coral reef teeming with tropical fish. A bright yellow fish the size of a football floated just above a smaller fish that was a deep royal blue hue. The vibrant colors drew her in and she put her finger to the cool glass. A swarm of tiny fish immediately flocked to her finger before swishing away in a choreographed routine.

"Did you see that?" she asked.

"Can you blame them? I'm sure most men come running with the crook of your finger."

Warmth swept from her heart up to her cheeks. He had to stop saying things like that.

"Did you know," he said, his voice suddenly casual, "the fish in the middle of the school control the school? The ones on the outside follow their lead."

That was better. The normalcy of his statement gave her a chance to regain her bearings.

"Look up," he commanded.

She did. A great white shark glided overhead; his sharp, lethal teeth, creepy gill slits, and smooth white belly provided an ominous sight. She gasped and her breath fled her body. Her muscles tightened and she stumbled back into a steady, protective embrace. He enclosed her in his arms and a sense of calm descended over her. She leaned into him and they stood together as her terror faded away.

Eventually, Katie returned. "If you'll follow me . . ."

She'd forgotten about the other woman. For a few moments she'd believed they were the only two people here and the reminder that they weren't helped. She inhaled and turned to Adam. "There's more?"

He nodded and took her hand, his strong grip giving her a feminine thrill. Katie escorted them to a large room where they could look down into a pit filled with stadium seating. A large screen rose from the front of the room and tilted up the wall and over their heads to some point behind them she couldn't see. It looked like a movie theater with the biggest projection screen she'd ever seen.

"Are we watching a movie?" Chelsea asked.

Adam smiled. "In a manner of speaking."

Down on the floor at the front of the theater sat an elegantly dressed table covered in white linen. Suddenly, the lights went out. Everything around her disappeared and stars burst forth all around them. She felt as if she were floating through space.

He slid a hand around her waist. "I thought we'd enjoy dinner beneath the stars."

Planets appeared and floated past. She recognized the redness of Mars, the serene blues and greens of Earth, the rings of Saturn. When he guided her down the stairs, she imagined them taking a stroll across the universe.

She'd always thought of herself as a strong woman, but she wasn't made of titanium. How could any woman resist this man? She pressed a hand to her chest, overwhelmed by the beauty she'd seen and the immense thoughtfulness of the man at her side. "I can't wait."

He pulled out her chair and, once she was seated, took his place across from her. A server materialized with their first course.

"The chef took the liberty of creating a specialized menu for you. Please, enjoy."

The food looked spectacular and smelled even better.

"Is this from Quartet?" she asked.

Quartet was one of the best restaurants in the city, home to a James Beard award-winning chef who specialized in Italian-and French-inspired cuisine.

Reservations were at least six months out. What kind of favors did Adam have to call in for their dinner tonight?

"Yes," Adam said. "The chef is a friend and I'm an investor in the restaurant."

The mystery of his incredible access solved.

"I didn't know that," she said, surprised and impressed. He was more a man of the world than she'd thought. "I'm excited to try the food. I've heard good things about it."

"It's a great restaurant. I wouldn't invest my money in anything less."

She pursed her lips. "But you said the chef is a friend."

"He is."

"So you'd want to help him, without regard to his talent."

His features tightened and his eyes hardened. "Are you questioning my integrity?"

She started to smile, thinking he was playing along, but his stilted tone caused her to rethink her initial assessment. "No, no. Adam, I was kidding."

His eyes cleared, his face relaxed and a sexy grin curled his lips. "So was I."

"Oh." She bit her lip and let her lashes fall to cover her embarrassment. "Good one."

Their shared laughter swept away any lingering tension.

"Did you become friends with the chef after your investment or did you know him before?"

"I met him in college."

"Wow." She swallowed. "Have you known Mike for that long?"

He nodded.

"Loyalty must be really important to you."

"Paramount." He lounged back in his chair and rested an arm on the table. "What made you choose a career in entertainment?"

She paused, her fork in midair. It was an innocent enough question, a variation asked by millions on first dates. But theirs wasn't a typical social outing. The man across from her was astute and had already proven his proficiency at detecting inconsistencies in her story. She needed to hold on to that fact and remember she couldn't afford to lower her guard any further and get personal with him. She ignored the part of her brain that flashed images of just how personal their joined bodies could be.

"I'm a people person," she said, giving him the stock answer she trotted out at parties and gatherings when asked a similar question.

"I intentionally seek shelter from the limelight. You bask in it."

"I wouldn't say I 'bask' in it. It's been reflected onto me because of my proximity to others. I understand it. I've learned how to use it to my advantage."

He nodded slowly, his brows furrowing, then releasing. He had a way of focusing on her with his complete, undivided attention. Like she was his current project and he was solving for x. Being the object of such intense scrutiny was flattering but a touch uncomfortable. Especially when she possessed information that needed to stay hidden.

"Have you always liked computers?" She took another taste of the mushroom and artichoke tortellini.

"Not in the stereotypical fashion that's always portrayed in the movies. I didn't dismantle them or create my own super computer. I was interested in video games. I liked to escape into worlds I could control."

She hadn't thought they would have anything in common, but she could relate to his teenaged self's need to escape his circumstances. There were numerous times growing up that she'd go to sleep at night praying her life was some never-ending nightmare from which she'd finally awaken. "Then, why not become a video game designer?"

"It was more than the software. I wondered how I could adapt the hardware. Find better uses for it in the world. My real-life fascination outgrew my interests in the make-believe world."

Some might say she chose a similar path. That she couldn't stay in her make-believe world where she wasn't the victim of her mother's choices, but needed to find a way to make living in the real world bearable.

"At some point you had to get into computers, right?"

"Of course . . ."

His eyes flashed as he discussed his work. She leaned forward, resting her chin on her palm, wanting to take it all in and not miss anything. He was a lethal combination of brilliance, good looks, and a relatability she hadn't been expecting.

Careful, Chelsea. You're teetering on infatuation.

Who wouldn't be? They'd spent an incredible day

together. Could she be blamed for succumbing to his charm?

He broke off abruptly, his gaze shifting sideways. "Sorry."

"For what?"

"Sometimes my desire to continue talking about a topic outpaces the interest of the person listening."

Her face relaxed into a smile. "Where have you been hiding him?"

"I—" He blinked. "I don't understand."

"This man in front of me. You aren't the same man I met two weeks ago."

His expression was solemn. "Yes, I am, Chelsea. I'm the same man and I have all of the same issues."

"Then, how do you explain all of this?"

He took her gesturing hand in his, and the friction of his thumb sliding across her skin spread quivers of sensation throughout her entire body. "I want you. This is my opportunity to show you I'm more than computers and routines and my mountain. I want you to see that my world can be fun. That we can have fun in it together."

She couldn't imagine saying this two weeks ago, but damn, he had a way with words.

He wanted her. Not Chelsea Grant, mover and shaker in PR, executive in one of the country's top PR firms, influencer in all things image related.

He wanted *her*, Chelsea Grant. The woman.

She wasn't even sure she believed it was possible. When was the last time it had happened? When she knew the man she was with was interested in her for who she was and not what she could do for them?

Adam's words about the movie she watched the day after the storm swept into her mind. *She lied to him. He doesn't know her.*

She may still be confused personally, but professionally she was more determined than ever to make sure his presentation was the best it could be . . . and not only for her promotion. She could list all of the reasons they shouldn't be together, the big one being the lie that hung between them like a two-way mirror, but his conviction touched her, fed the part of her unused to such regard. She would ensure his invention received the launch of the decade.

Her heart wouldn't permit her to do anything less.

Chapter Thirteen

THE LIGHTS OF the aquarium exhibit bathed Chelsea's smooth skin in an aqua hue, and Adam couldn't help but admire her profile while she studied the colorful marine animals. Her high cheekbones, the graceful slope of her nose, the addictive fullness of her lips. She entranced him more than any woman he'd ever known.

After dinner they'd made their way back to the underwater tunnel. There had been numerous revelations throughout the evening, but the most significant had been that the launch and his presentation weren't the sole focus of their conversation. Despite his fears, they'd engaged in an earnest and lively discourse about books, movies, and politics. He'd answered her questions about computers and the tech industry and she'd shared anecdotes about her experiences in entertainment.

She wasn't on his intellectual level—very few people were—but she was smart, perceptive, and possessed an aptitude for dealing with people. Rather than diminishing his attraction for her and confirming that the feelings he'd been experiencing were wrapped up in the circumstances of the storm, their interaction had left him determined to experience her kiss and her touch, again.

And that wasn't good news for the HPC, Computronix, or the launch.

She turned to him and smiled. "I had an incredible time tonight. No one has ever done anything like this for me. Thank you."

A remarkably serviceable word, *incredible*. He'd use it to describe the meal they'd consumed, the exhibits they'd enjoyed, and most fittingly, the short dress she wore that clung to her curves and emphasized her amazing legs. She'd pulled her hair off her face and neck and secured it with a jeweled clip. A few tendrils had escaped to curl around her face and one had claimed an enviable position at the top of her cleavage.

He'd been eyeing that curl for the past hour, the way it nestled against her skin. He'd never thought it possible to begrudge a lock of hair, but he now found himself rethinking that assertion. When her smile dwindled and she ducked her head, her lashes falling to cover her eyes, he realized he hadn't responded to her comment.

He cleared his throat. "You're welcome. I told you, I wanted you to enjoy yourself."

"Well, mission accomplished, because I did."

He gazed into her upturned face and cupped her cheek, the contact causing his palm to tingle. She was beautiful. Complex. Intriguing. He'd spent two weeks in her company and he'd yet to decode her, to unravel the enigma that hid behind her eyes. But he *would* figure her out. He could no more resist that compulsion than he could refrain from breathing.

The thumping of his heart blocked out all ambient sounds until Chelsea was his sole focus. She licked her bottom lip and swayed toward him, lifting her hand to rest her fingers on his forearm. He slid his hand from her face to grasp her nape, squeezing gently as he tugged her closer. Her lashes fell, shielding her pretty brown eyes. The heat from her body warmed him, her smell aroused him, and his eyes drifted shut as he lowered his head and—

"Mr. Bennett?"

His muscles went rigid and he opened his eyes. Chelsea stared at him, her lips parted, her lashes fluttering wildly. She pushed away from him and, reluctantly, he released her. They turned in unison to Katie, who stood across the room.

She clutched an iPad to her chest. "The culinary service team is cleaning up and the Academy's staff is waiting for us to leave so they can lock up."

He nodded, keenly aware of Chelsea standing next to him, smoothing her hair into place. Dammit. If he had his way, more of those curls would be spilling out instead of being tucked away. "Thank you for your assistance this evening."

"It was our pleasure, sir."

"Hey, what about me?" a deep voice asked. "Aren't I entitled to some of that gratitude?"

Adam laughed and walked over to Jonathan, his hand extended in welcome. "What are you doing here?"

"When I heard you'd booked our services for tonight, I thought someone was fucking with me," Jonathan said, clasping Adam's hand and bringing him in for a hug. "I couldn't imagine what would get you down off your mountain for a night in the city, especially considering our conversation a couple of weeks ago. I had to witness this marvel for myself." His gaze strayed over Adam's shoulder and he lowered his voice. "Is that the miracle worker? She's lovely, and quite different from the last one."

"Watch yourself," he muttered, while motioning for Chelsea to join them. "Chelsea, this is Jonathan Moran, executive chef and owner of Quartet. Jonathan, this is Chelsea Grant."

Adam placed his hand on the small of her back as they completed the formalities of the introduction. Jonathan was a brilliant chef, dedicated restaurateur, and notorious womanizer. He didn't want the man to create any notions about Chelsea.

"Nice to meet you," Jonathan said. He glanced at Adam's hand and grinned widely, his brown eyes shining. "Did you enjoy dinner?"

"It was perfection," Chelsea said. "I particularly enjoyed the duck with the chanterelle mushrooms."

"A woman with exquisite taste." Jonathan shoved his hands into his pockets and widened his stance. "Next time you're in San Francisco, have him bring you to the restaurant for the true Quartet experience."

"I'd like that."

"I'm looking forward to the presentation next week," Jonathan said, nodding as he turned to Adam. "I expect nothing less than having my mind blown."

It took a moment for Adam's mind to shift from the woman at his side to the presentation.

"Then your expectations will be met," he said.

"You'll be there?" Chelsea asked.

"I never miss a launch. How many people can say they know an actual genius?"

Jonathan's support remained constant long after Adam's initial investment in Quartet had been repaid. His loyalty was one of the many reasons Adam called him a friend.

"I've got to get back to the restaurant. Chelsea, it was an absolute pleasure to meet you." Jonathan took her hand and raised it, glanced at Adam, and then with a quirk of his mouth, settled for a handshake.

"So, he's the other friend you mentioned?" Chelsea asked as she stared at Jonathan's retreating figure.

"Yes."

"You surround yourself with very talented people."

Enough about his friends. He ached to return to their interrupted kiss. His heartbeat quickened as he laced his fingers through hers and gathered her close. With his free hand, he pulled a few curls loose and let his thumb sweep across her smooth dark skin. Her lips parted and her head tilted into his caress.

Gorgeous . . .

"Before we were interrupted, you were telling me how much you've enjoyed this evening. So I need to know—" His fingers continued to move over her cheekbones and across her delectable mouth. Desire swelled through him, heating him from the inside. As her lashes closed he leaned forward and whispered, "Is the evening over?"

He held his breath.

Her tongue darted out to dampen her full bottom lip and his cock hardened further as he imagined it sliding between them. She opened her eyes and met his gaze.

"No."

THE SENSE OF smell was a basic biological function. When odorants stimulated sensory cells in the nose, electrical currents were passed to the brain, which processed and interpreted the patterns as specific odors.

Adam knew this, but it was possible he'd confused basic with insignificant.

When he missed the first turn, he attributed the mistake to the late hour darkness. It was only after he zoomed past their second turn that he realized the road wasn't holding his attention. The sweet citrus scent of her skin filled the car's intimate interior, permeating every breath he took until she was his brain's primary pole-star. Although he'd driven up and down the mountain numerous times, the winding road still required his full consideration. Especially at night. Now he understood he was concentrating on Chelsea instead of the path ahead.

Spotting one of the mountain's scenic overlooks, he pulled the car onto the gravel turnout and engaged the emergency brake.

"Adam? Are you okay? Is something wrong with the car?" She faced him, her brows pulled together and her knees slanted in his direction, providing a moonlit view of her thighs.

His breathing accelerated and his nerve endings roused back to life. He unbuckled his seat belt and turned, his gaze inevitably drawn to that enticing curl that undulated with her deep breaths. He surrendered to the compulsion and reached for it, watching as it entwined itself around his finger. He rubbed his thumb against the soft texture and imagined her legs similarly wrapped around his body. His cock hardened.

Her gaze traveled his body and stayed on his lower regions for several moments. She nodded imperceptibly, then turned and flattened her palms on the leather center console, using it to leverage herself closer to him. Her tongue cleaved her lips, leaving a moist shimmer on the bottom one. She searched his eyes and what she discovered caused her to tremble.

"Adam?" she whispered.

He cupped the back of her head, looped his fingers in those magnificent curls, and slanted his mouth over hers. Other than his hand in her hair, their lips were their sole point of contact, and he found the restriction erotic. Kissing her was as heady and addictive as he remembered, and he could imagine no scenario where he tired of the feelings coursing through him. She tasted of the coconut

and guava of their dessert mixed with the berry fruiti-
ness of her Pinot Noir. It was a potent combination.

She moaned and tangled her tongue with his while
reaching one hand up to grip the front of his shirt. His
heart raced in his chest, thrilled with her passionate
response. He braced his arm against the steering wheel,
seeking a way to surmount the armrest and achieve
deeper contact. Only when his knee landed on the console did he realize his intent. He was seconds away from
pressing her into the passenger side seat and sinking his
body into hers. The all-consuming desperation shocked
him and he wrenched his lips away from hers, falling
back in his seat as he sucked in air and attempted to get
his bearings. What the fuck was he doing? He'd never lost
control kissing a woman before.

He rolled his head on the headrest and stared at
Chelsea, watched the rapid rise and fall of her breasts and
the puckered imprint of her nipples against her dress's
fabric. He leaned over and pressed his lips against hers
one more time, trailing his finger down her cheek.

"Without that kiss, I couldn't have guaranteed we'd
make it back up the mountain without incident."

Her smile was slow and sensuous. "Thank God for
road safety awareness."

He smiled and settled back into his seat, shifting the
car into gear. Twenty minutes later, he pulled in front of
his house and cut the engine. He'd driven past the turnoff to her driveway and had slowed down, waiting for an
indication from her of what she wanted.

"Your place," she'd said. And so, he'd headed home.

He knew what he wanted, had known from the moment her eyes had widened when she'd seen the underwater aquarium. What he was feeling toward this woman was different from what he'd felt for anyone else. But she hadn't said anything, hadn't moved since their kiss at the bottom of the mountain. He thought she felt the same way, but this was too important to leave to assumption. He needed to be clear before they could go any further.

Still staring straight ahead he said, "I want to make love to you."

"I know." Her voice floated out of the darkness.

"Is that want one-sided?"

Silence. Disappointment weighed heavily upon his shoulders. He hunched forward and gripped the steering wheel, his knuckles pale in the moonlight. What irredeemable faux pas had he committed between the turnoff to her house and his? Had she changed her mind? Or had he misread the signs and she'd never been interested? It wouldn't have been the first time, but the sting of defeat had never been so acute.

But she surprised him by bringing her hand to rest on his thigh, heating the skin beneath. She squeezed. "Let's go inside."

When they reached the great room, he shed his jacket, put his phone and keys on his desk, and hurried into his room to grab a condom from his nightstand. He wanted to be prepared, no matter where the mood struck. When he returned he found her standing in front of the window.

The image recalled their dinner at the museum. She was a celestial fantasy come to life, surrounded by the velvet backdrop of the starry sky. He was consumed by a need to not experience another moment ignorant of the feel of their merged bodies.

Walking over, he gripped her hips from behind and kissed the vertex created by the angle of her neck and shoulder. He inhaled deeply and his eyes fluttered, her scent making him dizzy. Her nearness threatened to short-circuit his brain function and accelerate his pulse beyond normal limits. She tilted her head and leaned back into him as he nuzzled her smooth skin. He indulged in the feel of her curvy ass pushing back against his cock. He ground against her, the heat from her body burning through the thin material of his sweater.

She pulled away and turned in his arms. He smoothed back a curl that had flown forward to touch her cheek.

"I can't wait to taste every inch of you."

Her mouth fell open. She caressed his cheek, then claimed his lips in a fierce kiss. He moaned and her hands rose to encircle his neck. Her lips were perfect, as if created specifically for his kisses, and he savored her like a rare and expensive delicacy. He intended to spend all night renewing his acquaintance with the angles and contours of her body. He had nowhere else to go, nothing else to do.

She felt so good. He vowed to do everything in his power to ensure he experienced this again. Just the thought of the forthcoming pleasure sent a tide of desire rushing through him. He deepened the kiss and used his body to propel her backward until she collided with the window.

"Oooh." She laughed. "That's cold."

"Not for long."

He braced a hand against the window and trailed his index finger from her clavicle down her sternum to the top of her breasts. Her silken skin gave way easily. Her head tilted back and she arched into his touch.

"Can I see you?" he asked.

She nodded.

He edged his fingers beneath the straps of her dress and drew them down her shoulders until the garment fell to her feet in a puddle of fabric. He crouched down, going on a visual journey from her flat stomach, the curve of her hip, her delicate pink panties, and her strong and supple thighs. She placed her hands on his shoulders and lifted one stiletto-clad foot at a time to step out of her discarded dress, which he instantly tossed aside. The pink of her panties against her dark skin was like a prettily wrapped treat and the scent of her arousal called to him. He pressed a kiss to the scrap of material covering her. Then he rose, his hands skimming up the sides of her body until he was once again standing. His blood raced through his body until he swore he could hear it coursing through his veins.

How did he get so damned lucky?

Peering closely he could see a clasp between the satiny cups of her bra. He flicked it open, baring her breasts to his gaze and he inhaled with reverence. His palms tingled as the heavy teardrop-shaped globes filled his hands. Her lashes dropped to half-mast and her lips parted as she watched him. He drew his thumb over the dark chocolate-hued tip.

Her breath hitched and, again, her back arched toward him.

"Do you like that?" he asked, forcing the words past a throat thickened with hunger.

"Yes," she said, her own voice husky.

He did it again, noting how she leaned into the caress. The nipple was an erogenous zone full of thousands of nerve endings sensitive to stimuli, and Chelsea liked being touched there. Wanting to please her further, he grazed his thumb over her other nipple. She moaned and the sound arrowed straight to his cock.

An audible response, suggesting a more heightened reaction. He tweaked her right nipple, then her left, flushing with heat when her lashes fanned against her cheekbones and she moaned again, swiveling her pelvis in a needy motion. While she enjoyed the sensation of both breasts being touched, her left nipple was extremely sensitive.

Using that information, he rubbed, tweaked, and licked until she moaned, twisted, and quivered in his arms. She was responsive to his every touch, her sounds of pleasure almost his undoing. He loved being the cause of such an intense reaction. He feathered his tongue up her neck and bit down on her earlobe. She gasped and bucked against him and he smiled, soothing the sting with his tongue. The heat of their bodies fogged the glass.

She slid her hands around his hips to grasp his ass, gyrating herself against him.

"Tell me how it feels," he said, yearning to know everything about her.

"Hmmm?" she moaned.

"Tell me how it feels."

"It's . . . oh God . . . slow and heavy . . . and thick . . ." She trailed off on another moan.

"Is it too much?"

"It's perfect," she whimpered, and his cock swelled.

He reached down to cup her through the silky material of her panties, then rubbed the heel of his palm against her, knowing the friction would feel good against her clitoris. She moaned and rotated her hips, grinding against his hand.

Ahhh baby . . .

He grabbed the waistband of her panties and yanked them down. The clitoris was the most sensitive female erogenous zone, but he didn't know if she'd enjoy direct stimulation. So he aimed for the area around it, using his middle finger to massage in slow circular motions through her folds. She arced into his touch and her hands gripped his shoulders, her nails biting into his skin with a pleasurable sting. When his finger was slick from her arousal, he dragged his thumb through the wetness and rubbed it back and forth against her clit before pressing it firmly. Her hips jerked and he captured the resulting moan with his tongue. He engaged all of his fingers to stroke her, alternating the pace and the pressure, noting her quickening breath, the rapid rise and fall of her breasts.

Having an idea of what she liked based on how she responded, he tweaked her left breast and stroked her clitoris. She undulated against his hand, her torso maneuvering against him. She began to tremble and her head tipped back, her moans issuing in an increasingly frequent staccato. He slipped two fingers inside of her, pressed against her front wall, and bit down on her earlobe. She cried out and came apart in his arms.

Fuck, he was about to explode. His body couldn't be equipped to handle this level of arousal. Watching her come was better than solving a thousand equations, better than developing next-gen software. What he'd done had comprised only one combination of moves to get her off. He wanted to play with her until he'd uncovered every combination to achieve that same result.

She leaned her forehead against his shoulder and sagged against him. "Good God," she breathed.

He unfastened the clip holding her curls and let them tumble down her back. "I refuse to let God take credit for that."

She looked at him wide-eyed, then laughed.

He smiled and kissed her, and it wasn't long before the playful embrace turned frenzied. Passion beat through his body, seeking release. She pulled on his belt, her fingers fumbling as she undid the clasp. She unbuttoned his pants, pulled down the zipper, and reached for him. He surged into the tightness of her hand. He was hard and hot and he covered her hands with his, pressing her grip tighter around him as he stroked in and out of her palms. He closed his eyes and his head lolled to the side. Having her hands on him was amazing, but it was a pale imitation of what he wanted from her.

"Do you have a condom?" she asked.

The thought of leaving her and walking the few feet necessary to grab the prophylactic from his desk seemed like torture, but he did it, returning a few seconds later with the packet in his hand. He put it between his teeth and tore it, quickly sheathing himself. She licked her lips.

"Next time I want to taste you," she said.

"Me, first," he said, aware that they were both acknowledging there would be another time.

He lifted her and wrapped her legs around his waist. His cock was inches away from the hot entrance to her body. He pressed her upper shoulders against the window, kissed the corner of her mouth, and surged inside of her.

He paused, his body aching as he strained to retain control. He was in serious danger of coming right then, but he willed it back, needing more time within her sweet body. He locked his legs, cupped her hips, and tilted upward, giving him deeper penetration as he stroked in and out. She moaned loudly and wrapped her arms tightly around his neck. Her heat pulsed against his cock, the suction warm and thick and threatening to drive him mad. He squeezed her ass and varied his strokes: shallow and fast, deep and slow. When he bent his knees to change the angle of penetration, she shivered, and her eyes slammed shut. He stared at her, wanting to remember the erotic pleasure etched on her face.

Far too soon the muscles of her inner walls began to pull at him, suck and massage him from the inside. His body responded with the telltale tightening at the base of his spine and tingling waves that radiated from his scrotum. A second later, she clamped down on his length and called out her release. He roared as his own powerful orgasm ripped through him.

"Can I give God credit for that?" she asked, panting, a few minutes later.

"No, but we can thank him," he said, managing a wheezy laugh.

After he caught his breath, he slid from her, lamenting the loss of her warmth. He kissed her and she snuggled against him, never opening her eyes. He carried her to his bedroom, laid her on the bed, and hurried into the adjoining bathroom to clean up. When he returned, she was lying on her side, turned away from him. He slipped into bed behind her and curved his arm around her middle, pulling her back to him. He hauled the duvet up to cover them. He thought she'd fallen asleep, so was surprised when she took his hand, kissed it, and placed it over her heart.

Only then did all the questions come tumbling forth. Had he sated his desire for her, now that he'd determined their chemistry wasn't created by circumstance?

Hell, no.

Tonight had been better than he'd imagined, but it wasn't nearly enough. He'd need more of her, and not just sexually. But how would that function? Had he managed to convince her that they could work well together, both in and out of bed? Or would the sunrise bring a choice he didn't want to make?

He could wait until after the presentation and then pursue her, but his body rejected that notion as soon as his brain thought of it. He didn't want to go another day without experiencing the pleasure of being inside of her. And then there was the issue of his diagnosis. When should he tell her? Did she deserve to know? And could he take it if she rejected him like Birgitta or his mother?

He shook his head. Today had been about spending time with Chelsea away from work and it had been one of the best days of his life. Tomorrow he'd figure out if things between them would change. He nuzzled her curls and drifted into a restful slumber.

Chapter Fourteen

CHELSEA WOKE TO sunlight streaming across her face. She stretched and the white, high thread count sheets slid over her skin in an echo of Adam's tenderest caress. She smiled. The man was talented. His touch, his kiss, his lovemaking was beyond anything she'd experienced before.

He played her body like a maestro discovering a new instrument, learning what movements she responded to and then repeating the series until she'd become a frenzied mass of pleasure. She'd never been on the receiving end of such studied focus. It was an experience she was eager to repeat.

She reached over and trailed her fingertips over the cool space. Adam must've been up for a while. He'd woken her in the early hours, making love to her again with the same quiet intensity she was learning he brought to everything he attempted.

Swinging her legs over the side of the bed, she looked around for something to cover her naked body. She definitely wasn't putting on the dress from last night. A gray shirt was neatly folded over the back of a chair in the corner. She stepped into her discarded panties and tiptoed across the room to grab it. She slid the large Henley over her body, the hem settling mid-thigh.

Walking into the great room, she found him standing in front of his desk, his chest bare, a pair of running pants slung low on his hips. A partially finished glass of his breakfast smoothie sat near the edge. Her lips parted and a swell of heat roared through her body. Her fingers clutched the wall near her for support and she leaned against it, taking in the arresting picture he made, his hair tousled, his body lean perfection. Navigating the haze created by her gawking, it took several moments before she realized he was talking to someone by speakerphone.

"We're stoked about Computronix's product launch. We've heard some amazing things," an excited voice rushed.

The product launch? Who was he talking to?

"The whispers you've heard will fail to live up to the reality." Adam stood in front of the window, his posture strong but relaxed, bouncing a small green-and-yellow ball between both hands.

"We won't hold you long." This from a different voice. "Our plan is to do a brief segment we'll insert into our podcast prior to the launch."

She looked around, positive she'd misheard. A podcast?

"I understand."

"Great. And now we're recording. Welcome to *Tech Today, Gone Tomorrow*. We're here with Adam Bennett, CEO of Computronix. How's it going, man?"

"Busy. Computronix's latest product launch is next week. It's our biggest one in five years."

"Can you give us any specifics?"

"Of course not," Adam said.

Absently, she smoothed her hair back and lifted the heavy mass, letting it sift through her fingers as she listened, trying to comprehend what was occurring. Adam was doing a podcast without her knowledge or guidance?

"You can't blame us for trying," Host A said. "If you won't answer specifics about your new tech, can you talk to us, generally, about the future of Computronix?"

She pressed a hand to her stomach. What in the hell was he doing? This was his first interview since they'd begun working together and he didn't think she should be notified, let alone involved? Quivering images of the *People* press conference scrolled through her mind as if the memories themselves understood what was at stake. She prayed the conversation would continue smoothly. That he'd consider his answers before he gave them. And when the interview concluded she was going to wring his neck.

"The future of Computronix? How much time do you have?" Adam laughed. "The world is changing quicker than previous generations are prepared to tolerate. Millennials are the largest generation in the country, representing a third of the population. They've matured during technology's massive growth and they want it seamlessly integrated into their lives. Meeting that aim is my singular focus in the next three to five years."

Chelsea's mouth dropped open. She couldn't have written a more comprehensive answer. What was more astonishing was Adam delivered it with ease and charm and without any prompt from her.

"We're creating a first-class experience for our users," he said. "We want them to associate essential innovation with Computronix."

He was gesturing widely, alternating between clutching the ball in his hands and playing a solo game of toss-up. He was in his element and his enjoyment of the subject matter was apparent. *This* was the Adam who needed to show up for the product launch. He was charismatic, relaxed, and, important for him, responsive.

She now had evidence that Adam Bennett could give a successful presentation. She needed to re-create this experience at the launch and lengthen it threefold.

"We appreciate you taking the time to speak with us," Host B said. "We're stoked for the presentation. We have one more question."

"Why not?"

"Are you concerned that the debacle of your last launch will contaminate this one?"

The muscles in Adam's back tensed. He caught the ball and set it firmly on his desk.

"No," he said, tersely. Gone was the agreeableness of moments ago. His posture was as stiff and inflexible as a newly Botoxed brow.

Shit.

Host A chimed in. "A few years ago, any device released by Computronix was an automatic buy. After the last one, insiders are skeptical. How do you plan to handle their loss of faith?"

Adam clenched his fingers into fists and dropped his head, exhaling sharply from his nose. Chelsea winced. This wasn't good. She wanted to step in, but that would make things worse. A good publicist stayed behind the scenes and never made herself a part of the story. Interrupting the interview shifted the story from the device to the developer. But what if he uttered an inflammatory comment? She rolled her eyes heavenward. None of this would be happening if he'd told her about the interview in the first place.

"Adam? Are you still with us? What's your response to our follow-up?"

"If podcasts were regulated by the FCC, my response would engender a large fine."

"You know we're fans," Host B said, "but it's the natural question to ask."

"And I have a natural response when I'm being attacked."

He clicked off his phone and tossed it aside.

"Fuck!" He shoved his hands into his hair and clutched tufts between his fingers.

That was the worst thing he could have done. "Call them back."

He whirled around. "Chelsea—"

"We'll tell them you were accidentally disconnected."

"But I wasn't."

"Who cares?" This wasn't the time for his Honest Abe routine. She charged across the room until they stood toe to toe. "Why were you doing an interview? Especially an interview I knew nothing about?"

"It was an industry tech podcast that Anya scheduled for me three weeks ago."

"So you had plenty of notice." She crossed her arms over her chest. "You should've told me about this. I'm supposed to help you prepare."

He cupped her cheek, then trailed his hands down her arms to grip her elbows, pulling her close to his hard body. Her breath caught in her throat at the blaze of emotion she saw burning in his hooded gaze.

"You looked so peaceful sleeping," he whispered. "So beautiful in my bed. I didn't want to disturb you."

She shook her head, as if the action would clear away the sensual cobwebs his presence was weaving. She pushed out of his embrace. "You should've awakened me."

What had she been thinking? One act on the personal side of their relationship may have undone them professionally. How many times had she handled a version of this story? She'd allowed incredible sex, dreamy eyes, and washboard abs to momentarily obscure the vision of her partnership. She was here for one reason only: to help Adam prepare for his presentation. How could she have forgotten that? She bowed her head and shook it slightly so that her curls swung forward to curtain her face. Pressing her hands to her cheeks, she imagined the burn of shame singed her fingertips. She didn't deserve the partnership.

He reached for her again, but she took a step back and his arms dropped to his sides. "I've recorded podcasts with them before and found them reasonable and fair. They're interested in my work, not boxers versus briefs or Team Edward versus Team Jacob, though I still don't understand that cultural reference." He rubbed the back of his neck and glanced at her from beneath his thick lashes. "I was certain I could handle it alone."

"Now we know better."

"I don't understand your response."

"I'm upset," she said, stating the obvious. "You were doing so well. Why didn't you use those deep breathing exercises I taught you?"

"I terminated the call. I didn't curse or break into a tirade."

Her back teeth became intimately acquainted as she ground them together. "You hung up on this interview, you walked out of your last one. Your media abandonment is now a trend. I swear, Adam, you're doing their work for them. The copy about you is practically writing itself."

She ignored the twinge of guilt that reminded her she owned stock in this colossal screw-up.

"This isn't significant enough to warrant your reaction."

"You don't know that. This isn't your field of expertise. It's mine," she said, hitting her chest with her hand. "And you're supposed to be smart enough to realize that fucking me wouldn't change that."

The vein in his forehead throbbed. "It appears I made a rare error in judgment."

"You lost your composure. You can't do that at the product launch. These guys were supporters of yours. At the launch you'll have allies in the audience, but there'll also be skeptics and people who want to tear you down. You've got to be able to respond better than you just did, or what the hell have we been doing? Wasting our time?"

"Nothing about the past two weeks has been a waste of time. I've met you and that makes this entire experience worthwhile."

She softened. Damn him and his way with words.

No.

She straightened and steeled herself against his earnest charisma, using the warm indignation of her anger as a shield. "What happened? Why did that last question rattle you?"

"I wasn't expecting it."

"Why not? You aren't the first company to roll out a product that underperformed. Surely you knew that might be an issue?"

He sighed and shook his head. "It wasn't the product's performance, although that was a problem. It was the timing of the release."

He sat in his desk chair and held out his hand to her. She hesitated, knowing they needed to have this conversation and not wanting to confuse her role again. This was Chelsea, the PR professional, trying to determine what had gone wrong during the interview. Not Chelsea, the woman, wanting to comfort the man with whom she was sleeping. But the downward tilt of his brows and the tension brackets around his mouth burrowed through her intent. She took his hand and allowed him to pull her down onto his lap. He wrapped his arms around her waist and leaned his head against her back. His words vibrated through her as he talked.

"Several years ago I conceived an idea for a mini video game console that would end hardware loyalty and allow you to play whatever game you desired, no matter the system for which it had been designed. Gaming was an arena I was interested in, but one we hadn't explored."

There was information on that device in the research Mike had given her. If she recalled correctly, Computronix released it over a year ago.

"Then I met Birgitta at a party Jonathan dragged me to in San Francisco."

Chelsea's chest tightened. This would've been less painful before she'd slept with him.

Adam and Birgitta had been a media sensation. His dark, vivid good looks and her pale, angelic beauty made them a photographer's dream. Their courtship and breakup had landed them on the covers of countless entertainment magazines. Chelsea wished she'd paid more attention, but she'd been in the midst of handling a public relations nightmare involving an athlete and allegations of performance-enhancing drug use.

"She was beautiful, amusing, and we began dating. What I liked most about her was her independence. In case you didn't notice"—Adam brushed her curls over one shoulder and placed a kiss on the nape of her neck—"I can get engrossed in my work. But she had her own life. Between fashion shows and international photo shoots,

Birgitta was away most of the time we dated. I found that schedule acceptable. Preferable, even."

Of course. Adam could focus on his work and still reap the benefits of a "relationship."

"Computronix had just released our newest mobile phone to great acclaim and economic success. I was subjected to a lot of press attention. Birgitta loved it. I did not." He sighed and tightened his arms around her waist. "I don't enjoy large crowds of people or being the center of attention. Birgitta thought that would change, that I would become accustomed to it and grow to glorify it as she did. When I assured her I wouldn't, and explained why, she told me she understood. It was a lie. Later she disclosed that she found my . . . quirks tiresome. She wanted to be with someone with less defects."

Chelsea narrowed her eyes. Just because he admitted he'd never be the life of the party? She pictured the lanky model-turned-professional-snowboarder currently sharing Birgitta's spotlight. A huge step down, in her opinion. She stroked Adam's arm where it rested on her hip.

"It was a relief," he continued. "The game console was turning out to be more difficult than I'd originally anticipated, but I relished the challenge. Birgitta was forgotten until I was besieged by requests for interviews. Reporters staked out the Computronix campus, harassing our employees, hunting for quotes. They wanted to know how the genius could be duped by the blonde bombshell.

"She was involved with someone else and they'd discovered she'd been screwing him the entire time she'd been with me. They'd been photographed together all around the world. They had evidence that she'd been with him in Europe the day before she flew back to the States to attend a gala with me. She'd been lying to me the entire time. Using me to take her career to the next level. Mike said the story would fade away, but it didn't. For weeks, new stories would emerge where the press depicted me as a moron."

The story would've died down and some new tidbit would've taken its place. It was the nature of gotcha journalism. Birgitta had probably been feeding information to the media, hoping to keep herself in the headlines.

"Afterward, I made it my mission to prove them wrong. I had to show I wasn't an idiot and that her lies and behavior hadn't affected me. But it had. I wasn't heartbroken. I barely knew her and that was the appeal of the relationship. But I needed a win. I had to salvage my reputation. I released the mini game console.

"It was the worst decision I ever made. It sold well initially, but it wasn't properly tested. It was years from being perfected. There were bugs and glitches and issues with the hardware loyalty aspect. It was a failure of considerable proportions."

Oh, Adam . . .

"I didn't salvage my reputation. I destroyed it. Before I let the media take anything else from me, I left Palo Alto and retreated here. I needed to focus on the basics, and that decision led to discovering the HPC."

He shifted her on his lap so that she could see his face. His jaw was set, his gaze direct. "That's what I reacted to when he asked me that final question. My last launch was a disaster. This one has to be a success. But you're right. I should've told you about the interview. I'm sorry."

Suddenly, his sought-after apology sat heavy upon her shoulders. How could she require his atonement when their entire association was based on a lie? She shook her head and tried to swallow past the sudden thickness in her throat. "You don't have to apologize."

"This isn't how I imagined our day beginning," he said, the tone of his voice changing. "I'd planned to wake you with a cup of coffee and sweet kisses here"—he kissed her right shoulder—"here"—he kissed her forehead—"here"—she shivered when he kissed the spot beneath her left ear—"and, finally, here."

His last kiss quickly turned passionate as his tongue danced with hers and his fingers clutched her hips. She leaned into him, trembling from the passion that blossomed in her body. Her breath quickened, her body loosened, and her muscles lost their tension as she opened for him.

How would his comfy chair creation hold up to an energetic session of sex?

Unfortunately, she'd never know the answer to the question. He broke the kiss and leaned back, smoothing a curl from her temple. He smiled his killer HPC smile, then slapped her lightly on the bottom. "I can still provide the coffee."

She exhaled and attempted to regain her composure. "I thought you didn't own a coffeemaker?"

"I don't."

Good Lord. He made conversations more laborious than her weekly curl detangling routine. "Then how will you make coffee?"

He frowned. "Easily. I'll heat the water in a pot, measure the grounds, and pour the water into the grounds. Then I'll strain the coffee into the—"

She kissed him, her smiling lips halting his flow of words. She pulled back and cupped his cheeks. "I take my coffee with cream and sugar."

As she watched him walk away, her own sexy barista, the smile fell from her face. Last night had been a personal revelation and a professional mistake. Adam was putting his career and his life in her hands. Hands that were full juggling opposing needs and wants. His launch. Her promotion. Her and Mike's secret. Her firm's entree into the tech world. The lines between her roles were becoming blurred, leaving her to wonder who she owed what. Her promotion was still her primary concern, but she suddenly wondered if it was worth the path she was taking. One wrong move, one false step, it could all come crashing down and she might lose everything in the end.

Chapter Fifteen

ADAM LOWERED THE backpack from his shoulder and
selected a patch of grass where they could admire the
panoramic scene of the mountains and the city below. He
unfolded a large blanket and anchored it with rocks he
found nearby.

"Who is insane enough to hike up the side of a
mountain? When I catch up to you, Adam Bennett . . ."
Chelsea's words were audible, though she'd yet to crest the
hill.

He smiled. He'd needed a way to apologize for his
decision to do the podcast interview without her, especially after he'd finally convinced her a sexual relationship wouldn't interfere with their business one.

He pulled four bottles of water and containers of
trail mix and dried fruit from his pack. She'd believed
he didn't have faith in her skills and nothing could be
further from the truth. He had no doubt that if he'd told

Chelsea about the interview, she would've foreseen that question and helped him prepare a suitable response.

But lately, he'd been feeling like a project. All of Chelsea's lessons required fixing some part of him, and while those things were necessary to ensure a successful launch, it's not the dynamic he wanted between them. He wanted her to see him as someone whole, regular, normal. After they'd slept together, he knew he'd achieved his goal. Unfortunately, his mistake with the podcast had set him back.

He heard her footsteps a second before she came into view. As always, he marveled at her beauty. Perspiration glistened on her skin and she rested her hands on her knees while she caught her breath.

"Son of a bitch." She straightened and whipped off the scarf she'd used to secure her curls. "That was not c— What's this?"

"A snack. It was a long hike." He considered the offerings of their rudimentary picnic. "There's trail mix and fruit, if you suffer from nut allergies."

"Ooh, I love trail mix." She dropped her smaller pack next to the blanket, then settled down and grabbed a handful of food. "You are full of surprises, Mr. Bennett."

He'd never thought of himself as surprising. In fact, he abhorred surprises, finding them inefficient and detrimental to order. But if Chelsea liked that about him, he'd have to consider cultivating that aspect of his personality.

"If I was guaranteed this view at the end of a trek, I'd actually consider hiking."

He stretched out beside her, extending his legs and

leaning back on his hands. "It's one of my favorites. When I'm not working, I spend a lot of time outdoors."

"I've never been an outdoor person. Which is odd, considering I grew up in a town on Lake Michigan. People did a lot of boating and camping, but I never did."

"Why not?"

She shrugged. "One, you needed money. And two, you needed someone invested enough to take you and share the experience. I had neither."

He blinked. They'd spent so much time focusing on the presentation and his needs that it occurred to him he didn't know much about her background. He intended to remedy that immediately. However, before he could question her further, she changed the subject.

"No offense, but don't most computer geeks spend an inordinate amount of time avoiding the outdoors? It's how they acquire their pasty pallor."

"Saying 'no offense' doesn't mean offense won't be taken, and it doesn't excuse your fault in causing it," he said. She slapped his thigh and he laughed, picking up several pieces of trail mix and popping them into his mouth. "I've always been active."

He didn't mention that playing sports was his way to atone for the son he could never be. But nothing he'd done had alleviated the biting disappointment always present on his mother's face.

"Always? Are you trying to tell me you were the star quarterback of your high school football team?"

"Not at all. I didn't enjoy team sports. I ran cross-country and wrestled."

"As I said, full of surprises." She bumped his forearm with her shoulder. "But isn't wrestling a team sport? Don't they call it a wrestling *team*?"

"There is a team of wrestlers, but when you're on the mat, facing off against an opponent, it's just the two of you. Unlike in football, where the mistakes of your teammates can affect your chances of winning, in wrestling my success or failure depended entirely on my own efforts. It's a physical version of chess, where my goal was to outmaneuver my opponent and gain control."

Considering the lack of it in his life at that time, seeking control was something he'd desperately needed.

"I bet your family came to all of your events. A genius and an athlete? They must've been proud of you."

Were they? "My life isn't governed by thoughts of my family's feelings about my achievements."

"That's evident. You don't talk about them and there aren't any pictures of them around your house."

His scalp prickled. "I don't need pictures to remind me of their existence."

"Are they coming to the launch?"

How did they end up discussing his family when he'd just noted his intent to learn about hers? "No. They don't enjoy visiting me."

She tipped her head to the side. "Is that what they said?"

"No. They just don't visit."

"Do you invite them?"

He narrowed his eyes. "Why would I invite them to my home when it's clear they dislike being here?"

She dusted her hands together. "Ugh, I've stepped onto your word merry-go-round again."

"My what?"

"Word merry-go-round. That's when we talk around the same subject, but our understanding of the subject is different. My point was maybe your family doesn't visit because you don't invite them."

Word merry-go-round. That was an accurate turn of phrase. He found it amusing. No one had ever described it in that manner before, though he'd experienced this ordeal numerous times.

"When I invited them to Computronix's first product launch, they complained about my schedule, then left during the festivities. They never mentioned a follow-up visit and I had no interest in putting any of us through that experience again."

"You said your father and sisters still live in Colorado. Is that where you're from?"

"Yes, about two hours west of Denver."

"Your father and sisters, but not your mother?" She paused. "Where is she?"

He shifted away from her on the blanket. "I don't know. I haven't seen her since I was fourteen years old."

"What happened when you were fourteen?"

His chest tightened and his skin alternated between feverish and chilled. And *he* was the one who was deficient in understanding social cues? Were his clipped responses not enough to telegraph his unease with this topic? "She left and never returned."

"Oh . . ." She jerked upward and pressed a hand to the

front of her sweatshirt, covering the letters spread across her breasts. "My God, Adam. I'm sorry."

He avoided her stare. "My mother really wanted a son, and after two daughters she was ecstatic when I was born. It wasn't long before she realized I wasn't going to be the kind of son she'd envisioned."

This wasn't why he'd brought her out here. He hadn't planned to have this conversation now.

"Are you kidding me? Look at what you've accomplished. Any mother would be proud to have you as a son."

He entwined his fingers with hers and squeezed. "Not when I was a child. I was different."

"Different how? Because you were gifted?"

If only.

"Because I was diagnosed with Asperger's Syndrome."

She stiffened and her head jerked back. "Like autism?" she asked, dropping his hand.

He stared at his abandoned hand and the trail mix sank heavily to the pit of his stomach. "It's on the autism disorder spectrum, although the term was dropped for a broader one two years ago."

"When were you diagnosed?"

This was harder than he'd imagined. He stared straight ahead. "When I was six years old. My genius had already begun to manifest itself and my mother was keen to have me tested. She got what she wanted, but not in the package she'd have preferred."

"That's no excuse for her to abandon you."

"Imagine feeling overwhelmed, exhausted, and distressed at the way your child's issues and needs have taken over your life. Schedules, decisions, and daily routines all seem to revolve around a child whose mind moves at a rate you can't fathom, who doesn't share your interests—or even pretends to—and who has a preoccupation with perfection and finds it difficult to establish an emotional bond."

He'd memorized the introduction of the parenting website, having found it after doing a search on the topic of raising a child with Asperger's.

"Is that because of the Asperger's or the genius?"

"For me, they're intertwined."

"That explains some of our miscommunication."

He nodded. "When I was younger, idioms were my undoing. Pulling my leg, butterflies in my stomach, shoes that cost an arm and a leg. It's estimated that there are over twenty-five thousand of them. It'll never come naturally to me, as it does to many people, but most of the time, I'm fine. When I'm distracted or stressed, it becomes more difficult."

"And this is why you asked for my help with the presentation?"

"Struggles with understanding social cues and uneasiness being the focus of attention in a crowd are not the traits inherent in a successful interactive presentation."

"I can't imagine how difficult it's been for you," she said, her voice soft.

Heat swept across the back of his neck. "I don't want your fucking pity."

"Hey!" She rose to her knees and scooted to face him.

"Pity is the last thing I feel for you," she said, her tone vehement.

He noticed he'd curled his hands into fists. He forced himself to relax. "There's always someone worse off. On the one hand, I have this condition that makes socializing challenging for me. On the other hand, I possess a drive, determination, and single-minded focus that has made me more successful than most people in the world." He offered her a small smile. "In the grand scheme of things, I've come out ahead."

She touched his leg. "And that part about it being difficult to establish an emotional bond. Is that still an issue for you?"

His gaze bored into hers, needing her to understand. "I can't speak for all people on the spectrum, but I have no problem establishing a bond with anyone who captures my interest." He sighed and looked away. "Are you angry that I didn't tell you before we slept together? I wasn't trying to hide it, but it's personal information I only share with a few people."

When she didn't respond right away, he hurried to clarify. "I swear I wasn't trying to deceive you. I don't respond to the social and vocal cues you instinctively notice when someone sets out to mislead you. It adds an extra layer of difficulty to conversations. I don't lie and I can't tolerate people in my life who do."

She sat hunched over with her eyes closed, rubbing the middle of her forehead. His heart slowed as he struggled to pull fresh air into his lungs. He'd been expecting this response, but he hadn't expected it to hurt this much. Now wasn't the time to wallow in self-pity. He had to think about his company.

"Are you still willing to help me?"

Her eyes popped open. "Of course. And now that I understand, I'll be able to assist you more effectively."

"I never wanted to be treated differently," he said.

"You *are* different, but that's part of your appeal and it makes you special. Anyone who doesn't recognize that, including your mother, isn't worthy of your care or consideration."

Her words fueled him, sending adrenaline coursing through his body. He reached out for one of her curls, hopeful when she didn't pull away.

"Why are you here?" he asked, scrutinizing her face, wishing that, just this once, he could automatically understand every tick, every nuance.

"You suggested a hike," she said, the corner of her mouth lifting.

"Not here with me. Here, in the mountains. When we first met you said you were spending a couple of months up here. This isn't the natural destination for a person who doesn't like the outdoors."

It was her turn to look off. "I needed some time away."

"From what?" Or whom?

"I—" She swallowed. "I'm close to a promotion but it requires me to do something I'm not sure about." She bent her head. "I came up here to think about it."

He recalled their earlier conversation. A promotion would epitomize the success she craved and her hesitation spoke volumes.

"Is it illegal?"

"No."

"But you're unsure. Is it unethical?"

"Let's not talk about it. What a horrible conversation to honor this wonderful view." She shook her head. "You know, if we'd attended the same high school, I would've come to your wrestling matches."

"Really?"

"Uh-huh. And when you pinned your opponent, I would've stood up and cheered."

He imagined looking up into the stands of his high school gymnasium and seeing Chelsea applauding his victory. "You would have been a costly distraction."

"I doubt it. You're one of the most focused people I know."

He smiled. Then, in one smooth, controlled motion, he hooked his hand beneath her knees and pulled her forward until she was lying flat on her back and he was braced above her. She squealed and her eyes widened.

He swept her hair off her forehead and pressed a brief kiss to her lips.

"You'd be amazed to learn the effect you've had on me."

"I'm no wrestling expert," she said, her voice breathless, "but I'm certain this isn't part of a regulation wrestling match."

"They'd alter the rules if all opponents looked like you."

Chapter Sixteen

Adam has Asperger's.

Chelsea closed the lid of her laptop and stared into the flames of the gas fireplace. It had been difficult to reconcile the man she was drawn to with the popular depictions of autism in movies and on TV, like *Rain Man* and *The Big Bang Theory*. But after her hike with Adam, she'd returned to the Anderson house and immediately began researching Asperger's and autism spectrum disorders. From what she learned, Adam fell on the side of the spectrum where his problems had more to do with social interaction than they did with cognitive disabilities.

She was humbled that Adam had chosen to confide in her, but what did she do with this new information? What did it mean for the presentation and what she was hired to do? More importantly, would it affect her growing feelings for Adam?

She needed to talk to her best friend. She picked up her phone and texted India.

Can you talk?

Her phone rang almost immediately.

"I've never had so much sweet tea in my life!" Indi said. "I swear they mainline it here."

"Welcome to the South."

"No kidding. So, how was your date with Adam Bennett?" She huffed out a laugh. "I can't believe I just uttered that sentence."

Chelsea smiled in remembrance. "It was amazing. He rented out a science museum and we had dinner under the stars."

"Now, that's something you don't hear every day. Sounds romantic. It's going well, then? You've reconciled him being a client and becoming involved with him?"

"Oh Indi . . ." She hated that her voice cracked.

"Chels, what is it? What's going on?"

She blinked rapidly, refusing to let any tears fall. "You can't tell anyone."

"You're scaring me."

"I'm sorry, that's not my intention, but I really need to talk to you, and the information is sensitive, and I—"

"I got it. And I wouldn't tell anyone if you told me not to."

Chelsea took a deep breath. "Adam has Asperger's."

"Oh. Oooh."

"I just found out about his diagnosis. That's the real reason why I'm working with him, why he needs my help."

"You just found out? Don't people with Asperger's exhibit obvious behaviors?"

"It's a spectrum. Everyone's different, although there are similarities in symptoms that help with diagnosis. When we first met, I thought he was an eccentric genius and a stubborn prick."

"An alpha-hole."

"Exactly."

"But that changed?"

"Yes, and despite my better judgment, I agreed to go out with him. And now . . ."

"Does finding out affect how you feel about him?"

"No. Wait, that's not true. It does. But not negatively. When I think of all he's accomplished, how much was stacked against him, and how little support he had, I'm in awe. He's the most incredible man I've ever known," she said, her breath catching. She lowered her voice. "And he can make me come just by crooking his finger. Literally."

Indi sighed. "That makes me miss Jeremy."

"Ewww. I told you I got rid of that showerhead. When I get home, I'll box him up and send him to you. Spark a reunion."

Indi's laughter blared from the phone. "I'd appreciate that." She cleared her throat. "So he's smart, gorgeous, rich, and a great lover. I'm not seeing the problem."

Chelsea's euphoria faded. "I'm lying to him. The way we met, why I'm here. It's a lie."

"You're one of the most honest people I know. Why would you do that?"

"It's a condition of the assignment. You know this promotion means everything to me."

"If it meant everything, you wouldn't be so conflicted."

"You know what I went through growing up," she said through clenched teeth. "How I was taken from my home and how my mother was harassed and bullied. I'm never going to be treated that way again. This promotion will give me a respectability that no one will ever be able to deny. I've worked toward this for years."

Her phone beeped. "Hold on. Shit," she said when she saw Howard's name on the notification. She couldn't wait until this assignment was over, if only to ensure she'd never have to answer to him again. "I've got to take this. It's my boss."

"For the record, you're enough, Chels. I've always thought so. You employ so much effort putting on a front, but you've never needed to prove anything to me. I *do* know what you went through. I was there. And I'm here. I'll always be here, even when there are miles between us. You don't need to lie or hide who you are to achieve respectability. I love you and I trust you'll make the right decision."

And then she was gone.

Dammit. She massaged her forehead. She didn't have time for an emotional breakdown. She called Howard back.

"Is everything on track for the launch?"

No, I've just been sitting around with my thumbs up my ass. "Yes."

"Good. It's generating a massive amount of buzz. Once Computronix acknowledges our assistance, we can look forward to a new revenue stream from the tech industry," Howard said, his glee unmistakable.

She regretted ever agreeing to this condition. Now that she knew about Adam's diagnosis and his beliefs, should she take her chances and tell him the truth? The lie plagued her, an accusing sound track to every moment they shared. Maybe she could convince Howard that she'd come up with an alternative that would be beneficial for everyone.

"I know you and Rebecca are excited about this account, but I think we erred with this strategy. If we'd approached him from the start and said Computronix hired us on his behalf—"

"Our client insisted on this course of action and he knows Bennett better than you do. It's been working so far, right?"

It was working for them. But she was getting royally screwed in the process. She'd crossed the line between personal and professional, all while committing the unpardonable sin of lying to Adam. All the justifications and exclamations of client confidentiality wouldn't make her deception any more palatable.

"Four more days. You're in the home stretch. Don't waver now. If you need motivation, picture your new corner office. And Chelsea? Keep me posted on his progress."

She threw the phone down and covered her face with

her hands. She wanted that partnership, craved the validation it represented, but at what cost? Losing Adam? Losing herself?

"I REFUSE TO participate," Adam said, not taking his eyes off his center monitor.

"You can't refuse. You need to do this."

"Can't you read the speech? Why do I need to perform it for you?"

"Because the more times you do it, the more comfortable you'll be. And remember, you aren't reading a paper, you're giving a presentation. Don't memorize your speech word for word. Learn broad talking points and then elaborate."

"This is absurd."

She took a deep breath, trying to summon her patience. "I know this is uncomfortable for you, but it's really important."

"That's easy for you to say. You're not being challenged to stand in front of a crowd and bare yourself to strangers."

"Hmm," she murmured. "What if I bared myself to *you*? Would that help?"

He swiveled in his desk chair and sat forward. "Absolutely," he said, his voice dipping to a husky register, "but not the way you intend."

"You don't know my intention. Maybe that's been part of our problem. I thought I knew your intention, assumed you had enough of your own motivation to help get you through this presentation. But maybe you need some outside motivation."

His eyes gleamed with interest.

After her phone call with Howard, she'd decided to put all of her focus on the presentation. It was much simpler that way. But the next time she'd seen Adam, he'd pulled her in for a panty-melting kiss, ruining all of her plans. She'd spent the past two days in a blissful mix of business and pleasure. Lessons on engagement and rapport were interspersed with sexual sessions in the master bedroom, the guest bedroom, on the couch, and against his desk of destruction. Still, she never got comfortable. The moments when she felt his gaze on her and looked up to find him staring, she knew it was all an illusion. If he found out she'd lied to him about how they met, that she'd been hired by the computer company to get him ready for the presentation, he'd never forgive her, and anything he was starting to feel for her would curdle into hate.

She raised her hand. "Mr. Bennett?"

He shook his head. "Chelsea—"

She pitched her voice high and waved her hand in a flapping motion. "Mr. Bennett?"

He exhaled, thumbed his ear, and answered. "Yes?"

"Mr. Bennett, Chelsea Grant from *Mountaintop Today* magazine." She worked hard to keep from smiling, though her muscles strained to show her amusement. "It seems like there are new tech items hitting the market daily. How is yours different?"

Adam waved her off. "This is ridiculous. It doesn't—"

He halted and considered her hand, which she trailed down the front of her shirt and used to unsnap the button on the front of her jeans. His eyes widened and his Adam's apple—ha!—bobbed as he swallowed.

"Mr. Bennett? How is yours different?" She held the fly's flap with her left hand while her right hand poised over the zipper.

His gaze jumped from her hand to her face and back again. "Since the first PC, very few products have been revolutionary. But in the same way the iPod changed the music industry, I believe the HPC will change the way we use personal computers."

Chelsea smiled. "Very good, Mr. Bennett."

She slid the jean's zipper down, the metal teeth separating the only sound in the room. She shook her hips—adding an extra shimmy for him—pushed the material down her legs, and kicked them off. She stood in a sheer maroon silk T-shirt, black panties, and nothing else.

Adam stood, but she held up her hand.

"Uh-uh," she chided, shaking her head.

"Chelsea." His voice was strangled and the evidence of his longing was imprinted against the front of his jeans.

"Not yet."

She winked, and with a tilt of her head, raised her hand. Would he play the game with her?

"You," he said, pointing at her. Lightness warmed her chest.

"Who is your target demo for this device?" She

gripped the bottom of her T-shirt in both hands, stretching the material away from her body.

"I think everyone will be able to use this device. It has the potential to replace your personal desktop or laptop computer."

She gave him an approving nod and whipped the garment over her head until she remained in her bra and panties. His gaze staggered her with the force of his desire. His chest rose and fell and his hands clenched briefly and released at his sides. Despite his obvious longing, he answered her question in a clear and concise manner. She wanted him so badly, she was ready to leap across the space and tackle him, but she also wanted him to be ready for the launch in two days.

"What will be a successful market share for your first year out of the gate?"

She'd thrown him with that one. It was more of an insider question and not an easy lob like her two previous queries. It took a moment for his mind to shift gears as he put on his tech hat and stuffed his lust back in the closet.

"There's a segment of the population who consider themselves tech people, even though they are not in this industry. If we can get a large number of them interested in our device, we'll have a real shot at carving out a place for ourselves in this market."

It would've been easy for him to throw out lots of figures and take minutes to answer the question. What he'd done was succinct and informative, without coming off as condescending and long-winded. What a transformation.

She hopped up onto the back of the sofa, reached behind her, and unsnapped the clasp on her bra. Her breasts sprung free, swaying slightly. Her nipples pebbled when the cold air hit them and she heard his audible intake of breath.

"You've convinced me, Mr. Bennett. Consider me a fan for life."

She'd barely got the sentence out before he closed the distance between them, grasped the back of her head, and kissed her.

Their tongues dueled and she wrapped her arms around his waist. He tilted her head back as he devoured her mouth. His hands roamed over her body, through her curls, down her back, around her front to cup her breasts. She moaned and he wrenched his mouth from hers and trailed kisses down her neck. Bending low, he took her left nipple into his mouth and suckled, pulling on the tight bud. Her core throbbed and moisture pooled between her thighs.

Adam knew her body as well as she did and she was learning that intensity was inherent to this man. When he focused on something, he gave it his full attention. And she was the latest lucky recipient.

He dropped to his knees before her, startling her. She clenched her fingers in his hair, the satiny strands soft against her fingers. He looked up at her and she froze. His blue eyes were wide and his pupils were dilated.

"Can I taste you here?" He placed his palm against her core.

He was the one genuflecting before her and yet

she feared he would eventually bring her to her knees. She shivered with need and nodded. He pressed kisses along her inner thigh, the heat from his breath teasing her sensitive flesh. She moaned and tightened her grip in his hair. He licked over her fabric-covered center, the surprise causing her to arch up and move closer to his mouth. He repeated it and she squirmed against the sofa, her abdominal muscles straining to keep her in place. She was ready to fall apart and he hadn't even removed her panties.

That situation was quickly remedied as he pushed the fabric aside, baring her to his eyes. The air in the room whispered over her heated flesh, goose bumps popping out on her arms. He leaned forward and stroked his tongue through her folds, and she jerked upward, bucking against him.

He loved her slowly and leisurely, as if nothing else was important and her pleasure was the only thing he cared about. He took his time, drawing out the sensation, making it last, and just when she thought she would come from the pleasure, he stopped. It was so close. She could feel it, taunting her. She squeezed her eyes shut. She was afraid to move, afraid that any movement would bring it on and she wanted to share this feeling with him. The feeling of standing on a precipice, with one foot out over the edge. Where she was equal parts safe and equal parts imperiled.

"Wait for me, sweetness."

She could hear him. Her closed eyes and existence in a sexual trance had heightened her other senses. She heard the shirt slide from his skin, the pull on the zipper descend, the heavy fabric hitting the floor, the tearing of the foil. Then he was touching her, hooking her knees over his elbows and pulling her toward him. This was it. She knew she wouldn't be able to hold out much longer.

"Chelsea. Look at me."

She did, opening her eyes and gazing into his heated stare.

"No confusion about who's claiming you. You're mine and I'm yours. Okay?"

"Yes," she whispered.

With a triumphant grin, he surged into her. Her breath caught in her throat at the rightness of the coupling. She clenched around him, welcoming him home as he repeatedly thrust into her. She wrapped her arms around his neck as she kissed his cheek, his ear, his jaw.

"You feel so good," he said, leaning his head on her shoulder.

She felt the abyss calling her, whispering to her, letting her know it was there, waiting for her to tumble into it. She answered the call, falling headfirst into pleasure unlike anything she'd ever experienced.

"Chelsea," he shouted, as he came inside her.

She clenched her legs around his hips and held him to her as waves of pleasure rippled along his frame. Finally, they were both still, their breaths feathering the other, their hearts beating strong. Adam lifted his head and pressed a kiss to her cheek.

"Can I request this same reward on the actual day of the presentation?"

She laughed and his answering chuckle rumbled through his body. She stroked his hair from his forehead and succumbed to the sensations enveloping her. The world could end at this moment, and she'd be content. Lying in his arms, there was no place she'd rather be. She thought about the moments of happiness she'd felt in the last few years. They usually involved work. How much brighter and more gratifying would it have been if Adam had been by her side, celebrating those triumphs with her?

In between one breath and the next, her world tilted on its axis and when it righted itself she knew she had fallen in love with him. The joy she felt thickened to sludge when she imagined him learning her secret. If he discovered she was lying to him before she had the opportunity to explain, he would hate her forever. But if she confessed now, how would that affect his presentation?

Sure, she was concerned about her own employment issues. She'd worked hard, and for a long time, to earn this opportunity. But Adam also deserved the victory that would come from a successful launch. And anything that divided his focus risked that success. Maybe if she had more time. The launch was two days away. There was no scenario where she thought she could confide in him now and he'd be ready to go on Friday. No, the presentation was the more pressing objective. She'd get him through it and then she'd tell him the truth.

And hope like hell he'd forgive her.

Chapter Seventeen

THE DAY BEFORE Computronix's product launch there was a tangible buzz in the Moscone Center. People scurried to and fro all around her, carrying bags, clipboards, and the ubiquitous tablets and smartphones. The sense of excitement was palpable.

Adrenaline raced through Chelsea and she squeezed Adam's hand, pressing her body against his arm. The lights, the energy, the chaos all reminded her of the various award ceremonies she'd attended. No matter the field, people were eager to be in the presence of greatness. As they took the steps to the lower level, everyone recognized the man next to her.

"There's Adam Bennett."

"Wow, the rumors are true."

"What is he doing here?"

"No one's seen him in over a year."

Chelsea bit her lip and executed a sideways glance,

but she needn't have worried. He was resolute, his entire being focused on the upcoming presentation.

When they reached the door to the main conference area, Adam showed his credentials to the guard. The man referred to his clipboard and granted them access to the room.

The inside was arranged in a manner similar to many other press conferences she'd attended. Recessed and stage lighting flooded the rows of chairs placed facing forward. At the front of the room, three large screens projected Computronix's logo. A stage had been constructed in front of the center screen, and a man stood there now, his body appearing minuscule against the backdrop of the thirty-foot surface. Two chairs sat on the left side of the stage and a podium was situated on the right side. Technicians scrambled around them fine-tuning the sound system, adjusting the lights, and taping down cords to avoid stumbling hazards.

"Check one. Check one." A familiar voice boomed through the speaker.

"There's Mike." Adam smiled and headed toward the front of the room.

Dread claimed residence in Chelsea's chest and she pressed a suddenly shaky hand to her midsection. She hadn't spoken to Mike Black since that day at Beecher & Stowe. She didn't know what he'd been told or if Howard had warned him that she'd be there, but she needed to speak to him before he could say or do anything to ruin her relationship with Adam.

"No delays with setup. We're running on schedule," Mike was saying to Adam as she approached.

"Great. There's someone I want you to meet. Chelsea?"

She stepped from behind Adam, her hands clasped tightly in front of her. Mike's smile dissipated from his handsome face and he stared at her with wide eyes. Not good. She rushed her greeting, ending the budding awkward moment and attempting to set the tone of their introduction.

"It's a pleasure to meet you," she said. "Adam has told me all about you."

Mike pulled on his bottom lip, his brows smashed together into a confused arc. "I can't say the same. He's been secretive where you're concerned."

"That's not true," Adam said. "Chelsea's the neighbor I mentioned."

She wasn't sure what Adam had told him, but based on his reaction it couldn't have been favorable. Mike stiffened, his shoulders going rigid beneath his black tee. His nostrils flared and he studied her with the same disdain an A-list celebrity gives the paparazzi. She smoothed her hand down the sides of her pencil skirt and shifted in her strappy heels. If only she possessed the ability to disappear.

"Sorry. She's not quite what I was expecting."

Adam slid an arm around her waist and pulled her to his side. "You're forgiven. Not only is she stunning, she's also extremely talented. Chelsea's in the entertainment business and she's been assisting me with the presentation."

"Really?" Mike said, his expression hardening like quick-set cement.

Her smile sat heavy on her face. Adam seemed oblivious to the tension in her body, conversing easily with his friend. Was it wrong of her to be slightly grateful that his Asperger's shielded him from the shame and guilt that seeped from her pores?

"She helped me with the *CGR* feature. The one whose continued incompletion had Anya labeling me as a terrorist."

Mike narrowed his light blue eyes. "I guess we should thank you on behalf of Computronix," he said, his tone caustic.

"It was no problem." She met his heated stare.

Please, don't say anything. I promise I'll explain.

Mike firmed his lips and glanced at Adam. "Some of the tech guys have a question about connecting the HPC to the large screen display. Can you walk them through it?"

Tears pooled in her eyes and she allowed her lashes to flutter closed. Thank God. It appeared he was providing her the opportunity for which she'd mentally begged.

"Chelsea?" Adam's soft grip on her elbow induced her to open her eyes. "I'm the only person who will touch the HPC until after the presentation. Do you mind?"

"Don't worry about Chelsea," Mike answered in her stead. "I'll keep her company. She can talk to me about what's she done to get you ready for the presentation."

Adam frowned. "Are you sure?"

"Yes." She forced a smile. "I'll be fine. I'll stay here and talk to Mike."

He kissed her. "I'll be fifteen minutes."

As he pulled away, she reached up and briefly touched his cheek, halting his escape. She stared into his eyes, memorizing every plane and angle of his sexy and intelligent face. God, she loved him. "Go get 'em."

One last kiss and he jogged off to the stage, a tempting sight in dark jeans and a merlot-colored cashmere sweater.

When Adam was out of hearing distance, Mike turned on her. "What the hell is going on?"

"I can explain."

"I wanted you to get him ready for the presentation. I didn't think sleeping with him was required to accomplish that goal."

She flinched as his verbal arrows hit their intended target. "It's not what you think."

"Really?" His tight smile reeked of condescension and rendered his attractive features anything but. "Are you telling me you haven't slept with him?"

"That's none of your business," she said, crossing her arms over her chest.

"I'm his best friend. I'm making it my business. If you knew him, you'd know how serious this is."

His concern deflated her indignation slightly and she sighed. "I do know him and that's the only reason I'm going to address that issue. I didn't set out to get involved with him. I fought our connection until . . . I couldn't."

"You've got to be kidding me."

"I'm not." She hadn't found anything humorous about this situation for a while.

"But he doesn't know the truth about how you two met. You're still lying to him."

Hello, hypocritical pot! She arched an incredulous brow. "I'm not the only one."

Mike pointed an accusing finger at her. "Don't compare our situations or motives. I did what I did because it was best for him and the company. You did it for a promotion."

"No. I neglected to tell him the truth in the beginning because you ordered us not to. After we became involved"—she shook her head—"I was afraid I'd lose him. I'm in an untenable situation, but we want the same thing: for this presentation to be a success. For Adam. We both know how much he deserves it."

She glanced over her shoulder and saw Adam gesturing as he talked to the tech guys on stage. He looked up and their gazes met and held. Her breath seized in her throat and everyone around her froze in suspended animation. Had it only been a few weeks since they'd met? He was so intertwined with her heart that she couldn't imagine not being a part of his life. He waved and she responded instinctively with her own greeting. He smiled and turned his attention back to the young man. She released her imprisoned breath.

And the world resumed around her.

"Adam has a thing about lying—" Mike began.

"I know. That's why this has been so difficult. I approached Howard numerous times about changing our tactics, but he refused based on *your* orders."

"Adam's been through this before. His last girlfriend lied to him and—"

"I know all about Birgitta and the rushed launch of the mini game console."

He shook his head. "I'm not talking about a typical person's distaste for lies—"

"He has Asperger's. I know," she said, at Mike's shocked expression.

He cleared his throat. "He told you about that?"

"Yes."

His mouth tightened. "So you know he felt betrayed and why. He vowed he'd never be in that position again. So to see him here with you like this . . . it's Birgitta two point oh."

That produced a bitter tang in her mouth. She recoiled, wrinkling her nose. "I'm nothing like her. I would never betray him."

"No, it's not in your financial interest."

Fuck him.

Irritation boiled her blood and she turned away from him, twisting her curls up and letting them cascade down her back. He was the one who'd started this with his insistence on hiding her identity from Adam. But she refrained from expressing her outrage, knowing she was the sole culprit for her current predicament. Investing in transferred emotion was counterproductive. Anger wasn't the antidote for Mike's suspicion. Understanding was the strategy for her success. She had to convince him they were on the same side. Plus, a part of her admired the other man for defending his friend.

She faced him. "This isn't about work or my promotion. Please, I don't want to hurt him. I love him."

He stared at her for a few tense moments. Was she wasting her time? Would Mike never trust her sincerity and decide to blow her cover with Adam? She replayed their conversation in her mind, wondering if there was anything she could've said or done differently to affect the outcome.

"I believe you," he finally said.

She exhaled and straightened, her conscience having shed thirty pounds. His approval was like whipped cream on dessert—not necessary, but nice to have. "Thank you."

"Don't thank me yet. You love him. But none of it matters until you tell him the truth."

"I know, and I promise I will, after the presentation."

"I'll give you some time, but then I'll have to step in. This lie is larger than you. I'm already lying to him about how you met, and now I'm part of the lie about your relationship and I—"

He stiffened and winced.

Oh, no. Please, God, no. Not like this.

She closed her eyes and her heart sank into the depths of her stomach. Slowly, she turned to find Adam standing behind her, his once-heated gaze gone glacial, the vein in his temple twitching frantically.

Chapter Eighteen

A RUSH OF coldness hammered Adam's midsection. His muscles tightened and his head drew back as Mike's words echoed in his mind.

I'm already lying to him about how you met, and now I'm part of the lie about your relationship.

Mike lowered his gaze and rocked back on his feet. Chelsea shook her head, her palm covering her lips. No one with his quantifiable intellectual prowess could fail to accept the truth of the situation before him.

He'd been used. Again.

"Your arrival at my house wasn't coincidence." It wasn't a question.

Her beautiful eyes were wide, luminous with the sheen of unshed tears. "Adam, please. I know what it sounds like, but you have to let me explain."

How had he thought he'd been cold before? His heart pounded in his chest and his body burned.

"You planned this before we'd ever met. What was your endgame?"

"Listen to me—"

He advanced on her. "Did you sell me out? Auction off the HPC blueprints to other companies? Is someone going to come out with a cheaper version before ours gets to the market?"

"No! Of course not. I—"

He grabbed her forearms and shook her. "What did you do, Chelsea? What did you do?"

"Hey," Mike interrupted. "Let her go—"

Anger swirled within him, fueling him, inoculating him from the hurt and disappointment that would surely overwhelm him. He swung his arm to dislodge Mike's grip and pivoted to face him, clenched fists raised to strike. "Stay the fuck out of this."

How had this happened again? What was it about him that attracted unreliable women into his life? First his mother, then Birgitta, and now Chelsea.

"Adam, all I did was get you ready for the presentation, which is exactly what I'd promised you."

He lifted his hand, as if his flesh could stem the tide of her excuses. Her betrayal threatened to fracture his armor, but he ignored the pain and sought relief in analytics, letting his mind sift through the options and follow each to its logical conclusion. Had he left any of his research lying about for her to examine? Had she ever seen him input his password? What about when his files were unlocked and vulnerable? Did she go through them, email some to his competition?

Her hands trembled as she reached for him. "Listen to me—"

"Why? So you can lie to me again? Pacify me to get a head start on my next invention?"

"It wasn't like that."

"I'm not interested in anything you say unless you start telling me the truth. You owe me that."

"You needed to accept my help of your own accord. That was my job." She dashed away her tears with the back of her hand.

He hated seeing her cry, despised seeing her in pain. What she said made no sense, but he fixated on her last two words. "Your job? You're in the entertainment industry. What does your job have to do with me?"

She bit her lower lip and he refused to surrender to his instinct to assume that task himself. That had been part of the problem. Her presence had weakened his common sense. There'd been numerous instances where her words hadn't added up, but he'd ignored his inner mathematician, succumbing to emotion. He waited, knowing he wasn't going to like what came next.

"I don't work in entertainment in the way I led you to believe. I work in public relations."

"You're in PR?" He hadn't expected *that*.

"I'm the Executive Managing Director of West Coast Entertainment for Beecher & Stowe Public Relations."

"Hence the entertainment," he said, muttering to himself. She'd probably assuaged her guilt by telling herself she'd partially told the truth. "And who gave you 'me' as an assignment?"

"I did."

His head swiveled to Mike, who'd remained standing several feet away, his brow lowered, arms crossed over his chest.

"What?" Now he was really confused.

"I gave her the assignment. She was there because of me."

"What are you talking about?"

Mike glanced around. "Can we talk about this somewhere private?"

Adam followed the trajectory of Mike's gaze and for the first time he noticed their melodrama had garnered an audience. Fucking fantastic.

"*I* introduced *you* to Chelsea," he told Mike. "You'd never met her before today."

"You needed help with your presentation. After the last launch, you were having problems, whether you'd admit it or not. A successful launch was key to a profitable initial rollout of the HPC. So I hired Chelsea's firm to get you ready for the launch and, as a condition of the job, she couldn't tell you about my involvement. If you knew what I was doing, you would have thwarted her efforts at every turn."

Adam felt blindsided. Lied to not only by the woman he was involved with, but his best friend and business partner. Remembered humiliation bubbled in his midsection. This was why he preferred solitude on his mountain. In fact, if he'd turned her away the night of the storm, he wouldn't be in this situation. He walked away.

Not wanting to endure the crowd on the escalators, he headed for the elevators.

Damn his Asperger's. A normal man would've figured it out. A normal man would've read their body language, seen the clues, felt . . . something in the air. A normal man wouldn't have been fooled. Again. He laughed bitterly. What would it take before he accepted he wasn't normal? Was he or was he not a fucking genius?

"Adam, wait." Chelsea gave chase and caught up with him. "We're not finished."

"There's nothing else to say."

She grabbed his elbow. "The hell there's not."

He jerked away from her touch. The doors opened and he stepped onto the elevator. She followed, bestowing a fierce glare on the people attempting to enter behind her. They let the doors close without further efforts to board. Adam pressed the button for the lobby.

"You have to listen to me," she said.

He'd actually accepted he'd live his life alone.

Until her.

"Did I miss something? Didn't Mike hire you to prepare me for the launch? Have you not been lying to me from the moment we met?"

The anger seeped from her face and she hugged her waist. He was an idiot and should be retested. He knew the truth, *knew* it, yet he needed her to say the words, so there was no confusion.

"Chelsea?"

Her gaze shot to his and she nodded. "Yes."

It was impossible for the stomach to literally drop, and as the elevator was steady, there were no motions to affect his center of gravity. But that's what he experienced. He didn't shy away from it, hoping this time he'd learn his lesson. He let the sensation imprint itself in his mind and on his heart.

He would never go through this again.

"I will explain everything, I promise—"

"You don't have to explain anything," he said, studying the control panel, refusing to look at her. "I have the ability to fully comprehend the situation, once my questions are answered. The night of the storm, when you came to my house, you knew who I was?"

She sighed. "Yes."

"And that meeting was part of your plan? To get in my good graces?"

"It's the reason I was on the mountain, although I hadn't anticipated the weather. Mike hired our firm but I was the one who decided how to approach you."

At least she wasn't denying it. Which shouldn't surprise him. She'd always been a straight shooter. Or was she? He didn't know the real Chelsea.

"Was it part of your brilliant business scheme to sleep with me?"

"It wasn't like that and you know it. I didn't plan to sleep with you. I certainly didn't count on falling in love with you."

He flinched and shook his head.

"I love you, Adam. That's why I can't apologize for taking this assignment. Because if I hadn't, I'd never have met you. I only wish I hadn't agreed not to tell you who I was, or that I'd told you earlier." She paused. "But I didn't."

"No, you didn't," he said, finally turning to face her. "Why is that?"

Her account was still illogical. He was missing an important fact. Why would she go through all of this for her job? He swallowed, wanting to banish the sour taste that suddenly materialized at the back of his throat. From his memory, their conversation on the mountain popped into his mind. His stomach roiled and he hunched forward, his shoulders curling inward.

"What was your prize upon the successful completion of your mission?"

"What?"

"You aren't slow, Chelsea. Don't insult us both by pretending that you are. This," he said, motioning to the space between them, "is the ethical dilemma you were pondering. The task you had to complete to get your promotion."

Her hands trembled and she shoved them in the crook of her elbows when she crossed her arms. "This has nothing to do with my partnership—"

"Oh, it's a partnership. Impressive. So now we know the going rate of betrayal: a new title and a high six-figure salary."

"I deserve that. But you have to understand, Adam. This job, this partnership, was the most important thing to me. I told you a little about my upbringing, but not all of it."

"That appears to be a pattern with you."

Her mouth tightened at the corners, but she continued.

"My mother raised me. I never knew my father. It wasn't the most normal upbringing. She kept trying to replace him. She'd take her paycheck and run off with her latest boyfriend, leaving me to fend for myself for a week. And when that boyfriend left her, she'd descend into a depression that left no room for taking care of me. Then she'd meet another guy and the cycle would start all over again."

Despite his anger, he listened, the information giving him an insight into her he'd never had. It explained a lot about her, but it didn't excuse her behavior.

"When we met in the beginning it didn't matter; you were just a job. I didn't know anything about love. My mother said she loved me a thousand times, but her love didn't pay the rent, put food in my belly, or clothes on my back. Her love for me couldn't make her show up for meetings at school, it didn't stop me from being bullied because of her reputation, and it didn't make her fight to keep me when the state took me away. By the time I recognized that I loved you, it was too late. I was afraid you would hate me."

"You just told me how important your career is to you and what that promotion would mean. So don't tell me that keeping the truth from me was about being afraid that I would hate you. What scared you was the possibility that I wouldn't go through with the presentation and you wouldn't get your partnership."

The elevator dinged and the doors opened. Two men

wearing lanyards and carrying iPads stood waiting. They took one look at them and stepped back.

"We'll take the next one," the taller man said, waving them off.

"What about us?" Chelsea asked, when the doors had closed again. "You can't let this one mistake negate our entire relationship."

"There wasn't an us because I don't know who *you* are."

"Yes, you do. I never lied about the important things. Think about our moments together. Playing video games, our mountainside hike." She lowered her voice. "Making love. Those weren't fake."

"How can I believe you?"

"Because it's the truth," she said, her voice increasing in volume and intensity.

Didn't she understand? "I thought what you told me before was the truth. How can I trust anything you ever tell me again? I told you how I felt about lying and you smiled in my face and deceived me behind my back."

"Oh, my God," she said, clenching her hands into fists. "People aren't computers, Adam. We're complex creatures. I'm not saying I didn't lie to you in the beginning, but things changed. I thought making partner would compensate for my mother and my upbringing, but I was wrong. The partnership means nothing to me if I lose you because of it."

"Then you did all of it for nothing."

Tears coursed down her face and fell from her quavering chin. The acid in the back of his throat threatened to choke him.

"We always seem to get stuck on this verbal merry-go-round," she whispered. "I love you. I will never lie to you again. Doesn't my word mean anything?"

He considered her. Her vibrant curls, her glassy eyes, her smooth dark skin, her full lips.

"For a time, it was everything."

When the elevator doors opened again, he stomped out, the sound of her sobs following him. He didn't care where he was or where he was going. He couldn't be near her one moment longer. Her presence was a painful reminder of her deception and his disability. Pressure pricked behind his eyelids, emphasizing the tightness in his throat and the hollowness in his chest.

Was this what heartbreak felt like?

Chapter Nineteen

I LOVE YOU. I will never lie to you again. Doesn't my word mean anything?

Adam stared out the floor-to-ceiling windows in the living room of the presidential suite at the St. Regis Hotel. The sun had yet to set and the surrounding stone, metal, and glass skyscrapers that comprised San Francisco's cityscape seemed to sparkle from its rays.

He missed his home. If he were standing in his great room, studying his usual vista, he'd see mountains instead of buildings, sky instead of lights, trees instead of people. That's the lesson he should learn from this ordeal. Life had been better on his mountain, developing new technology without distractions, keeping his own vigil.

He swung from the polished scene and glanced over the large, well-appointed room. Chelsea said she'd reserved it because it boasted a "meticulous decor with timeless elegance," and it was close to the Moscone

Center. He'd agreed the space had seemed perfect when he'd planned to share it with her. But when he'd returned to the suite, he'd discovered her bags gone and any trace of her presence erased. Now the room felt barren. He was alone.

Again.

He glanced at the clock on the wall. He'd missed sound check hours ago. It was for the best. He doubted his ability to concentrate. Their fight was probably the topic of the convention center and he'd dreaded facing all of those people. It was shades of the *People Magazine* debacle all over again.

For the fortieth time he rued his faulty judgment. He'd vowed to never place himself in this situation again and here he was, on the eve of another presentation, pondering deception by a woman.

And not just any woman. Chelsea.

It was quiet. Too quiet. Guess he'd enjoyed having Chelsea around.

The lock on the outer door clicked and his heart revived in his chest, pounding painfully.

Chelsea?

His body had skirted the wooden side table and leather club chair before his brain recalled he didn't want to see her. Still, he held his breath.

The door swung open and Mike entered, dressed in a dark suit.

Adam's heart stuttered. Great. "What do you want? I've had my fill of liars today."

"You missed sound check." Mike shoved his hands

into the pockets of his slacks and shrugged. "I was worried."

"How did you get in here?"

Mike nodded to the small plastic card emblazoned with the hotel's insignia that he'd flung onto the console table by the door. "Chelsea gave me her key."

Hearing the other man utter her name and recalling their hushed voices and guilty expressions fortified Adam's earlier weakness. His jaw tightened. "I'll make sure the hotel reprograms the lock."

"I know you're upset—"

"You've proven your knowledge is inaccurate and unreliable. If you *knew* me, you would know that I find lying an unpardonable sin."

"I do know you and how you feel. But I did it for your own good."

"I'm not an infant. I don't need to be coddled."

"Don't you?" Mike slashed a hand through the air. "How many times did I ask you to consider using a PR firm? To let me bring in someone to help you with the presentation?"

"I didn't need—"

"Yes, you did. And you would've known that if you'd stopped being so goddamned stubborn and listened to somebody else for once." Mike rubbed the back of his neck. "You know, you talk a good game about trust, but in successful relationships, the trust has to flow both ways."

Nice try. He wasn't going to let Mike absolve himself of his responsibility for this situation. Adam raised a brow. "I trusted you and you lied to me."

"This company is important to me, too. I've been with you from the beginning, through the highs of our initial success and the lows of Birgitta's betrayal. I've given you my unwavering support. This one time I asked you to trust *my* skills, to have *my* back, and you couldn't." Mike straightened and lifted his chin. "I did what was best for Computronix, and if you can't understand that, then screw you."

Adam frowned. Mike had been his best friend since college. Making friends had been exceedingly difficult for him, yet Mike was one of the few people who'd seen beyond his idiosyncrasies to the person beneath. Was he willing to throw away their relationship and the business they'd built for this one mistake?

"Come on, Adam, we need to get past this." Mike splayed his hands wide, palms facing upward. "Do you want to hit me? Will that make you feel better?"

He considered it. A little Pavlovian classical conditioning? Anytime Mike thought about lying to him, he'd recall the feel of Adam's fist against his jaw.

"This can't happen again," he finally said, choosing to forego physical assault.

"I won't go behind your back. But you have to promise to be more open-minded. To listen to, and consider, ideas that originate from others."

He hesitated then said, "I can't promise success, but I'll make an earnest attempt to try."

Mike grinned. "Your earnest attempt is better than ninety-nine percent of the world's."

"True." He sighed. "I only wish you could have found some other way that didn't include Chelsea."

Mike's grin disappeared. "I bear some responsibility for the Chelsea situation. As a condition of the contract, I instructed them not to tell you about me. I do believe her when she said she loved you and was planning to tell you everything after the presentation."

"After she received her promotion."

"She could've handled this better. We all could've. But she didn't get to her position at Beecher & Stowe without hard work, loyalty, and ambition. When she took this assignment, she didn't know you personally. She only knew that the reward for its successful completion was a partnership."

"You're excusing what she did?"

"You don't have to forgive her right away. Take things slow. Give her a chance to regain your trust. Don't cut her out of your life entirely, when doing so would make you both miserable." Mike's phone dinged and he pulled it from his inner coat pocket. "I'd hate to see you waste two more years of your life, up on your mountain, pushing everyone away." He checked the display and headed for the door. "I'm late for cocktails before dinner. Do what you need to do to feel better, but I want to see your ass at the Moscone Center tomorrow morning, 10 a.m. sharp."

His stomach shifted and his pulse raced. He couldn't go through with the presentation. He'd possessed plenty of confidence earlier, knowing he had Chelsea's support. But now?

Heading to the bedroom, he stopped just inside the doorway. The king-sized bed, with its plush comforter and mounds of pillows, taunted him. For dinner he'd reserved the private dining room at Quartet and for dessert he'd imagined spending the night before the launch reveling in the sexy heat of Chelsea's body. Instead, he was facing the real possibility he'd never see her again.

People aren't computers.

The sting of her words returned. He knew people weren't computers, but that didn't stop him from preferring they were. He understood computers. People, especially women, were significantly more difficult. Was it too onerous to expect not to be lied to by the person who proclaimed to love you?

I'd hate to see you waste another two years of your life, up on your mountain, pushing everyone away.

How had Mike known that'd been his initial instinct? Because that's what he'd done after Birgitta? He'd checked out of life, afraid of being hurt, but what had been hurt more than anything had been his pride. When he'd proposed to her, he'd been polishing his image of a successful life. His business was thriving; a beautiful wife would be a natural garnish.

No one would dare call him a disappointment.

But he'd had no real attachment to Birgitta. They rarely spent time together, she'd never been to his house on the mountain, she didn't know about his family. He'd shared more of himself with Chelsea in three weeks than he had with Birgitta the entire two years they'd been together. That's why it'd been easy to let her go. But the idea of living without Chelsea?

That existence seemed untenable.

Chapter Twenty

QUESTIONS ABOUT LOVE and trust, combined with the memory of Chelsea's sobs as he walked away, haunted him and he couldn't ignore the hypothesis that the issues highlighted by her and Mike started before he'd ever met them. That theory induced him to leave San Francisco, the night before the most important event of his career, and head east.

Three hours later, under a full moon in the starry Colorado sky, Adam rang the doorbell of his father's home and waited to be admitted. Numerous times—in the helicopter, on the private plane, in the car from the airport—he'd questioned the prudence of his decision, but he proceeded, intent on seeking answers.

The porch light illuminated above him and the door opened. Rick Bennett stood blinking in a hastily belted robe, his short graying hair tousled, a long cast covering his left leg from just below his knee. They spoke concurrently.

"What happened to your foot?"

"What are you doing here?"

Adam strode across the threshold, closing the thick wooden door behind him and taking his father's arm. "Let's get you settled."

He helped the older man into the open family room, the rhythmic thump of his cast against the wide planked floors a somber accompaniment. Adam settled him in his favorite recliner and engaged the padded footrest. Pulling the Aztec fabric ottoman closer to the chair, he perched on its corner and rested his elbows on his knees. "What happened?"

"It was stupid. I broke my ankle playing softball," Dad said, bracing against the armrests and shifting in the chair.

He exhaled and bowed his head, allowing himself a tiny measure of relief. At least he hadn't been assaulted or injured in an accident. "You're still playing?"

"In the town's senior softball league."

In his formative years, Adam had been heavily influenced by his father's active nature. Skiing, hiking, rafting, Dad always emphasized physical endeavors.

"When did it happen?"

"About three weeks ago."

Three weeks? *What the fuck?*

He crossed his arms and averted his head, unable to meet his father's gaze. It didn't take a genius to understand why the majority of his significant relationships were broken. "I didn't know."

"I'm fine. There was no need to worry you."

He cleared his throat. "Should you be walking on it?"

"I usually don't. I keep it elevated most of the time and Sarah comes over and checks on me during her breaks from the hospital. But when someone rings your doorbell at nine at night, it tends to get the adrenaline pumping. I acted without thinking."

Though he was grateful both of his sisters lived nearby, it annoyed Adam that Sarah hadn't called to inform him of the situation. He could've arranged for a private nurse. He made a mental note to contact local agencies after the launch.

"How is Sarah?"

Dad smiled. "Doing well. She and Douglas just bought a house over in Rippon Landing."

"And Amy?"

"Still working at the bank. Been dating a local fire-fighter. I think it's getting serious." Dad leaned forward and crossed his hands over his stomach. "But I have a sneaking suspicion you didn't fly over two hours, the night before your big product launch, to ask me about your sisters."

Adam's gaze flew to his father's. "You know about the presentation?"

Dad laughed. "We live in Colorado, not outer space."

Adam frowned. "Would that be a 'yes'?"

"That would be a 'yes.' Are you excited?"

His pulse accelerated. "The new device we're unveiling is cutting-edge. It's the best thing I've ever worked on."

"The girls are coming over tomorrow and we're watching it on the computer. I wish I could be there with you, but getting around in this thing"—he knocked on the cast—"is a pain in the ass."

Adam raised a brow. "You would've come to the launch?"

"Of course."

But— "The last time I extended an invitation, you left before the event ended. I thought you regretted attending."

"I could never regret the chance to see you. But I underestimated the demands on your time. You were so busy and . . . it didn't feel like the appropriate time to visit. I should've checked with you, but we left, assuming that's what you'd want." Dad pulled the edges of his robe together. "I figured you might still be mad about that."

"I'm not angry," he said, his voice low.

Chelsea had been right. Another instance of his word merry-go-round, except not much talking was done. Just assumptions made.

"So, what's going on?" his father asked.

"I—" Adam took a breath and started again. "Do you— Did you ever wish I was normal?"

The words spilled from him and seemed to be augmented by the resulting silence.

Dad's head jerked back, grooves appearing in his forehead. "Where is this coming from?"

"I need to know."

His father stared at him for a long, uncomfortable moment. "Raising you was . . . challenging, exhausting, humbling."

The dizziness caught Adam unawares. He dropped

his head and fought to draw air into his constricted lungs. Having doubts was one thing, but knowing you were right . . .

"It was also exhilarating, wondrous, and awe-inspiring."

Adam looked up.

"Son, there's no such thing as normal. We all have our issues."

"Not like mine."

"It wasn't always easy, but I wouldn't change you. I'd change myself. I could've done better. When you began to pull away from us, I could've fought it. But I was ashamed that I hadn't done a better job of protecting you. From your mother and the world. How could I protect you? I could barely keep up with you. By the time you left for college, you'd put us in your rearview mirror . . . and I let you. One of the biggest mistakes of my life."

Adam shook his head dismissively. "You don't have to say that."

"Yes, I do. Because it's the truth."

He hung his head. "If it were true, if I were so damned 'awe-inspiring,' why did Mom leave?"

"Oh, Adam." Dad surged forward, collapsing the padded footrest and bringing both feet to the floor. "So that's what this is about. You haven't asked about your mother in a long time."

"Ten years." The last time he'd just sold his first company for over four million dollars. The acquisition had made national news. Surely his mother would hear about his success . . . He massaged his temples, suddenly wishing he'd remained in San Francisco. What had caused him to unearth these issues when he'd dealt with them years ago?

"There are things a parent wishes to never share with their child." His father sighed. "Your mother and I were having problems before you were born."

Adam stilled. That was new information.

"We almost filed for divorce several times. But then she got pregnant again and we learned we were finally having a boy. We wanted to make our family work."

His stomach churned. "Only I didn't turn out to the boy she wanted."

"There was a hole in your mother's spirit that none of us could fill. It wasn't just you. It was the same with your sisters." Dad rubbed the back of his neck. "With me."

Adam ingested this new familial data.

"You were six the first time you solved a quadratic equation. Your mother couldn't believe it. She sent me out to buy a high school math textbook and you zipped through it like you were reading a Dr. Seuss book. That experience . . . it energized your mother." He winced. "That was probably unfair to put on a child, but she seemed to have a purpose. A special identity."

"Then I was diagnosed."

"Yes," Dad said. "She started zoning out, looking for something else. I recognized the symptoms and I'd had enough. I told her she needed to get help or leave. She chose to leave."

Adam pressed his thumb and forefinger against his eyelids to stem the tears. "I always believed it was my fault that she left. That I was weird and unlovable. I thought you, Sarah, and Amy blamed me, too."

His father squeezed his shoulder. "It wasn't your fault, son. No one ever blamed you, not for one moment."

He let his hands drop and stared at his father through tear-spiked lashes. "She's my mother. If anyone is supposed to love me, it should be her." And the scariest part— "If she couldn't, how can I trust anyone else to?"

"You've got to let that go. You are not defined by the mistakes of your parents."

"Aren't I? Mom, Birgitta and now Ch—" He clenched his teeth. "I'm the common denominator."

"Love isn't logical, Adam."

"Then how do you trust it?"

"It may be hard for you to believe, but I think you're uniquely qualified to figure that out. Say you have strong feelings for a woman. Some would assume that's enough and give in to it. But there has to be a rational component and that's where you excel. Is she a good person? Does she have goals? Do you have things in common? Can you carry on a conversation with her? Does she make you feel good about yourself? Because the initial euphoria will wither away. And it's the answers to those questions that will feed the fire and keep it going."

Adam sighed. "Not only are you utilizing metaphors, Dad, you're mixing them."

"How about this? If you're lucky enough to find some-one who appeals to you, both physically and intellectually, then you owe it to yourself to give it a shot. So"—his father pursed his lips—"who is she?"

"Who?"

"Only a woman can cause a man to start questioning his life."

"Her name is Chelsea. But I hurt her, Dad." He recalled her tears and pleading. "Badly."

"You're the smartest person I know. When you care, there's no problem that can stand between you and the solution. The question is, do you care?"

More than he ever thought was possible. Chelsea had shown him that even a genius had things to learn. And instead of making him feel shame for his differences, she understood and accepted him. Even the "lessons" she'd offered had enhanced who he was, instead of changing him as he'd feared. Getting the new clothes had been a good idea. Learning to relax and imagine others' perspectives had only made engaging with others easier. In fact, when he thought back through his entire association with Chelsea, he realized everything he'd learned from her had augmented his life, not weakened it. The antithesis of his experience with Birgitta.

He settled for a simple "Yes."

"Then you'll figure it out." Dad hesitated and his eyes watered. "This is the longest conversation we've had in years. Whatever happens between the two of you, she'll always have my gratitude for that."

It was half-past eleven when Adam landed back in San Francisco. He'd succumbed to a moment of impulsivity when he'd headed to Colorado over six hours ago, but it turned out to be a judicious use of his time. It had allowed him to begin mending the relationship with his father, after years lost due to incorrect assumptions about their feelings. He was determined to visit again soon, and spend time with his entire family.

But first, he had a presentation to deliver.

He turned his phone back on, startled to see missed calls from Mike and Jonathan, as well as numerous ones from a number he didn't recognize, tagged Los Angeles, CA.

Chelsea?

No, it wasn't her. Her number and picture were programmed into his phone. What if it was *about* her? Before he could access his voice mail and listen to the messages left, his phone rang and the caller ID displayed that same Los Angeles number.

"Yes?"

"Mr. Bennett, this is Howard Richter from Beecher & Stowe."

Beecher & Stowe. That was the fucking company Mike had mentioned, the PR firm where Chelsea worked.

"Why are you calling me?"

"I apologize for disturbing you at this hour the night before your presentation, but I needed to speak with you."

"I don't know Chelsea's whereabouts. Try her cell phone."

"Chelsea Grant is no longer an employee of our company, so she isn't our concern. You are. Mr. Black hired us on behalf of your company and our job was to prepare you for the launch."

He'd ceased paying attention after the man's first sentence. Chelsea no longer worked for them? "What do you mean she isn't an employee?"

"Ms. Grant handed in her notice. We're mortified that she left you without guidance for your presentation, but we've already assigned someone from our office here in LA to—"

Chelsea resigned? Why would she do that? Her job and the partnership meant everything to her.

The partnership means nothing to me if I lose you because of it.

It was all within her grasp and she'd relinquished it. Because of him. She'd told him he meant more to her than the partnership, but they both knew more than words were needed to decipher a person's true intentions. Chelsea had buttressed her words with the one action guaranteed to prove she'd meant what she'd said.

He squeezed his eyes shut and pinched the bridge of his nose. He was an ass. Had he lost her for good? Or was her resignation a way of communicating that he still had a chance? He chose to believe the latter option. He sure as hell didn't deserve her, but she loved him and he needed that hopefulness if he had any chance of winning her back.

He interrupted the man who was still talking. "I don't want a new PR rep. I want Chelsea. If you want to keep Computronix as a client, you'll make sure she's at the presentation tomorrow."

He disconnected the call and hurried to his waiting car, his brain formulating a plan. Being a genius had its advantages. He couldn't afford to lose more valuable time.

Chapter Twenty-One

CHELSEA STOOD IN the back of the large room and catalogued the assembled audience. Reporters from tech blogs, computer journals, and twenty-four-hour news outlets rubbed shoulders with reporters covering pop culture, entertainment news, and financial trends. Howard had been right. This launch was big news and everyone was excited to see what Computronix was promoting.

"It's about to start," she told Indi, clutching her cell phone to her ear. She cleared her throat, trying again, without success, to dislodge the boulder that sat squarely mid-trachea. Her eyes were gritty after a sleepless night and hours of crying, and it had taken a deft and skillful hand with her makeup to mask the effects of yesterday's breakup with Adam. She was grateful her outside appeared poised and confident, even though her inside was an unruly, chaotic mess.

"Why are you attending the presentation? You can leave right now. Come visit me in Nashville," Indi said.

"Howard asked me to stay," Chelsea said.

Indi scoffed. "I'm calling bullshit."

It wasn't bullshit . . . not exactly. Late last night she'd received a surprising phone call from her former supervisor asking her to stay for the presentation. Despite her resignation, Beecher & Stowe still had a stake in the outcome. They hoped if things went well, and with the offending party gone, Computronix would continue to use their services. She'd told him she'd be here, but not on their behalf.

"You're staying for him, aren't you?"

There was no place she'd rather be.

She needed to see the presentation. She hoped Adam hadn't let what happened between them derail his progress. What she hadn't admitted to Indi was that she was determined to convince him to give her another chance. She had no reason to believe he would, but she had to try.

He'd been so cold in the elevator, his expression closed, his stance rigid, his arms crossed across his chest, keeping her at a distance. He'd erected a brick wall between them and with each plea she uttered he'd mortared another stone into place. She should've followed her instincts and told him the truth from the beginning.

Was she so desperate to be accepted that she was willing to give up her integrity? Even if she'd gotten away with it, her soul would've been forever stained. She used to pride herself on being honest with her clients, but she'd never be able to make that claim again. And why? For more money and a corner office? For the outer trappings of success that would say she'd arrived? That she was worthy?

Was she really any different from the woman who'd given birth to her? Her mother had lost herself in a succession of men. Had she defined herself by them? Had being with them made her feel better about herself? Was she—Chelsea—suffering from the same affliction? Had she looked to a job and a partnership to validate who *she* was? Had she actually ended up like her mother, just in a different tax bracket?

Why hadn't she realized—before it was too late—it didn't matter what she had, in the end it was about who she was? Hadn't she seen that lesson replayed over and over with her clients? She dealt with some of the best in the entertainment field. People who were lauded, worshipped, and had loads of money. Yet they were some of the unhappiest people she knew. She refused to follow that path, to spend the rest of her life embracing power and pulchritude at the expense of her principles.

"I love him," she said, simply.

"Then do what you have to. If you need anything, you call me. And the invitation to visit is open."

The telltale stinging pressure began and through sheer force of will, Chelsea held the tears at bay. No more tears. If she lost any more moisture, she'd begin to prune.

"Thanks, Indi," she said and disconnected the call.

She inhaled deeply, expelling all of her fears and doubts. Clutching her bag close, she moved down the aisle, searching for an available seat in the back. The lights in the room were up and the stage was lit, though empty. She wondered where Adam was and what he was doing. Was he nervous or calm? Was he using any of the relaxation breathing she'd taught him? Was he even here? She spied an available seat on the inner aisle and headed toward it when someone called her name.

She turned. It wouldn't be unusual for someone here to know her. She dealt with the press often and there was certain to be entertainment reporters present that she dealt with during her time at Beecher & Stowe. But when she discovered the source of the call, surprise froze her to the spot.

"I heard what happened. Are you okay?" Adam's friend, Jonathan Moran, stood before her, a sad smile marring his handsome face. She recalled the chef saying he planned to attend the launch.

"Bad news travels fast," she said, attempting to lighten the mood. She wasn't sure what the man knew or heard and she wasn't keen on rehashing everything in such a public place.

"The Friends of Adam Bennett club is pretty small, so . . ." He shrugged, his brown eyes kind. "Seriously, are you okay?"

"No, but I will be."

He squeezed her shoulder. "I'm glad you're here. It means you haven't given up on him. What happened took him by surprise, but the man *is* a genius. It won't take him long to realize how happy you make him. Come on, I grabbed us a couple of seats up front."

Her mouth was as arid as the Sahara. She swallowed

and let her gaze dart around the room. "Oh, no, I couldn't. I planned to sit back here—"

"Nonsense." He took her elbow and guided her down to two prime seats on the front row. They'd just settled in when the lights dimmed and an excited murmur surfed the crowd. A swarm of butterflies nose-dived in her stomach and she placed her hand there, wrangling them.

You can do it, Adam.

A spotlight illuminated the far side of the stage and Mike stood at the podium in a dark, slim-cut suit, his fair hair gleaming. Disappointment tore through her with swift surgical precision. She lowered her head and pressed her lips tight to prevent crying out. Adam wasn't here. He hadn't been able to get past what she'd done.

This doesn't mean anything, Chelsea. You always knew they were both doing the presentation.

Mike flashed a charming smile and rested an arm on the dais. "Apple did it in 1984. They invented the Macintosh and changed the computer industry."

Behind him, a picture of the aforementioned computer appeared on one of the large screens.

"In 1985, Nintendo introduced the Nintendo Entertainment System and revitalized the home video gaming market. Apple did it again in 2001 when they created the iPod, transforming the music industry, and again in 2007 with the introduction of the iPhone. Amazon did it with the creation of the Kindle, as they shifted the publishing industry. Computronix is proud to join this distinguished list of pioneers."

A spotlight on the side of the stage closest to her high-lighted Adam standing there.

Those butterflies soared in flights of fancy. She leaned forward, a smile blooming on her face. He wore dark jeans, a navy V-neck sweater over a crisp white-collared shirt and a pair of his favorite sneakers. Stubble covered his strong jawline, giving him the look of a brawny intel-lectual. Not *GQ*, not geek chic. But all Adam. And he was gorgeous. She clasped her hands together and pressed her knuckles to her lips.

No one would necessarily say he was comfortable, but he was calm. He inhaled and she saw his lips moving. He was counting and doing the deep breathing exercises she'd taught him. He exhaled and began.

"What if you could check your email, update your status, conduct your business, all without being tied to bulky hardware? What if you could seamlessly incorpo-rate your conventional and technical worlds? What if the only element you needed to access your computer was air?

"For the past two and a half years I've dreamt about this day and it's finally here. My name is Adam Bennett and I give you the Holographic Personal Computer, or the HPC."

The stage went black. Whispers and nervous titters tore through the audience like a dry brush fire. On the stage, a holographic image appeared in front of Adam. The audience gasped. Chelsea experienced the same thrill of awe and amazement as she had the first time Adam had demonstrated it for her, in his house on the mountain.

"Today, we change the way you'll interact with personal computing."

Thirty minutes later he completed his portion of the presentation. The auditorium erupted in sound as people leapt to their feet and began clapping. The applause was loud and lengthy. Adam smiled his "sell-a-million-HPCs" smile and raised his fist in the air.

Mike rejoined him on stage. "Thank you. We'll take questions now."

A dizzying cacophony of sound accompanied the numerous hands flying upward. Mike handled the questions about availability and price points, but Adam fielded the ones about the technology.

Would other Computronix devices have a holographic interface?

Was the processing efficient?

How long was the battery life?

Would speech recognition come standard?

He stayed calm and appeared relaxed, answering the questions clearly with no lapses of condescension, employing all the lessons they'd worked on. Tears stung her eyes. She was so proud of him. He'd done a great job. This was going to be a success.

"Our viewers want to know if the Sexiest Man Alive is wearing boxers or briefs?"

Chelsea stiffened at the question from an entertainment news channel's fashion police.

Adam smiled. "I'm no longer the sexiest man alive. I believe that title was passed to another genetically blessed individual. However, I *can* report that I'm going commando."

Laughter followed his response. This was better than Chelsea had ever imagined. She should've known to never underestimate him. He'd proven more than once that he could do anything he put his mind to.

Except forgive you.

Adam stepped to the front of the stage. "I'm going to beg your indulgence for a moment. There's someone here who asked me some questions yesterday and I didn't answer them to the best of my ability. I'm ready now." He shielded his eyes and peered into the audience. "Is Chelsea Grant from *Mountaintop Today* here?"

Blood rushed from her face to her heart, then turned around and made the return trip just as fast, leaving her light-headed. Had she heard him correctly?

Beside her, Jonathan stood and she stared up at him, dumbfounded. His dark hair fell charmingly over his forehead and a large smile brightened his face. He held out his hand and she took it, rising to her feet.

"Showtime," he said, and walked her over to the right side of the stage, away from Adam.

A random thought popped into her head. She didn't know what was about to happen, but at least she looked her best. The coral dress with its asymmetrical hem emphasized her long legs and the color popped against her skin.

Mike met her at the stage and took her hand from Jonathan. He helped her up the stairs. "If you make him happy, then I'm happy," he whispered in her ear.

Then her brain went blank, as she stood alone on the stage, with Adam.

After several moments of silence, his eyes widened comically and he looked at the audience in apprehension. "Aren't you going to say something?"

She leaned toward him. "I don't know what to say."

"Ask me a question."

"Here? In front of all of these people?"

He smiled. "Aren't we both tired of worrying what other people think of us?"

It suddenly struck her that she was part of a press conference. Where she'd used to love watching as a spectator sport, she had now become the participant. It wasn't as enjoyable.

"Um, what will be a successful market share—"

He shook his head. "Not that type of question."

She could hear the audience murmuring, but they couldn't be more confused than she was. What did he expect her to do? *Think, Chelsea. Mountaintop Today*, questions from yesterday . . .

There was only one thing she cared about and it wasn't the HPC or Computronix's profit share. But could she do this? Here, in front of all of these people? She'd often made her clients issue apologies or address their behavior in a public arena, for money, to save their career, or rehab their reputation. Wasn't her future happiness and the love in her heart more important than those superficial goals?

She tried to call on her years of professional poise, but it refused to answer. This was too personal. She had too much at stake. She licked her lips. Her heart was beating so loud she was certain everyone in the room could hear it.

"Your last launch didn't go well, but today's was a success. You were granted a second chance. Do you grant them in your personal life, or is it always one strike and you're done?"

The room fell quiet, waiting for his response.

"It used to be. Recently I was told people aren't computers. They make mistakes."

"So you'd consider forgiving that person?"

"Under the right circumstances."

"And what are those circumstances?"

He moved closer to her and cupped her cheek. "Our circumstances."

She exhaled shakily as lightness engulfed her being. It wasn't over.

"Can I ask *you* a question?" he said, surprising her.

"Of course."

"Do you know who Gottfried Leibniz was?"

It was like a cosmic needle scratch on a blissful moment. "No."

"He was a German mathematician and philosopher. His best-known contribution to metaphysics is his theory of the monad," Adam continued, despite her puzzled expression. "He posited that monads are the ultimate elements of the universe and that all substances, no matter how big or small, are made up of an infinite number of monads."

"Uh, Adam? I think you're getting a tad bit off track."

He laughed, his beautiful blue eyes warm, clear, and shining, and she was willing to listen to a thousand lectures if it meant he would continue looking at her that way. He cradled her face between his palms, his thumbs skimming over her skin. Like an affectionate suntan, his regard warmed her, marked her as his.

"You asked me what your word meant to me and I said it meant everything. I was wrong. I put so much focus on what you *said* to me that I let it eclipse who you *are* to me. *You* are everything. I love you, Chelsea Grant. And I know that because every monad in my soul and body scream out your name, every waking moment of every day. I'm sorry for hearing you but not listening and I'll do whatever it takes to make it up to you."

A silly grin lifted her lips as he kissed her. Her pulse raced and a feeling of pure satisfaction ran through her body. God, she loved this man. This sexy, intelligent, caring, literal, challenging, exasperating man. *He* was everything and he was all hers.

"Can we go now?" he said in her ear, over all the commotion. Now that the two of them had finished with their spectacle, the reporters hurried to get the information about the HPC—and his shocking declaration—to their readers and viewers. "You know, center of attention and crowds . . ."

She pulled back and stared at him. "Are you kidding me? You were fantastic. But if it bothered you that much, why did you do it in front of all of these people? I would've been happy with just the two of us in a dark room."

He smoothed her curls and kissed her forehead. "I thought you'd approve. It's the perfect PR move."

She laughed. "It wasn't enough to release an innovative device, you also had to give them a love story. Going out of your way to make sure no one is talking about anyone other than you this week?"

"This was a success because of you. I couldn't have done any of that without you."

"You could've, but thank you for the appreciation." She grimaced. "Can you hold on to that feeling? I'll have to depend on your hospitality for a little while longer. I quit my job."

"I know. Your boss called me. That promotion meant so much to you and you were willing to give it up for me." He stroked his fingers over her cheekbones and her lips. "But you don't have to. Why don't you give them a call? We'll tell them it was all a misunderstanding."

She shrugged. "If I call them now, they'll just put me to work on another assignment." She wrapped her arms around his neck and kissed him. "I could use a vacation."

"Are you sure?"

"Yup. I'll let them sweat awhile. Besides, I have a little leverage. I happen to personally know the CEO of Computronix."

"Ummm, how fortunate for you."

"You have no idea."

"I bet I do. I'm kind of a genius."

Chapter Twenty-Two

THOUGH THE SEPTEMBER sun shone brightly through the tops of the trees and spilled into the great room through the floor-to-ceiling windows, Chelsea only had eyes for Adam.

Her pulse raced and her heart thundered a bit out of control. She crossed her arms, leaned against the far wall and watched him circulate among their guests.

It wasn't his dark good looks, although faded jeans clung to his strong thighs and he transformed a plain white T-shirt into a lethal weapon. No, his considerable sex appeal paled in comparison to the effort he put into entertaining their families. Despite their personal affiliation to everyone in the room, Chelsea knew the small crowd still made Adam uncomfortable. But he did it.

Because she'd asked him to.

"Stop mooning over him. It's embarrassing," Jonathan said, coming over and draping an arm around her shoulders.

"Jealousy isn't an attractive trait."

"It is on me."

Oh, Lord. "You're too charming for your own good."

He stood with his jean-clad legs spread apart, his light blue shirt making his brown eyes flash. "Is that possible?"

She rolled her eyes. "Trust me, it is. You could have someone moon over you. It only requires you to look at a woman the way you look at your ovens at Quartet."

"My ovens will do anything I ask them to. Can you say the same thing about women?"

She punched his arm.

"Ouch!" He grabbed his bruised limb. When a couple of people swung in their direction, he straightened. "Quick, look happy. Adam will have my ass if I upset you."

On cue, Adam's narrowed gaze landed on them and he frowned.

"Shit, I'm in trouble."

"You're fine." She blew a kiss to Adam, who eyed them for a long moment, before allowing his "sell-a-million-HPCs" smile to spread across his face. He nodded and returned to his conversation.

"It's great his dad and sister could make it," Jonathan said.

"Yeah."

It was the first time she'd met Richard Bennett in person, though they'd FaceTimed on several occasions since the HPC product launch. They'd taken Rick—as he'd insisted she call him—and Adam's oldest sister, Sarah, to dinner the night before, after their flight from Colorado. His youngest sister, Amy, stayed behind in

Colorado, her doctor declaring her grounded eight months into her pregnancy.

In his early sixties, Rick was a handsome man. His thick dark hair was threaded with strands of silver and fine lines fanned from his hazel eyes and bracketed his smiling mouth. During dinner, it was clear to see their temperaments were worlds apart, but there was no mistaking how much the older man loved his son.

"Adam said you're close to opening the restaurant."

"I am. I'm really excited about it. We're in a great location. I hope you guys can fly out for the opening."

"We wouldn't miss it."

"Miss what?" Indi asked, coming up on her other side. After spending several months in Nashville, Indi had tired of sweet tea, cowboy boots, and country music and had decided to work her way back to the West Coast, gracing them with her presence. Her sister's look was ever-evolving and since the last time Chelsea had seen her, Indi had traded in her twists for long, beachy waves.

"The opening of Jonathan's new restaurant in DC."

Indi tilted her head and twined her fingers through the ends of her hair. "Really? If it's anything like Quartet, I'm there."

He leaned toward her, lowering his voice. "You're a fan of my food?"

Were they any other people, Chelsea might be concerned about her sister flirting with one of Adam's best friends. If they got involved and it didn't work out, the aftermath could create a potentially awkward situation. But between Jonathan's devotion to his restaurants and

Indi's aversion to responsibility, there wasn't potential for anything serious to develop between them.

They were two peas in a commitment-phobic pod.

"So I can expect you with Chelsea and Adam?"

"Sure." Indi stroked his forearm and smiled at him through her lashes. "As long as Jeremy doesn't mind."

Jonathan lifted a brow, an uncertain smile hovering. "Who's Jeremy?"

"Shoot me now," Chelsea muttered, rolling her eyes. She caught Mike's gaze, who stood on the other side of the room, watching them. She crossed the floor toward him, her knee-high brown leather boots clicking on the hard surface.

"Having fun?" she asked.

"Loads," he said, his voice indicating otherwise. He rolled a highball glass between his palms and stared into its contents.

Chelsea shifted her weight onto her back foot and inventoried the man before her. His navy slacks, white dress shirt, and slate-gray blazer were impeccably tailored and the flawless fit emphasized his urbane leanness. But his blond hair was mussed and his blue eyes seemed haunted with a solemnity that didn't fit the celebration.

"Everything okay?"

"I just have a lot on my mind. Work."

"I thought work was going well?"

Computronix sold eighty million HPCs during the past quarter, making it the most profitable quarter in Computronix's history, and according to Adam, it showed no signs of slowing down.

"We owe much of that to you. I knew it was an exceptional product, but your work with him ensured that others would know it, too."

"He created the device, you knew he needed help. I played a small part."

"Can we agree on small but significant?"

"We can."

They shared a smile and Mike raised his glass to her. "Congratulations on your promotion."

"Thank you."

Once Beecher & Stowe understood that she and the Computronix account were a package deal, she accepted their sweetened partnership offer with a bump in compensation and the responsibility to run their new San Francisco office.

"We're looking for a place in San Mateo," she continued. "It's a good halfway point between San Francisco and Palo Alto. I'm not interested in driving an additional thirty minutes up the mountain each day."

"It's been great having Adam back on the company's campus. We've missed him." He motioned to the room with his tumbler-occupied hand. "What about this?"

"The house?" At his nod, she continued, "We'll keep it. Adam made me promise we'll escape up here for a long weekend once a month. And I'll make it happen. I know how much he needs it."

Mike pressed a brotherly kiss to her forehead. "He's a lucky son of a bitch."

"He is, but so am I."

"Why does every man in this room feel the need to

fondle my woman?" Adam asked, twin grooves appearing on his forehead. He nuzzled his nose in the mass she'd pulled into a high ponytail. "I love your curls."

She leaned away from him and smoothed her fingers over his features, quivering with pleasure when his teeth grazed the pads of her thumbs. "No one is fondling me."

"I hope not," Indi said, popping up again. "My impressionable eyes couldn't endure it."

"You could leave," Mike said, his voice tight.

Chelsea's eyes widened and silence smothered the buoyancy of the past several seconds.

Indi recovered first. She shoved her hands on her hips. "I could, but I'm not. In fact, I'll be staying here for a few months, until I can get on my feet."

Adam's head ricocheted in her direction. "She's joking, right?"

"Yes, my love," Chelsea said, even as Indi glared at Mike and mouthed the word "no."

Where had that come from? What was going on with Mike? She shot Indi a questioning look. The other woman shook her head, her full lips pursed.

When Adam slipped away from their guests and headed into the kitchen, she followed, gasping when he grabbed a tray of champagne flutes out of the refrigerator.

"When did you do that?" she asked.

He winked at her. "I have my surprises."

She cupped his cheeks in her hands and pressed a kiss to his lips. "I'll have to find a way to surprise *you* later."

"I hate being on the receiving end of surprises, but I

love you. I can't wait," he said, stealing a kiss the same way he'd stolen her heart.

Stealthily and before she'd known what was happening.

She smiled, appreciating his proficiency in making her feel special. It wasn't always easy. They both had demanding jobs and making their relationship a priority took work. She sometimes found his literalness exhausting, and he got frustrated when she didn't plainly state what she needed. There were word merry-go-rounds and misunderstandings, but she would do anything for him and he loved her more fiercely and with more devotion than she'd ever experienced in her life.

She wouldn't trade what they'd found for all the partnerships, million-dollar salaries and corner offices in the world.

Once everyone was in possession of a glass, Adam came and stood by her side. He inhaled deeply. "Thank you all for coming up to our home on the mountain. We wanted to celebrate everything that's happened to us in the past six months with the people who matter most. We're fortunate to be surrounded by old friends, make the acquaintance of new ones, and reconnect with family."

He placed his hand over his heart and nodded at Sarah and Rick, whose chin trembled in an effort to rein in his emotions.

"So here's to great friends and family. They know you well . . . and still choose to like you!"

Everyone laughed and a chorus of "Cheers!" rang out in the large space.

"Where did you find that toast?" she asked, raising her glass and accepting a kiss from the man who was truly the love of her life.

"The internet," he whispered in her ear, not even bothering to pretend he didn't understand her question. He stared into her eyes and kissed her once more. "Only one thing could top off this extraordinary moment."

Adam collected her champagne flute, placing it next to his on the counter. He gathered her hands in his and she began to tremble as she realized what was happening.

"The day you swept onto my mountain was the best day of my life. I love you and want to 'emotionally bond' with you forever."

He reached into his pocket and pulled out a box. Opening it, he presented her with a breathtaking three-carat, round-cut diamond flanked by five sapphire accent stones on each side.

"It reminded me of the underwater aquarium from our date at the science museum. So, Chelsea Grant, will you marry me?"

Her hands flew to cover her mouth.

Oh. My. God. "Yes!"

He barely had the opportunity to slide the ring on her finger before she was whisked away from him by Indi and Sarah, both women gushing over her ring. Above their bent heads, she watched Adam accept hugs and well wishes from his father and best friends.

A little over six months ago, she'd believed a promotion would be the best thing that could happen to her. Now she knew how foolish she'd been. She'd spent years on an endless quest to acquire things. But what she'd told Adam had been true: it all would've meant nothing if losing him had been the cost to acquire it.

"How did I do?" he asked, when they managed to steal away for a moment alone.

Brimming with love and happiness, Chelsea flung herself into his embrace and closed her eyes when his strong arms enclosed her. She had loyal friends, a job she could be proud of, and the man she loved. It should be unfair for a person to possess this much bliss.

"You were amazing. But I'd expect nothing less from my very own genius."

Acknowledgments

THIS STORY WAS born from love . . . a love letter to me and my love for my eldest son.

My husband wrote me this incredible letter when we were dating in law school. It was so unique—who quotes a dead mathematician and philosopher as a way to explain all-encompassing love? I kept that letter for twenty years, and when I knew I was going to write about a computer engineer, I knew I would use that letter as a way for the hero to profess his love to the heroine.

I've also been thinking a lot about my oldest son, who is a total cutie. He's smart, talented, and he has Asperger's. I'm a romantic, and I want my son to experience the same kind of love I share with his father. It takes a special person to see beyond the outer quirks to the person within and I wanted to write this story for him. I'm glad I did. It's my favorite of the ones I've written so far.

Thank you to my family for understanding my need

to write, especially my kids, who will tell everyone their mother is an author before I will. To my agent Nalini Akolekar, for her support and guidance, and to my editors, Chelsey Emmelhainz and Tessa Woodward, for their encouragement and belief in me and the stories I want to tell.

Huge thanks to the LaLas, Sharon, Annette, Petra, Leigh, Ashley, Nellie and Chrissy for keeping me company as the miles steadily increase and to Mary and Alleyne for nourishing my writing life.

And, as always, none of this would mean anything without the love of my life, my husband, James. Every monad in my body and soul screams out your name. Now and forever.

Don't miss the next sparkling and
sexy contemporary romance
from Tracey Livesay!

Coming October 2016 from Avon Impulse!

About the Author

A former criminal defense attorney, TRACEY LIVESAY finds crafting believable happily-ever-afters slightly more challenging than protecting our constitutional rights, but she's never regretted following her heart instead of her law degree. She lives in Virginia with her husband—who she met on the very first day of law school—and their three children.

Give in to your Impulses . . .
Continue reading for excerpts from
our newest Avon Impulse books.
Available now wherever ebooks are sold.

ONE LUCKY HERO
THE MEN IN UNIFORM SERIES
by Codi Gary

STIRRING ATTRACTION
A SECOND SHOT NOVEL
by Sara Jane Stone

SIGNS OF ATTRACTION
by Laura Brown

SMOLDER
THE WILDWOOD SERIES
by Karen Erickson

An Excerpt from

ONE LUCKY HERO
The Men in Uniform Series
By Codi Gary

Violet Douglas wants one night where she can be normal. Where she can do something for herself and not be just her siblings' guardian. So when she spies a tall, dark, and sexy stranger, she's ready to let her wild side roar. The last thing she expects is to see her one night stand one week later, when she drags her delinquent kid brother to the Alpha Dog Training Program.